For Two Thousand Yea

Mihail Sebastian is one of the most important Romanian writers of the twentieth century. Born Iosif Hechter to a Jewish family in 1907, he grew up in Brăila, Romania, an ancient port on the Danube. He studied law in Bucharest from 1927 to 1929 and in Paris from 1930 to 1931, then worked occasionally as a lawyer while publishing articles, novels and plays, and being part of an influential literary circle that included the historian of religion Mircea Eliade, the playwright Eugene Ionesco and the philosopher Emil Cioran (who was the model for Ştefan D. Pârlea in *For Two Thousand Years*).

During his lifetime, his most famous book was the novel *For Two Thousand Years*. Published in 1934, it sparked a furious debate in the newspapers for its ambiguous political stance. Critics on the left accused Sebastian of being anti-Semitic although he was Jewish, while those on the right attacked him for being a Zionist. At the core of the novel is the year 1923, when a new constitution gave citizenship to ethnic and religious minorities. The first edition of the novel included a foreword by Sebastian's mentor, the philosopher Nae Ionescu, who made a series of anti-Semitic remarks and was in fact the model for the character of Ghiţă Blidaru. Critics wondered why Sebastian had decided to include Ionescu's words and whether he agreed with him or not. Sebastian replied in an essay titled *How I Became a Hooligan* (1935), where he explained why he felt the need to think as lucidly as possible at a time when everything was politically charged.

His other books, written after this incident, include less political novels influenced by French modernists, such as *The Town with Acacias* (1935) and *The Accident* (1940), and plays like *Holiday Game* (1938) and *A Nameless Star* (1944). As the fascist Iron Guard rose to power, Sebastian was prohibited from work as a journalist and was abandoned by his circle of friends – an experience chronicled in the diary he kept from 1935 to 1944 and which is similar in style and tone to *For Two Thousand Years*. Having survived the war and the Holocaust, he was killed by a truck as he crossed the street in May 1945, as he was going to teach his first university lecture on Balzac. He was 38.

When his *Journal* was finally published in Romania in 1996, it became a bestseller, generating a heated controversy over responsibility for war crimes and the country's history of anti-Semitism. The English translation has been hailed as 'a humane masterpiece' and compared to Anne Frank's diary.

Philip Ó Ceallaigh is the author of two collections of short stories, *Notes from a Turkish Whorehouse* and *The Pleasant Light of Day*, both published by Penguin. His work has been translated into ten languages and adapted for cinema and he has received the Rooney Prize for Irish Literature. He lives in Bucharest, Romania.

MIHAIL SEBASTIAN

For Two Thousand Years

Translated by Philip Ó Ceallaigh

PENGUIN BOOKS

PENGUIN CLASSICS

UK | USA | Canada | Ireland | Australia
India | New Zealand | South Africa

Penguin Books is part of the Penguin Random House group of companies whose addresses can
be found at global.penguinrandomhouse.com.

First published as *De doud mii de ani* in 1934
This translation first published in Penguin Classics 2016
003

Translation copyright © Philip Ó Ceallaigh, 2016

The epigraph translation on p. 1 is taken from the Penguin edition of Montaigne's *De l'art de
conférer*, titled *On the Art of Conversation*, translated by M.A. Screech

The moral right of the translator has been asserted

Typeset in 10.5/13pt Dante MT Std by Palimpsest Book Production Ltd, Falkirk, Stirlingshire
Printed in Great Britain by Clays Ltd, St Ives plc

A CIP catalogue record for this book is available from the British Library

ISBN: 978-0-241-18961-0

www.greenpenguin.co.uk

J'ose non seulement parler de moy, mais parler seulement de moy: je four-voye quand j'ecris aultre chose, et me disrobe a mon sujet. Je ne m'aime pas si indiscretement et ne suis si attaché et mesle a moy, que je ne me puisse distinguer et considerer a quartier, comme un voysin, comme un arbre.

– Montaigne, *De l'art de conferer*

I not only dare to talk about myself but to talk of nothing but myself. I am wandering off the point when I write of anything else, cheating my subject of *me*. I do not love myself with such lack of discretion, nor am I so bound and involved in myself, that I am unable to see myself apart and to consider myself separately as I would a neighbour or a tree.

PART ONE

I

I believe I've only ever been afraid of signs and symbols, never of people or things. My childhood was poisoned by the third poplar in the yard of the Church of St Peter, a tall, mysterious tree, its shadow on summer nights falling through the window, over my bed – that black band slashing across my bedcovers – a terrifying presence I could not understand and did not try to.

And yet, I walked bareheaded through the deserted streets of the city when it was occupied by Germans: a white trail in the sky marking the passage of planes, bombs falling all about, even close by, the short dry thumps echoing across the open country.

And yet, with cold, childlike curiosity I calmly observed cartloads of frozen Turks passing by the gates in December, and not even before those pyramids of bodies stacked like logs in a woodpile did the presence of death make me tremble.

And yet, I crossed the Danube in a damaged boat, taking in water, to Lipovan villages, just rolling up my sleeves when it seemed the rotten bottom could no longer hold out. And God knows what a bad swimmer I am.

No, I don't think I've ever been fearful, even though the Greeks from the big garden, who pelted us with stones when they caught us there, shouted 'Cowardly Jew!' at me daily from the moment they knew me. I grew up with that shout, spat at me from behind.

I know, though, what horror is. Horror, yes. Little nothings which nobody else noticed loomed before me menacingly and froze me with terror. Vainly would I approach the poplar across the road in the light of day, caressing its black bark and, with bloodied nails, breaking splinters from the wood exposed between the cracks. 'It's just a poplar,' I told myself, leaning back against it, to feel it right against me so as not to forget. But by evening I had indeed forgotten, alone in my bedroom, bedded down as always at ten o'clock. You could still hear the steps of passers-by from the street, muffled voices, occasional shouts. Then that familiar silence, arriving with the usual pace, in the usual stages. If I made an effort, I could perhaps recall those three or four internal beats with which my night began, real steps which I descended physically in darkness and silence. Then the shadow of the poplar found me once again tensed, with fists clenched and eyes wide open, wanting to shout out but not knowing how or to whom.

*

Made a curious discovery yesterday at the second-hand bookshop. George Gissing. *La rançon d'Eve.* From around 1900, I think. Absolutely nothing about the author (probably English). Passed a good four hours.

When I'd finished it, I went into the street for an evening paper. More fighting, at the faculty of medicine in particular, and in our own faculty. I didn't attend today. Why bother?

*

Marcel Winder stopped me in the street to tell me they'd beaten him up again.

'That's number eight,' he told me, not specifying whether it was his eighth fight or his eighth injury. He had a black bruise under his left eye. He was chatty, almost cheerful. Superior at any rate. I've certainly never aspired to that kind of thing. I've steered clear. It looks like the lads are getting ready for 10 December, but Winder didn't want to tell me too much about it.

'Not your sort of thing, pal. You've better things to worry about. And coincidentally, just coincidentally, they stop you getting into trouble with us. Just a coincidence.'

Winder is wasting his time. He's flogging a dead horse: I don't have that kind of vanity.

*

In a letter from Mama I received today:

> . . . And, in particular, don't go to the university. I've read in the paper
> that big fights have broken out again, and the milliner's son, when he
> was home, told me it's worst of all at your faculty. Leave the showing
> off to the others. Listen to your mother and stay home.

'Leave the showing off to the others.' If Mama could know how that
sounds.

*

Can that be it? This morning I went to the class on Roman law. No
one said a word to me. I took notes feverishly, in order not to have to
lift my eyes from my desk. Halfway through the lecture, a ball of
paper falls on the bench, beside me. I don't look at it, don't open it.
Someone shouts my name loudly from behind. I don't turn my
head. My neighbour to the left watches me carefully, without a
word. I can't endure his gaze and I look up.

'Out!'

He barks the command. He stands up, making space for me to
get by, and waits. I feel a tense silence around me. Nobody breathes.
Any gesture from me and this silence will explode.

No. I slide out of the desk and slip towards the door between two
rows of onlookers. It all happens decorously, ritually. Someone by
the door lashes out with his fist, but it is a glancing blow. A late
punch, my friend.

I'm out in the street. I see a beautiful woman. I see an empty
carriage passing by. Everything is as it ought to be. A cold December
morning.

*

Winder sought me out to congratulate me on yesterday's events. I
don't know who told him about it. And he gave me a ticket to go to
the student dormitories the day after tomorrow. A group is being

organized for every faculty. The boys are determined to attend lectures on 10 December. A matter of principle, Winder says.

The whole thing bores me to death. I'd like a big, clear, severe book with ideas that challenge all I believe in, a book I could devour with the same intense passion with which I first read Descartes. Every chapter would be a personal struggle.

But no: I'm involved in a 'matter of principle'. Ridiculous.

*

10 December. Walking straight ahead, head uncovered, in the rain, blindly, looking neither right nor left nor behind, without crying out, to avoid crying out, above all, and allowing the noise of the street, the people who are watching, and this hour of confusion, to wash over me. There. If I close my eyes, nothing remains but drizzling rain: I can feel the fine droplets on my cheek, trickling from my eyebrow towards my nostrils and from there falling suddenly to my lips. Why can't I be profoundly, imperturbably calm, like a horse drawing an empty cart through mud, through a storm?

I've been beaten. That's all I know. I'm not in pain and, apart from a punch to the thigh, none of them were severe blows. He had a strange expression, under his cap. I hadn't believed he was going to strike me until I saw his raised fist. He was a stranger: perhaps it was the first time he'd laid eyes on me.

I've been beaten and the world doesn't stand still for such things. Italian-Romanian Bank, paid-up capital, 50,000,000. Where Minimax guards, fire doesn't spread. The capital of Iceland is . . . Liebovici Isodor, what happened to you? If he found the door to the secretariat, he escaped. If not . . . But what the hell is the capital of Iceland? Not Christiana, for God's sake, and not Oslo either, because they're the same place . . .

If I cry, I'm lost. I'm still self-possessed enough to know that much. If I cry, I'm lost. Clench your fists, you fool, if necessary, believe yourself a hero, pray to God, tell yourself you're the son of a race of martyrs, yes, yes, tell yourself that, knock your head against the wall, but if you want to be able to look at yourself in the mirror and not die of shame, don't cry. That's all I ask of you: don't cry.

*

If I thought it would do any good, I'd rip out that page I wrote the other day. One more pathetic outburst like that and I'll give up keeping a diary. What matters is whether I can understand calmly, critically, what is happening now to myself and others. Otherwise . . .

People say that this afternoon they'll decide to close the university indefinitely.

2

Yesterday, on the platform, as I was getting off the train, Mama looked thinner and older than ever under the weak station lights. It was probably only her usual nerves, in our first hour of being together again.

Her nerves ... 'Have you got all your parcels? You didn't leave anything on the train? Button up your collar properly. Now, to find a carriage ...' She talks a lot, hurriedly, about so many little things, and doesn't wipe the tear from her lashes, afraid I'd notice it.

*

First walk in town. Triumphal procession down Main Street, between two rows of Jewish shopkeepers who salute me loudly, each from his own shop, with discreet knowing nods.

'It's nothing, lads, keep your chins up, God is good, it'll pass.'

'For two thousand years ...' says Moritz Bercovici (manufacturing and footwear), trying to explain to me the cause of our persecution.

At the barber's, the owner himself takes the honour of cutting my hair and asks during the operation if I have any bruises, scars ... if you know what I mean, sir.

'No, I've no idea.'

'Well, the fighting.'

'What fighting?'

'The fighting at the university. Didn't you get beaten up?'

'No.'

'Not at all?'

'Not at all.'

The man is perplexed. He cuts my hair grudgingly, unenthusiastically.

* * *

A family evening. My cousin Viky has returned with her husband from their honeymoon. Seems she's pregnant. An uncle finds the matter amusing.

'You've been hard at work, you two!'

Viky is embarrassed, her husband serious.

'Well, young fellow, there you go! You're done for now! Whether you like it or not, feel like it or not, you have to . . . You know the story about the train?'

He tells the story about the train. Everybody laughs loudly. In the corner, Mama looks at me, confused . . .

I might have ended up like the rest of them, a fat married shop-keeper, playing poker on Sunday evening and talking dirty to newly-weds. You know the one about the train?

I sometimes ask myself, fearfully, if I have wholly succeeded in escaping them.

* * *

I asked Mama if we could stay at home. She works, I read. I look up from the book from time to time to see her, beautiful, calm, with the most peaceful forehead I know, with her eyes a little tired with age. Forty-three? Forty-four? I'm afraid to ask her.

'How are you getting on in Bucharest?'

'Fine. Why do you ask?'

'No reason.'

She continues working, without looking at me.

'You know, Mama, if sending me 4,000 is too hard . . .'

She doesn't respond. I go to the other side of the table, take her right hand in mine and squeeze it inquiringly.

'It's late, son. Time for bed.'

I should have guessed. Things have not been going well at home. There's no more money. I've told her that from now on I'll manage on 2,000 a month. I'll stay in the student dormitories. It's fine there too, it's warm and clean and comfortable. (She doesn't seem to believe me – and I talk quickly, surprised at the positive qualities that I've suddenly discovered in those barracks in the Jewish quarter in Văcărești.)

*

I can hear her breathing in the next room. I'm well aware that she can't sleep and deliberately breathes as if she's sleeping to fool me so that I won't be worried.

Such childish nonsense. I should be ashamed of it, but I am not. At my age, unable to leave home for three months without that feeling of something clutching at my heart, without that great yearning overwhelming me just as I am about to be embraced goodbye. If I weren't ashamed, I'd go and kiss her now, as I would in the past, when I woke in the night from a bad dream. The bad dream: that suitcase packed for the journey.

3

The voluptuousness of being alone in a world that believes it owns you. It's not pride. Not even shyness. It's a natural, simple and unforced sense of being left to yourself. Sometimes I'd like to leave my own body and from a corner of the room observe how I talk, how I get worked up, see what I'm like when I'm cheerful or sad, knowing that none of those things is me. Playing at having a double? No, that's not it at all.

*

I ate at the canteen between a bad-smelling loud-talking Russian and a thin girl with chapped hands and badly applied lipstick. A concrete floor, the cold, a coat thrown over my shoulders, a plate shoved before me, a tin fork on the ground.

I'm never going to be a social revolutionary, I who in that moment somehow managed a cheerful smile.

There are eleven boys in the room, including me. Sadigurski Liova, my neighbour to the right, shaves with the old razors given to him by Ionel Bercovici, my neighbour to the left. I'm still guarded in my interactions here. I fear greater familiarity.

Towards morning, whenever I happen to wake, I like to listen to the chorus of breathing of the ten people around me, in this long, cold room: the rasping breath of the polytechnic student by the door, his neighbour's fluting whistle, Liova's sighing, the bumblebee buzz of someone towards the back, by the window and, above them all, the loud, penetrating, animal snore of Ianchelevici Şapsă, the giant.

*

I watch how they return in the evening from the university, in dribs and drabs, or singly, worn out. And each one grimly enumerates the fights he's got into, like a billiard score, so that a competitor won't steal their points.

Marcel Winder is up to fifteen. The other day his hat also got ripped, which puts him well ahead on the road to martyrdom. Loudly, in the middle of the yard, he points out each of his wounds. This one and this one and this one . . .

*

Today they removed Ianchelevici Şapsă's mattress. He hasn't paid his bill for three months and they're taking action. He watched calmly, leaning against the wall, without protest. In the evening he laid down on his bed board and uttered a choice curse. I threw him one of my pillows. He sent it sailing back, high through the air, nearly smashing the lamp, and turned over to face the wall.

*

It was a tough day. It's been decided that we absolutely have to get into the civil law faculty, where they grade you for attendance. Up until now we've only been going in scattered groups of three people at most. This avoids major confrontations, but it achieves nothing as they usually identify us all and kick us out.

So today we had to change our tactics. We entered in a compact group and sat in the front rows, by the lectern. We don't respond to minor provocations, but defend ourselves if we're attacked. 'Until the end' – that was the slogan.

It's a bad strategy, I think, but I'm not going to tell the boys that, so thrilled are they with today's success. We gave as good as we got, perhaps, but did nobody notice Liebovici Isodor, jammed in the corner by the blackboard, with his coat ripped and a bloody split lip? Ianchelevici Şapsă did wonders: he was pale and serious, holding the leg of a chair he had broken off for the fight.

Evening. Marcel Winder made a list of those who were beaten up, to give to the paper. I told him to rub my name out: I don't think I received more than two blows and, more to the point, Mama doesn't need to find out.

*

Calm exteriors. Perhaps antagonism has acquired a certain style.

'Dear colleague, would you kindly show me your student identification card?'

Three of them surround me, waiting. I take out my student card and display it to the one who spoke.

'Aha! Please vacate the lecture hall. Come along.'

He points the way.

*

Liebovici Isodor got badly beaten up. Again. I wasn't there, but heard from Marga Stern, who was.

I'm rather fond of his curt manner, his proud, firm reserve.

'Again, Liebovici?'

'Again, what?'

'They beat you up again.'

'No.'

'Of course they did.'

'All right, they did, then . . . You seem to know all about it.'

He turns and leaves, irritated, head bowed.

I lost my gloves in the scuffle or they were taken. And the weather is icy . . . Damn.

*

15

No, I'm not the tough kind. Where are the oaths I made two years ago, on the freshly shut cover of Zarathustra? Why did I wander aimlessly in the street last night, alone, miserable because I was unable to cry and terrified at the same time that I might have been about to? Why in the evening, when I lay my head on my pillow, is it like collapsing in exhaustion after being chased?

Imbecile. Three times over.

What depresses me most is the feeling of losing, with each day, the refuge of solitude, of finding myself in solidarity with Marcel Winder and Ianchelevici Şapsă, descending the stairs together, united in common feeling, becoming one with them, the same as them, a fellow sufferer and sympathizer. Jewish fellow-feeling – I hate it. I'm always on the brink of shouting out a coarse word, just to show that even though I'm in the midst of ten people who believe me their 'brother in suffering', I am in fact absolutely, definitively alone.

Listen, Marcel Winder, if you pat me on the shoulder one more time, I'll punch you out. My business if I'm hurt, your business if your skull gets cracked. I've nothing to share with you, you don't need anything from me. You go your way and I'll go mine.

*

We've had no fire for three days. We're out of wood and awaiting a promised subsidy.

Liova is sick, a fever of 39 degrees. An intern from Caritas came to see him and promised to take him there as soon as a bed becomes available.

The polytechnic student has got frostbitten ears and a big yellowing bandage covers his entire cheek. It turns my stomach at mealtimes in the canteen, along with the tattered cotton wool and gutta-percha.

Ianchelevici Şapşa has washed his socks and hung them on the edge of the bed to dry. A girl was looking for him today. I think she'd come from a market in his town and she brought him a bag of walnuts. He laughed awkwardly: I think he was embarrassed to receive her in front of us.

Am I not ridiculous here, with my fussy judgements, and minding how I 'carry' myself? An aesthete. That's what I am. 'Decency, reserve, solitude' – worthless virtues that oblige you to grin through the pain.

Unshaven for four days. It's too cold to spend a quarter of an hour in front of the mirror.

*

Things could have gone badly today. I was coming down from the administrative offices, where I'd gone to get warm, and was two steps from the door when Ştefăniu went out ahead of me. He hadn't noticed me. I've just realized that. But I lacked composure and foolishly spun about to avoid him, and that's when he saw me. He could only reach me with his walking stick (a good blow on the right shoulder). I ran from him, though this risked attracting the attention of the others, and took a left into the hall. With him in pursuit. I went through the upper gallery, towards the senate, calculating I could stop in the chancellery. But there was no key in the door and I wouldn't have been able to hold it shut indefinitely with my shoulder. Luckily the door to the senate steps was open. Once out in the street, I supposed he wouldn't pursue me. And he didn't.

And I should write to Mama this evening. But what?

Ten in the evening. A while ago the Bessarabian medical student brought two pieces of wood in the pockets of his overcoat. But since we haven't had a fire for so long the stove smokes and now it's gone cold again and the acrid smell in the room chokes Liova.

Somebody went out and left the door open. Nobody gets up to close it. Ionel Bercovici is playing poker on his bed with Marcel Winder and two others whom I don't know.

You can hear Liova coughing from time to time. Somebody is beating his hands together, either because the coughing annoys him or because he's cold.

> Saturday evening
> Every Jew is a king
> And every corner of the house rings with laughter
> And everyone's happy

Ianchelevici Şapsă is singing. Leaning against the wall, overcoat draped over his shoulders, hands in pockets. He has a heavy, drawling voice that has trouble with the high notes and he stumbles a little at the end of each verse.

'... *A ieider i-id a melah* ... Every Jew is a king ...'

It's a melody I've heard before somewhere, long ago. At home, perhaps, in Grandfather's time.

My eyes feel hot. It's nothing, kid. Nobody can see you. And don't you feel it does you good, infinitely more good, than proudly gritting your teeth and holding it in?

Sing, Ianchelevici Şapsă. You're a big fellow, twenty-five years old, and haven't read a book in your life, you've passed through life aware of everything around you and steady on your fine animal feet, you wash your own socks and eat a quarter of a loaf of bread and three walnuts for lunch, you talk dirty and laugh to yourself, you've never looked at a painting or loved a girl, you swear like a trooper and spit on the ground, but look at you now while we, the rest of us, watch you silently as though by the roadside, you alone Ianchelevici Şapsă, dispirited, sullen and starved though you are – you alone are singing.

*

I'd gone to the rector's office to ask something. On returning, the vestibule – empty ten minutes before – had been invaded. I didn't recognize anybody. But it had all the makings of a nasty fight.

So – I'm trapped. I'm noticed by somebody, or so it seems to me. I go up the stairs three steps at a time, slam behind me various doors, hit walls as I veer left and right. On to the second floor, then left, and I don't feel I can keep going much longer: I stick to the walls and with a trembling hand seek a door. In trepidation, I push a handle. It's open.

A small, uncomfortable classroom. Ten or twelve in attendance. A very young man is at the lectern: a student or assistant. He's talking. Probably it's a seminar.

My head is spinning and I don't know if I'm afraid of those outside or embarrassed before those inside. I have to do something to occupy myself and compose my nerves. I take out my pencil and pad: I make notes. Mechanically, absently, simply to behave coherently and get a grip on myself. I don't know what the man at the lectern is saying. I record like a stenographer, like a machine. Involved only in the motion of pencil on paper, indifferent to everything said, completely detached from what's going on.

And now, this evening, I find this strange piece of paper in my hand:

There is something profoundly artificial in the entire value system underpinning our lives. Not solely in political economy, where the stresses are visible and the evil easy to locate. Financial instability is the most obvious, though not the most acute, crisis of the old world. There are breakdowns that are even more serious, and even sadder agonies. We will understand nothing about the economic crisis we are studying if we get bogged down in technical details. These are secondary. Absolutely secondary. It's not a financial system that is collapsing today, but a historical system. A structure is being razed, not a handful of forms, facts and details. A crisis of concepts of value in economics and finance is not an isolated fact, as it partakes of a general crisis on all levels of modern life. We live with too many abstractions, too many illusions. We've lost the ground beneath our feet. It's not only the gold standard that has been lost, but any fixed relationship between our symbols and ourselves. There's a gulf between man and his context. These expressions that you see have become dehumanized. Or, perhaps more accurately, they have become inhuman.

Take any of our institutions, ideas, attitudes, skills or shortcomings, take them one at a time and sound them out. You will notice that they ring hollow. Life has fled from them, the spirit has left them. Why? I don't know why. The result, perhaps, of the abuse of intelligence. I'm not joking. We have made for ourselves a civilization based on intelligence as the basic value, and this is an expensive luxury and a terrible presumption. Between ourselves and life, we have posed ourselves as arbiters. That is a tragic conceit. We are nothing and it was Descartes who believed otherwise. See now how we pay the price, three hundred years later.

I fear the hour of the fools is upon us. Rather, I don't fear it at all. I'm glad. Because I have seen what intelligence has done and where it has taken us. Now we turn back, penitent, embittered and with three centuries of weariness, heading back into the forests of foolishness and real life.

You can call that obscurantism. All the better.

*

He's neither student nor assistant. He's a professor of political economy. This year he's teaching a course on 'the concept of value in the history of economic doctrines'. His name is Ghiță Blidaru. The boys just call him Ghiță. He's come from Munich or Berlin, I'm not sure which. He looks much younger than his thirty-five years. He has a long, drawn, asymmetrical face, with something shy in his smile and commanding, joined eyebrows. He speaks in an offhand drawl, interrupting himself at times with a 'no?' like a fiery full stop.

From today's lecture, a passage that was just a parenthesis:

To be logical? To be logical is not, as is stated in our books, to think according to formulae and equations, but to think according to the essential nature of things. If you really require a definition, try this one: logic is the systemization of intuition.

And laugh.

*

The lecture on Adam Smith:

If you were to ask me what we are doing here, in a class in which the parentheses are longer than the treatment given to the subject of the course, I might respond as follows: we are disposing of values. Clearing them away like dead wood. Intelligence, individualism, free choice, positivism . . . And we are looking for a single 'value', one that contains them all. That is called, if I am not mistaken, life.

*

Mondays and Fridays, from six to seven, Blidaru's course. We're a small group of regulars, and we know each other but don't talk. Sometimes, a new figure appears and takes a seat at the back. I like to look around from time to time and observe, as the lecture progresses, the growing surprise on the face of the new arrival.

*

He spoke today of the superiority of the physiocrats over all the modern schools of economic thinking. Too broad for me to transcribe my course notes here. He spoke stridently, aggressively, with sudden twists in the movement of the argument. (The effect is that of an intelligent agitator working a crowd.) We were waiting, intrigued, for the denouement – when a military march struck up outside our window. A passing company with its colours.

He jumped from the lectern, sprang towards the window, opened it and stood there watching, nodding his head to the rhythm of the big drum.

He then turned to us.

'Isn't the street wonderful?'

*

The third lecture on the physiocrats. Blidaru's course rearranges hierarchies with the greatest of ease. Only a couple of words on what the textbook considers sacrosanct, then ten furious lectures on what the textbook despises most.

There is an element in physiocrat economics which is more powerful than any of their naiveties. Of course, those old men of 1750 had no idea of the mechanism by which goods circulated and what they imagined in this realm is romantic and fantastic as well as false. But for all these errors, there remains one intuition worth incomparably more than any dry statistic. Their economics starts with the earth and returns to the earth. Behold a peasant idea, a simple idea of life, an idea that comes from nature, from the most natural everyday human intuitions. Nothing can demolish such a simple, clear truth.

Disoriented as we are, we will perhaps one day find the truth that returns us to the soil, simplifying everything and installing a new order. One not invented by us, but grown by us.

*

They're talking again of closing the university. The fighting has intensified. The faculty has been under military occupation for a week.

What remains is Ghiță Blidaru's course, hidden in that obscure room on the second floor, where nobody goes because nobody knows about it.

Evening. The dorms as silent as a snowy wasteland. From time to time, in the corridor, tired footfalls, a door closing, a cry that goes unanswered.

You can work well in this silence. I re-read an economic treatise with Ghiță's notes in my hand. An impassioned confrontation.

*

It's worrying. There were too many people at the lecture. Strange hostile faces in the front rows.

Blidaru, brilliant. Success is ultimately achievable, perhaps. But if things don't work out? We'll see.

No, this is one thing I won't give up. I've left civil law, left the aesthetics course, left and will leave any course you want, history, sociology, Chinese or German, but I will not give up Ghiță Blidaru's course.

I received two punches during today's lectures and I took eight pages of notes. Good value, for two punches.

Some of them stopped me at the door.

'Student ID.'

It would have been stupid to present it. I tried to rush past them. They knocked me to the wall with a single blow. I watch them from the corner into which they have pushed me. The door was ajar. Laughter, voices, shouts from one bench to another could be heard. Five minutes to six. Ghiţă will enter now. If I could get in too . . . If I go to those idiots at the door and talk to them, perhaps they'll understand. Good God, a seat in the back row . . . It's hardly too much to ask . . . No, that's an idiotic idea . . . Silence. Then applause. He's entered, surely. The door closes. One of them, the only one who has remained to guard the lecture hall, stares at me.

'What's up, pal?'

'What's up? I'm terribly ashamed of you and the others, I feel a head taller than you, because you'll never know the sad pride of defeat, alone against ten thousand. And I'm going to see Ghiţă Blidaru and I'm going to talk to him.'

*

I can't re-create the scene. I'm powerless to remember it all now. It was brusque. Just two or three words and a puzzled glance.

Ghiţă was leaving the secretariat. I went up and spoke to him. I don't know what I said. I swear I don't, and that this isn't a ruse to spare myself one more moment of self-disgust.

He interrupted me.

'Young man, what do you want?'

'Professor, they threw me out and . . .'

'Well, and what do you want me to do about it?'

He walked off without waiting for a reply.

I should run for hours through the streets, or chop up a wagonload of barrels with a hatchet, to collapse in my bed in the evening and sleep and forget.

*

Third night playing poker. We played in the library, around a candle, until three or four in the morning.

Yesterday I won 216 lei and then treated everyone to some girls, where we went in two at a time.

Ionel Bercovici kissed me. 'Hey, and we all thought you were stuck up.'

A disgusting dive. That vinegary white wine is really pretty awful. The first few glasses make you wince. Then in the end it works.

It goes on until late in the night. At The Cross, at Mizzi's, that whore from Cernăuți, who for an extra 10 lei will do anything.

We walked between bayonets all day. There was a small group of us downstairs, at the secretary's office, when compact bands arrived from the faculty of medicine. We were surrounded on all sides and only got out between a line of police two-deep. They escorted us through the streets like that, closely followed. We changed direction several times, hurried on, ducking into courtyards in the hope of shaking them off. Until nightfall. Until now.

If it weren't for the consolation of the bitter-tasting nights of gambling, the dizzy pleasure of poker, what would life be?

Then there's another matter. The voluptuousness of being dirty, your secret pride in letting yourself go. Today you give up brushing off your hat, tomorrow you don't change your shirt, the day after you don't repair your worn-out heels. To sink down deeply, irrevocably in filth and to love it for its dirtiness, for its familiar smell, for its dry crusts of bread, for the intimate warmth of humiliation. And to know that you are once and for all rudderless, that control slipped from your hands one morning when you didn't change your collar, because you couldn't be bothered.

Haven't they always told us we're a dirty people? Maybe it's true. Perhaps our mysticism, our asceticism, our piety is just that – dirtiness. A way of getting down on your knees, a form of slow, voluptuous self-mutilation, ever further from the white star of purity.

★

This morning, in the yard of the dormitory blocks, Marga Stern said to me, awkwardly, as if the news had nothing to do with me:

'Look, spring is on its way.'

I fled. Two weeks ago, on a day when I told myself I had to choose between being the fourth hand at poker or living. I fled, and I'm glad, because it was hard.

It's a small room. A garret. But it's mine. A chair, a table, a bed. Four white walls and a high window, through which the tops of the trees in Cişmigiu Park can be seen.

The formula is simple and I wonder why I didn't discover it earlier.

Two thousand lei per month: 1,000 for the room, 300 lei for thirty loaves of bread, 300 lei for thirty litres of milk, 400 lei remainder.

I'm going to write to Mama asking her to embroider a handkerchief with the motto I've discovered: LIFE IS SIMPLE!

Fourteen days on my own. I'd like to know exactly how many people in this city, in the wide world, are freer than me.

I found a superb Montaigne for 60 lei in a second-hand bookshop, from 1760, with fine matt paper and amazing footnotes. Impassioned. The more impassioned he is, the more of a libertine, sceptic and artist he is. Me? I'm just tortured.

What a break. And I never, ever guessed, fool that I am, that such a holiday were possible.

I've put up a big map of Europe on the wall facing the bed. I need a globe but I haven't enough money.

Maybe it's childish, but I need to draw upon the symbolism of this map and to read off the cities and countries on it. It's a daily reminder of the world's existence. And that every kind of escape is possible.

*

It was beautiful just now in Cişmigiu, with that white metallic sun, the water green with vegetation, the still leafless trees, naked like a herd of adolescents drafted into the army.

People are so ugly in their out-of-season coats, their hats worn out from winter, with their sun-scared smiles and heavy, trudging steps. I watched how they passed and pitied them their graceless lack of awareness.

*

A young, smartly dressed girl stopped on the boulevard in front of the window of a fruit shop. I said the first nonsense that entered my head. She laughed and agreed to walk with me.

She didn't ask where I was taking her. She ascended the stairs, and undressed readily once the door was closed. A small body, pleasant rather than beautiful, very young. We made love in the middle of the day, the window open, both of us naked. The girl cried from pleasure and afterwards walked through my bedroom with my clothes over her shoulders, curious, looking through the papers on the desk, opening books, closing them loudly.

'Will you come here again?'

'I will.'

She didn't ask me for anything. I forgot to ask her name.

The pleasure of being naked. Feeling yourself recovering your animal poise, to feel it concretely and bodily, hearing the sure surge of your blood, knowing the voluptuousness of lifting an arm and letting it fall, having a sure sense of your solitary physical life.

This should be inscribed in the eulogy of love.

*

A curious meeting with Ştefan D. Pârlea. It was he who stopped me. I wouldn't have dared, though I retain a dram of affection for him since high school, without really knowing why.

A bony, hard, scowling fellow, with a mighty handshake, the eyes of a vulture, a virile ugliness that is almost a form of beauty.

'Hey, look, the sun is shining . . .'

We wandered about together, through various neighbourhoods, finding it odd not to come across our old familiar Danube. He told me what was going on at Blidaru's course, which he too discovered some time ago.

We talked a lot, about a thousand things, about books, memories, women. We stopped at a bakery, past the end of the bridge, to buy sesame pretzels. We ate in the street though people looked at us.

'You know, Pârlea, we could be friends, if we weren't divided by so much nonsense.'

'No. You're wrong. The pair of us can't be friends. Not now or ever. Don't you get the smell of the land off me?'

There was something absurd and terrible in his eyes.

Don't you get the smell of the land off me? Yes, indeed I get it. And I envy you for it.

I have an immense longing for simplicity and unawareness. If I could rediscover some strong, simple feelings from somewhere centuries back – hunger, thirst, cold – if I could overcome two thousand years of Talmudism and melancholy, and recover – supposing one of my race has ever had it – the clear joy of life . . .

But happiness, for me, is a strange, tumultuous feeling, composed of endless evasions, always in danger of collapse.

I was happy three days ago. Today I'm depressed. What happened? Nothing. An inner crutch slipped. Some poorly suppressed memory rose to the surface.

At twenty years of age, healthy and without any personal handicaps, I feel that I have been destined to be divided in ten parts and negated in each of them.

No, we're not an easy-going people. I am so ill at ease in my own company: how badly another person must feel being with me. We're impulsive. We're more than we can deal with. And on top of that, we're impure.

We: meaning me. Ianchelevici Şapsă. Marcel Winder.

He smells of the land, lucky man.

I regret that, in this internal conflict, I retain some sympathy for myself. I'm sorry I catch myself loving my destiny. I'd like to hate myself, without excuses or forgiveness. I'd like to be an anti-Semite for five minutes. To feel an enemy in myself who must be vanquished.

*

The girl from a week ago came. I didn't invite her in.

'Didn't you ask me to come?'

'Yes. And now I'm asking you to leave.'

Something tells me that we are unable to live any of life's moments fully. Not one of them. That we eternally stand at a remove from what is happening. A little above or a little below things, but never at their heart. That we don't experience feelings or events fully, and then we drag these unresolved matters after ourselves. That we have never been complete villains or complete angels. That the fires we lit to offer up our hearts smouldered out too soon. That we have lived through an eternal compromise between fortune and misfortune.

*

It's better this way, working fourteen hours a day. The exam is just an excuse. But I feel good in this prison of books, into which nothing penetrates from without or within.

I could have done with a dose of typhoid just now. Maybe this exam will be a substitute. The important thing is to forget myself, to have an exhausting, mechanical activity that absorbs me completely, and to hell with the world's problems.

Marga Stern has paid a friendly visit to my garret. She was wearing a red dress, and her hand was warm and calm and she playfully placed it on my brow.

Not quite a seduction, dear girl.

*

Marcu Klein, you're an ass, and if I had you in front of me I'd embrace you and then box your ears mightily four times so you wouldn't forget.

You weren't on your own. There were between forty to sixty of us with you, awaiting the civil law exam. From eight in the morning, from when we were called, until eleven in the evening, when Mormorocea, the professor, finally entered. He was clearly drunk and half asleep. We all saw it, just as you did, you smart-ass. We were all tired from that long, wasted day. But we took our places submissively, and perhaps a little disgusted. And you clenched your fists and continued frowning.

The professor mumbled a question and nodded off. The boy beside you answered clearly and very precisely. When he finished, there was a moment of silence. Mormorocea grunted, annoyed that the silence had disturbed his sleep.

'You haven't learned anything. Next one!'

You were 'the next one'. You stood up. I closed my eyes, because I knew – do you hear? – I knew what was going to happen.

'Professor, this is disgraceful.'

Why, Marcu Klein, could you not have kept quiet? Who pushed you, you lunatic, alone among forty, to speak for everybody, to condemn and avenge? What absurd need to denounce injustice inspires you to cry out? From what ancestral education in humiliation and revolt? What perverted instinct requires you to stop and investigate unpleasantness, instead of passing by? Do you not know how little it takes for people to turn against you? I'm furious with you because I can't hate you enough and because I, along with you, belong to a race that can't accept things and shut up.

*

Telegram to Mama: 'Passed exams. Happy.' Happy? I don't know. All I know is that at home, on the right bank of the Danube, there are twenty metres of warm sand and, before me, an entire river to swim in.

PART TWO

PART TWO.

November, the most beautiful month! Walking the streets, enveloped in a general lazy drizzle, shut off from the details around you, rendered impermeable, alone ... You leave home with a pipe and your thoughts and walk the streets for hours, seeing nobody, stumbling into people, trees and shop windows, arriving home late, like a ship to port.

My time of the year, November. The month when I re-read books, leaf through papers, gather notes. It's a kind of hunger for work, for activity, for taking up all the old tasks once again.

And that damp organic smell in the morning when I go out – and the warm halos of lamplight in the evening when I return ...

*

In a bookshop, where I'd entered to browse the magazines.

Somebody slaps my back. I turn around. Ghiță Blidaru.

'You missed the opening lecture ...'

I'm surprised, or very happy, or afraid of saying something impertinent. In any case, I say nothing.

'Why don't you pay me a visit? Look, Thursday evening, half past four, my place. What do you say?'

He bids me farewell with a comradely tip of the hat and leaves.

*

He has three rooms full of books and an empty fourth one where he sleeps: a simple bed, almost a camp-bed – and nothing else. On the wall by the door, a neat reproduction of a winter scene by Brueghel.

Almost half the front wall is taken up by an immense rectangular window made of a thick pane, more crystal than glass.

It's a bare, stark, frugal interior, yet it has an inexplicable air of intimacy, even warmth.

I'm so intimidated I can hardly move. Behold this man, whom I loved and envied. He has become enveloped in so many layers of legend in the past year, since that first evening I heard him, above in the university.

Here he is, his assured lordly demeanour, his rough joined eye-brows, his languid but commanding hand, here in this house that is just like him in its clean lines, its total precision, the starkness of its every detail. In a dressing gown, a wool scarf around his neck, his head inclined slightly towards the lamplight shining from the right, there is something monastic in his bearing, and in his frown, now softened a little by a smile smouldering in shadow.

I listen to him with a certain panic. Panic that he might fall silent at any moment and that I will be required to speak. And about what? Good God, what could I possibly say in response? And how would I say it? The pressure of his presence unnerves me more than it gladdens me, though I know it makes me very happy indeed.

Has he perceived something of my panic? He rises and fetches his pipe-tobacco, lights up, then goes to the window and stares out, as if watching for something in the fading evening.

*

I'd rather not see him again. I feel ashamed. Seldom have I been so utterly stupid and dull. My intelligence! A certain youthful attitude of mind, that's all it amounts to. And when you don't even have that, nothing is left. How else can my total vacuity yesterday be excused? Two hours of conversation, two hours of me being silent. I partici-pated with 'yes' and 'no' in a conversation from which I had wanted everything. I don't know what I mean by 'everything', but I must mean a lot by it, because I feel so acutely that I completely wasted my visit to Blidaru's home.

*

On Monday he spoke at the Foundation, as part of the Social Institute's series of lectures. There was no risk of me being seen in that immense crowd, in my seat in the second balcony.

What charm and simplicity the man has. His style is terse and angular, rough and digressive. He throws out a word, opens a secret door, kicks a stone he's picked up along the way. Spontaneously, and somehow trusting all to hazard. And then, when the hour is up, and you look despairingly at the field of thought that has been devastated, suddenly – I couldn't tell you how – matters begin to resolve themselves. The disconnected ideas strewn about over three-quarters of an hour return home in the final quarter, clear, quiet, necessary, utterly compelling, and completing a cycle of reasoning as though it were a symphonic arrangement.

I will understand later, when I'm older, what kind of a thinker Blidaru is. But I already know he is a great artist.

*

He caught up with me in the lecture hall as I was leaving and took my arm in a simple, friendly fashion.

'Let's take a stroll.'

I walked with him as far as his home, and several times along the way tried to talk to him. But it wouldn't come. His fault this time rather than mine, though, as he wasn't in a mood for chatting. He just wanted to walk, hands in the pockets of his long raincoat, hat over his eyes and his nose in the air, taking in the smell of rain and wet trees – the smell of the last days of November.

I walked nervously beside him, eager to cut through his small-talk to interject the questions I wanted to ask, the things I didn't clearly understand but which seemed so compelling. Several times I tried to start a sentence and gave up. Several times I formulated one in my mind but was unable to take it anywhere.

He must have sensed how worked up I was there, to his right, tongue-tied yet bursting to speak, because he suddenly halted in the light of a shop window and looked straight at me, in surprise.

'What's wrong with you?'

'Professor, what I want to say is . . .'

But I did not continue.

'I know what you want to say. You want to say it all. Which is the simplest and the most complicated thing in the world. Forget it. What's the hurry? There's none, believe me. We wanted to take a walk: so let's walk. We'll talk another time, when it occurs. Only those things that "happen" are worthwhile.'

He gave me a cigarette, took my arm and led me onwards, changing the subject.

2

The university was closed the day before yesterday, 9 December, in anticipation of the 10th. Quiet days, however: the occasional scuffle and an unremarkable street demonstration.

In any case, things have settled down. I've re-read, from the green notebook, the page from this day last year.

How young I was! Someday I'll manage to accept hurt without it affecting my personal calm in the slightest. Perhaps this is the only way to be strong. Anyhow, probably many blows lie in store for me.

I ask myself if fleeing from the dorms and my fellow students, even for this rough sort of life I lead, was in fact an act of courage or one of cowardice.

I ask myself if I have the right, for the sake of my solitude, to laugh at the cheap heroism of Marcel Winder, who still today luxuriates in enumerating the beatings he gets. Though he goes off at the mouth and I restrain myself, the fact remains that he's the one facing adversity while I turn my back on it. My way might be more elegant, but is it fair?

And don't forget Liebovici Isodor, still out there on the front line, patient and silent, inexpressive, without illusions or vanity.

A visit to the dorms. Black, black misery. Nothing has changed here. The same stoves, either cold or smoking, the same long rooms with their cracked cement, the same people. A few new faces – first-year boys.

Liova is gone. He died over the summer. He was somehow made for death, that boy, and seems to me to have fulfilled his destiny through tuberculosis in the same way others fulfil theirs by writing a book, building a house or completing their work. I talked to our old dorm-mates from last year about him. Nobody had much to say.

'He had these yellow boots, nearly new, that he left here when he went away,' said Ianchelevici Şapsă. 'But they're no good: too small.'

Liova, poor boy, your death did not even do that small good.

This building, despite being warmly called a 'shelter', is strangely apathetic, horribly icy . . . And yet several hundred young people live here. And only one room is alive, bustling, and breathing passion: 'the social issues room'. That's what they call it, with irony, because Winkler, the old medical student, has his bed here. Winkler has been kept from his exams by Zionism and by S.T. Haim, a mathematics student at the polytechnic and a fiercely argumentative Marxist.

The pair of them quarrel endlessly.

'I'm going to report you both,' shouts Ionel Bercovici, despairing of ever getting to the end of a page on constitutional law.

'Idiot,' replies S.T.H. (who is referred to by his initials, for some reason), 'you want us to hold back the march of history until you've passed your exam?'

Neither Winkler nor S.T.H. can have a very good opinion of me. They regard me as an outsider. At any event, they felt I was a fence-sitter, someone who observed in passing, neutrally. I listened quietly in a corner to their confused disagreement without intervening, enduring stubbornly the hard, flashing glances they shot at me over their shoulders.

'Dilettantes, that's what you are,' shouts S.T.H., 'dilettantes in all you do, in all you feel or think you feel. Dilettantes in love, when you think you're making love, dilettantes in science when you dabble in science, dilettantes in poverty, when you live in poverty. Nothing is seen through to its conclusion. Nothing heroic. Nothing unto the death. Everything for a cautious, compromised life. And you call yourself a Zionist, but you haven't a clue if there really is a land called Zion. I don't believe in it, you do. So why don't you actually go there, set foot on that land? You sit here agitating, which consists in cutting out receipts for membership fees for ten thousand people as smart as you are, and they too reduce a drama to a membership card.'

'And you?' asks Winkler, ever calm.

'Me? I'm here, where I should be. Wherever I am, that's where I should be, because I'm serving the revolution. By the simple fact that I exist, the simple fact that I think. My every word is a protest, my every silence is a shout rising above your receipt-books and your smile . . .'

And he suddenly turns to me, pointing an accusatory finger, putting an end to my quiet corner, because my reserve clearly irritates him and because, in the end, he can't stand the presence of an additional person who is neither friend nor foe – who is simply paying attention. S.T.H. needs an audience, an adversary, to feel he's up against something.

Now, having issued the challenge, he waits for me to take it up, his eyes flashing cold fire. Fire 'from the head', I'm sure, and not from the heart. He's tense as a folded razor, trembling in anticipation of being unsheathed. But I meet his gaze, and return it, though I feel it burning, and keep quiet. I let the silence grow, until it must shatter under its own weight.

He awaits a gesture, a sign, the start of a reply, something that will let him explode without being silly, but I'm determined not to help him out in any way, and all his violence, all his fury, is vain, useless.

But S.T.H. does not lose the match. Anybody else in his situation would have, but not him. He shakes off a lingering frown, passes his hand over his head, steps towards me and, in a tone that is surprisingly melodious and friendly after his previous vehemence, says:

'Won't you join me at the pictures this evening?'

S.T. Haim, my good friend, how well we play our roles, and how sadly.

*

I took my leave of S.T.H. last night and at seven-thirty this morning he was knocking on my door (when did he sleep? when did he get up?) so that I'd see the message he'd slipped under it . . . Then I heard him stomping down the stairs.

I wish to disturb you. Your complacency horrifies me. Montaigne, of whom you spoke last night, is heresy. Stendhal, a frivolity. If that's all it takes for you to sleep peacefully, all the worse for you. I wish you long, dark periods of insomnia.

'I wish to disturb you.' If he's taken that from Gide, he's ridiculous. If he came up with it himself, he's doubly so.

S.T. Haim, charged by destiny to summon me to my duty! S.T. Haim, called to shake me up and to remind me of the tragedies I've run from, Montaigne under my arm!

The messianic impulse and psychological insight are incompatible. S.T.H. is a missionary with no notion of what is going on in the people around him.

He wishes to disturb me. And I'd like to find a stone on which to lay my head.

Had I a sense of mission like his, I would do my best to bring calm to the situations and consciences around me. And most of all to that of S.T.H., who is a weary lunatic, a child under the spell of illusions.

'S.T. Haim,' I would say to him, 'you're worn out. Stop, sit still for an hour. Look around. Touch this and observe that it's a bit of stone. Hold this in your hand and know it's a piece of wood. Look, a horse, a table, a hat.

'Believe in these things, live with them, get used to regarding them normally, without looking for shimmering phantoms in them. Return to these sure, simple things, resign yourself to living with them, with their low horizons, in their modest families. And look around, entrust yourself to the seasons, to hunger, to thirst: life will get along fine with you, as it calmly does with a tree, or an animal.'

But who will say these same things to me? And who will teach me how to teach the others?

*

Let's presume that the hostility of anti-Semites is, in the end, endurable. But how do we proceed with our own, internal, conflict?

One day – who knows – we may make peace with the anti-Semites. But when will we make peace with ourselves?

*

It's not easy to spend days or weeks running from yourself, but it can be done. You get into mathematics and Marxism like S.T.H., become a Zionist like Winkler, read books as I do, chase women. Or play chess, or else beat your head against a wall. But one day, in a careless moment, your own heart will be revealed to itself, as though you had turned a corner and collided with a creditor you had sought to avoid. You behold yourself and perceive your vain evasions in this prison without walls, doors or bars – this prison that is your life.

You can never be vigilant enough. Some are better at pretending than others. Some keep it up for years, others for just a few hours! It ends for all in an inevitable reversion to sadness, like returning to the earth.

For some reason, after so many years, last night I was remembering my grandfather on my mother's side. I see him at his work-table, among thousands of springs, screws, cogs, and the faces and hands of watches. I see him leaning over them, a watchmaker's monocle clamped as always in the socket of his right eye, an exacting master casting spells with his long-fingered hands over the world of mechanical wonders he ruled, putting it in motion.

On that monstrous table, which as a child I was forbidden to go near (a missing cog meant the onset of chaos), he organized tiny autonomous worlds, tiny abstract entities from those minuscule dots of metal, which came together as a precise, strict, ordered harmony of hundreds of rhythmic voices in fine, ticking music. Under the glass of every watch-face lay a planet with its own discrete life, indifferent to what went on beyond it, and the glass seemed specially made to separate it from that 'beyond'.

Though I sensed he was restless, the old man was truly enviable for the peace he enjoyed among the metal beings his hand created. He lived under their spell for hours, days, years. Yet his craft was surely also an escape, a refuge. And perhaps he ran from himself, and was in terror that he would never encounter his true self.

And so, in the evening, when darkness fell and he had risen suddenly from the workbench over which he had sat silently all day, there was no pause, no restful smile on the face that gentle man. He was always hurrying. Why was he hurrying? Where was he hurrying to?

He would get his hat and coat and walking stick, say something in passing and hurry into the street, leaving the door open, and to the synagogue across the road. There he would rush about with the same harried air, shaking hands here and there, and finally come to a stop before his prayer stand. There he would recover his composure, leaning over an open book, as tensed and silent as he was before the tiny wheels of a clock. Many times I watched him there, reading. He seemed immersed in confecting more tiny mechanisms, and the letters in the book – terribly small – looked like more tiny parts to be organized by his eye, to be called forth from nothingness, from stillness. At home were clocks, here were ideas, and both were abstract, cold and exact, subject to the will of a man trying to forget himself. Did he succeed? I don't know. His face was at times illuminated from beyond, in expectation of what – or despairing of what – I am unable to say.

At least sixty years of life and twenty of death separate us. Even more – many more. He lived in the Middle Ages and I live today. We are separated by centuries. I don't read the books he read or believe the things he believed in, I am surrounded by different people and have other preoccupations. And yet today I feel I am his grandson, his direct descendant, heir to his incurable melancholy.

*

Why do we, who rebel against ourselves so often, for so many reasons, never revolt against our taste for catastrophe, against our kinship with pain?

There is an eternal amity between us and the fact of suffering, and more than once, in my most lamentable moments, I have been surprised to recognize the mark of pride in this suffering, the indulging of a vague vanity. There is perhaps something tragic in this, but to the same degree it also shows an inclination for theatricality. Indeed, in the very hour when I am deeply sad I sense, subconsciously, the metaphysical tenor of my soul taking the stage.

Perhaps I'm bad to think this way, but I will never be sufficiently tough with myself, will never strike myself hard enough.

*

I would criticize anti-Semitism above all, were it to permit me to judge it, for its lack of imagination: 'freemasonry, usury, ritual killing'.

Is that all? How paltry!

The most basic Jewish conscience, the most commonplace Jewish intelligence, will find within itself much graver sins, an immeasurably deeper darkness, incomparably more shattering catastrophes.

All they have to use against us are stones, and sometimes guns. In our eternal struggle with ourselves, we have a subtle, slow-working but irremediable vitriol in our own hearts.

I can well understand why a renegade Jew is more ferocious than any other kind of renegade. The harder he tries to shake his shadow, the tighter it sticks. Even in disowning his race, the very fact of his apostasy is a Judaic act, as we all, inwardly, renounce ourselves a thousand times, yet always go back home, with the wilfulness of one who desires to be God himself.

*

I'm certainly not a believer and the matter doesn't concern me, doesn't really trouble me.

I don't attempt to be rigorous in this regard and acknowledge quite frankly the inconsistencies. I can know, or say, that God does not exist, and recall with pleasure the physics and chemistry textbooks from school that gave him no place in the Universe. That doesn't prevent me from praying when I receive bad news or wish to avert it. It's a familiar God, to whom I offer up sacrifices from time to time, under a cult of rules established by me and – I believe – corroborated by him. I suggest typhus for myself, instead of a flu He was thinking of sending to somebody dear to me. I indicate certain ways in which I would prefer him to smite me or show me mercy. Anyway, I cede to him much more than I retain, as what I give him comes from myself, but what I retain belongs to the others, the very few others, that I love.

And I doubt our conversation troubles him, as He doesn't quite see it as a transaction and is aware of the good intentions with which I approach him.

All the same ... Sometimes I feel there is something more, beyond that: the God with whom I have seen old men in synagogues struggling, the God for whom I beat my breast, long ago, as a child, that God whose singularity I proclaimed every morning, reciting my prayers.

'God is one, and there is only one God.'

Does not 'God is one' mean that God is alone? Alone like us, perhaps, who receive our loneliness from him and for him bear it.

This clarifies so many things and obscures so many more ...

3

·A long conversation with Ghiță Blidaru. In the end I told him 'every-thing', that same everything I feared and which he had intuited at a glance. All I've been thinking about lately, everything written in the notebook, all I haven't written . . .

I spoke impulsively, quickly, and a great deal, in fits and starts, jumping from one subject to another, doubling back. I expressed myself badly, in my nervous disorder. But he has a way of listening that seems to simplify your own thoughts, however poorly you express them. His mere presence creates order around him.

'You should do something that connects you to the soil. I still don't really know what. Not law anyway, or philosophy, or econom-ics. Something to give you back your feel for matter, if you've ever had one, or that'll start to teach you, if you never have. A craft based on certitudes.'

I shrugged, despairing of such a vague solution. And, anyway, had I really been seeking a solution?

But he continued:

'Can you draw?'

'Yes.'

'Can you draw well?'

'I'm pretty bad at what they call "artistic drawing" at school. Quite good at technical drawing.'

'How are you at maths?'

'I don't love it. I was good at it at school, though unenthusiastic.'

I had no idea what he was getting at and replied more in puzzle-ment than from curiosity. What happened next was astonishing.

'Why don't you become an architect?'

I said nothing. Is he joking? Performing some kind of experiment? Attempting to demonstrate to me how vain my 'problems' are? Setting me up somehow?

Perplexed, I keep quiet – and he doesn't press it, and immediately changes the subject, leaving open the possibility that we will return to it.

'Anyway, think it over seriously. It's worth it.'

*

I'm very well aware that the professor's proposal is full of risks. I've never been overly concerned about my 'career' as I'm convinced that I will always be poor and accept that with good grace – and yet, though what he proposes I do is not exactly an adventure, it certainly is imprudent . . . Are the psychological motives impelling me to take such a leap really strong enough for me to carry it through?

I'm confused and can hardly believe that he has created these difficulties for me out of the blue.

*

'Changing tack.' Old emotional bonds that I can't break. In the end, what he's asking me to do is quite easy. I had settled on the idea of becoming a lawyer. Why? I don't know. From habit, from being tired of choosing, from lack of interest in a profession – any profession.

With a little effort, I could get used to seeing myself as an architect. A simple matter of mental training.

I wouldn't have done anything great in a courtroom, and I won't do anything great on a construction site. But it might not be impossible for me to find there what I certainly would have missed out on: the feeling of serving earth, stone and iron.

It should give me a feeling of fulfilment, of calm. Perhaps the tranquillity I've been looking for.

*

No, I can't do it. I have exams coming up, classes, papers – too much for me to throw it all aside and start anew yet again.

I went to tell Ghiță my decision, but didn't find him home, which I was glad of, I have to admit, because, however determined I was to reject his proposal, I was sorry to eliminate all other options with a categorical response. *Il faut qu'une porte soit ouverte ou fermée.*

I didn't find him home, and so I allowed myself to keep the door half-open.

*

I'll do it anyway. I lacked the courage to utter a straight 'No', and I put forward all kinds of objections. He disposed of them, one by one.

Isn't it too late now, in the middle of December, two months after registration?

No, it's not. He'd take care of it personally. He has good friends in Architecture and can manage it.

Won't it be too hard for me to catch up with the syllabus? Aren't the classes too far advanced? Aren't the exams too near?

No, it won't be hard. But if it is hard, all the better.

The matter settled, there was nothing left for me to say. I belong to architecture. He shook my hand heartily.

'You know, I'm pleased we did this. You'll learn to tread solid ground. Very important in life. You'll see.'

4

Yesterday's encounter in the train seems the more miraculous the more I think about it. That short, lively man with darting eyes who twitched oddly when he spoke, as though in the midst of an unsettled dream – that man loaded with parcels in the corner of the third-class compartment – was Ahasverus himself.

As soon as he came through the door, preceded by two suitcases and followed by some three more, and innumerable packages large and small, badly wrapped in tattered newspaper, I felt a sudden rage towards him.

'Just what I need!' I'd just been congratulating myself on finding such a good seat, on such a day, in the Christmas holiday rush, in a train overrun by students and soldiers heading for the provinces, and behold our Jewish friend, dragging an entire household behind him, opening the door wide to let in the cold air, pushing my suitcase aside, stepping on my toes, flinging his overcoat over mine and then pressing his way on to the bench between myself and my neighbour, begging pardon with his eyes, though no less tenacious for that in his determination to secure a seat, as guaranteed by his ticket, which he held ostentatiously between his fingers.

Everyone smiled at this comical apparition, and I tried to do the same myself, which took a certain effort, as I pitied him for being ridiculous and was at the same time deeply anxious not to appear friendly to him. I can't say exactly why, but I felt a strange sense of complicity, which I had an urgent desire to renege upon. I hurriedly sought my diary and acted busy with calculations, suddenly absent from all that was going on beside me. But I monitored my unfortunate neighbour from the corner of my eye.

He had calmed down, secure in the seat he'd occupied, shooting timid glances of gratitude about, carefully assessing each of his fellow-travellers and finally stopping on me. He was still not entirely sure of me, yet offered me the beginning of a cordial smile: a sign he had recognized me.

This suddenly infuriated me even more. It felt that this look, this sense of familiarity, identified me with him, with his silly appearance and awkward presence.

I raised my head and gave him a fierce stare, to make it clear I wanted nothing to do with him. I felt I would die of embarrassment if he spoke to me.

But my hostility didn't disarm him, and he continued to look at me, nodding his head and blinking frequently.

'No need to get upset, young fellow. The Jew is a man with baggage. Many troubles, and baggage to match.'

I immediately loved him for these words, and experienced such a wave of shame for how cowardly I had been, towards him and myself, that I felt a need to punish myself, good and proper.

I replied straight off with deliberately exaggerated eagerness, speaking loudly, in order to be heard by everyone in the compartment, so that they'd know that I wasn't ashamed of this odd old man, to acknowledge that we were friends, that his Jewish accent didn't bother me, that I wasn't bothered by his snow-laden boots, that his rude packages didn't trouble me, that, far from it, I was right at home with everything and had no idea why anyone would consider it comic or want to laugh.

The old man spoke Romanian correctly, with a slight Moldovan-Jewish inflection, so I too deliberately made myself speak with that questioning lilt that comes from Yiddish. This had never happened to me before, but I was determined to punish myself properly, to redeem my earlier cowardice.

I suppose my old Ahasverus understood the game I had fully entered into – his steady, indulgent smile hovered over me like a beam of light from a pocket torch.

'Forget all that,' his smile seemed to say, 'you don't have to do that on my account. I know you and know you're not as bad as you wanted to be a moment ago or as good as you're trying to be now. My journey is long and what do you want me to do with the stones you cast at me or the hands you extend? I, who have time neither to receive them nor respond to them since, well, somewhere out there, far, far away, someone is always waiting for me and I have to travel this path, though my journey may never end.'

He was smiling with this distrust, nodding his head, and I understood that indeed I could do nothing for him, and others could do nothing to him.

He told me his name was Abraham Sulitzer, which disappointed me, since for the symbol to be intact he would have had to have been openly called Ahasverus.

'What business are you in?' I asked him. 'What do you do?'

'What does a Jew do? I wander.'

He seemed to think that this reply was good enough.

Abraham Sulitzer wanders. That's his trade. He's a vendor of Jewish books. In the dozen suitcases, trunks and packages he drags about, he carries all kinds of books: Bibles, Talmuds, commentaries, Hasidic histories, stories from the ghetto, Hebrew poetry, Yiddish literature . . .

He's the link between German and Polish publishers and readers in the Moldovan ghettos. He knows every town in Bukovina where books are still studied seriously, all the Bessarabian households where serious thought is given to Talmudic texts, all the neighbourhood synagogues where a problem is still commented on according to Jewish thinking. He has an extensive mental catalogue of all the Jewish manuscripts and publications in the country, knows what town they're in, and which house. He could close his eyes and tell you exactly who possesses such and such a priceless copy of *Megillat Afa* by Shabbatai HaKohen, the Lithuanian, a book printed in Amsterdam in 1651. He thinks for a moment and tells you precisely which rabbi, from where, could clarify the great Talmudic dispute in Barcelona of 1240 or of Tortosa in 1413 . . .

He knows it all, has accumulated it all there behind that narrow forehead, behind those eyes that blink often and questioningly.

This is the first time I am hearing of these books, manuscripts, authors and issues, strange words, names from other centuries, dates from a history I never guessed at. Abraham Sulitzer carries it all with him, just as alive as it was centuries ago, in the mind of the person who wrote and pondered it. He lives in their presence, in their eternal passion, and it is of no account that hundreds of years have passed over these truths, that the face of the world has altered, and that so much time has melted to nothing: these old lights are still shining, these old passions are still burning.

And Abraham Sulitzer carries them everywhere, in the service of their eternal lives.

I bought from him a Yiddish Bible with photographs, for my grandmother, and a history in German by Şapsă Zwi, for myself. I had the impression that it was hard for him to let them go: he seemed to wonder if they were falling into the wrong hands.

*

A terrible snowstorm. In the morning I tried to go down to the Danube, having heard it had frozen over. I would have enjoyed crossing by foot to the far side, but it was impossible to get down to the docks. Great waves of snow were gusting up from the port and into the town.

I decided to have a family get-together. I gathered the grandmothers – Grandmother and Grandma – around the terracotta stove.

Grandmother is Father's mother. Grandma is Mother's. Grandmother is about eighty-five, while I don't think Grandma is over seventy. She's younger and livelier: still proud, vain and coquettish.

She was very beautiful in her youth and she knew it. The glory of that time still remains in her clear blue eyes, along with a rather proud and mischievous glint.

She wears a hat of straw and silk, tries a dress on three times and tells the seamstress what she needs done. She frequently checks herself in the mirror and gives herself just a touch of powder when nobody is looking. As Grandfather was a watchmaker and jeweller, she has held on to big diamond earrings, a gold chain and a ruby bracelet from their time together.

She wears them all with an air of importance, clearly flattered at the memory of having been a beautiful woman.

Grandmother, on the other hand, has entered old age resigned to everything, without regrets or lingering vanity. For as long as I have known her, she has had the same simple, decorous black dress with ordinary buttons of bone. White-haired, tired, calm – she's a storybook grandmother. She speaks the rough country-Romanian of a Muntenian village. She was born here, in this town, in the period of the Russian protectorate and has lived her long life in this county. For years her father worked on an estate in Gropeni, managing the accounts, and later her husband, my paternal grandfather, worked in the port. She has lived in the company of the Danube. When I ask, and have time to listen, she tells of the wonders of the past century, about the city and the townsfolk, and about high society in those years. In particular, she talks about a ball, her first, which must have been a sensation in the life of the town. From a few details she has given me, I suppose it was in 1848, perhaps around the time of the Proclamation of Islaz. And so history and the chronicles of my family are intertwined.

There are some very strange aspects to our family tree. On father's side, there is at least a century of Romanian life, in town and country, living alongside Romanian neighbours, working with them, mingling with them. For how many tens of years we were here before, or how many hundreds, living as an isolated community, I do not know. But my great-grandfather's name appears clearly in the census of 1828. Certainly, we cannot speak of a process of assimilation, but I sense a certain resilience in this branch of my family, which must have something to do with the Danube since four consecutive generations have grown up beside it. That great-grandfather of 1828 – Mendel of Gropeni, as he was called – spoke and wrote Romanian, wore boots and a traditional Romanian waistcoat. As for my grandfather, I can still remember his strange look of a boatman when he returned in the evening from the docks. He wore heavy metal-studded boots, his hands were calloused, and he would be white from head to toe from the sacks of wheat and corn which he breathed his whole life, four-teen hours a day, from dawn to dusk. There was something rough and ready about him: something of a boatman, a cart-driver, a day-labourer. On the evenings of holy festivals he also read from some immense Hebrew books, but didn't read with the same trembling passion I sensed in the other grandfather, Mother's father. One was an intellectual, the other not, though he too was – they say – well read.

He lived in the fresh air, exposed to the wind, his feet upon rock and earth, gazing at a horizon saturated by pools of water, raising his voice above the rushing river, the sirens of the boats, the rattling of the hoists. A man of the Danube.

Mother's family, on the other hand, didn't leave the ghetto until much later. From Bukovina and northern Moldova, they were all people who lived indoors, in lamplight, over books. They have always lived close to the synagogue. From there perhaps they get their black eyes, their long thin hands, the pallor of their cheeks. Their delicate, easily disturbed constitutions are sustained more by their nerves than by bodily strength.

Bad news or a sleepless night or a tense wait devastates them immediately: black circles around the eyes, pale lips, hot cheeks. The toughness of Father's family seems like coarseness alongside this peculiar glasshouse sensitivity. This explains perhaps the deaf incom-prehension that has always divided them, the reckless from the deli-cate. What's vigour to one side is boorishness to the other. One side's sensitivity is the other's fussiness.

The divide between the Danube and the ghetto.

*

I keep thinking about that great-grandfather of 1828. He must have been born in the last decades of the eighteenth century. The French Revolution, the American Revolution, Napoleon ... Something about his existence strikes me as fabulous and I've tried, without much success, to discover details from some elderly aunts who knew him in his final years.

He was born here and lived here all his life. A lifetime working his fingers to the bone, almost an entire century.

One fine day – he was well past ninety – he gathered his things, convoked his children, shared out among them what there was to share, and kept for himself a few gold coins, a few books and maps, which he packed into a knapsack. He said he was leaving. Where to? To Eretz Israel! Home. With whom? Alone.

The idea of a 100-year-old man deciding to do such a thing seems so wild to me that I asked Grandmother a thousand questions to find out exactly what was at the root of this flight. The truth is that he wasn't running away. It was absolutely simple. The old man just woke up one morning with the idea – and that was it.

They implored him, tried to restrain him forcibly, struggled to make him at least accept an escort to Jaffa – one of his sons would have taken him there and found him a home – all in vain. He would not be swayed. He gave them all he had, put the little he retained on his back and went down to the docks, followed, like in a scene from the Bible, by his sons and daughters and grandchildren, all bewailing him, he alone calm, collected and at peace.

Wintry old man. He died in Jerusalem, a few months after arriving. Grandmother claims he appeared to her in a dream that night, in the white shroud of the dead, saying: 'Behold, I have died. You will bear a son and you will give him my name.'

That was in 1876. With that information, perhaps it would not be hard for us to find his gravestone someday, if he managed to be buried with one.

It's much more likely he lies in an unmarked grave, among other unmarked graves.

Nobody in the family has a photograph of the old man. He refused to partake of such foolishness. A short time before, a German had arrived in town with a complicated machine and installed himself on the corner of the main street. On his way to the docks, says Grandmother, the day he departed, they all stopped there and begged the old man to leave them that small reminder: a photograph. He shook his head, annoyed. No.

*

Had I the time, it would be revealing to trace my family's migrations on a map. It seems very few of them have moved away.

Though members of my family can be wild, crazy and unstable as individuals, as a group their spirit is slower, more sedentary and tenacious.

Some broke away, left, became lost. The roots remained here, though, their traditions undisturbed, in enduring unity against those who ran off.

I find it significant that our people form two compact groups – my father's side of the family here, in the bend of the Danube, and my mother's family up in northern Bukovina. There have been few migrations and even those have been within a very small radius. In any case, the family's centre of gravity remains constant in each person's consciousness, and it only requires a family event – a death, a birth, or some trouble – for everybody to come together, either in happiness or alarm, and fall back into line.

All of this makes the escapees all the harder to explain, however few and far between they've been.

I've heard speak of an uncle who as a youth ran off to Vienna in midwinter by sled, in the last century, after a woman. A vague love story and the only one, I think, in a family of people who are sensual but not passionate in such matters. I've also heard of a brother of Mother's who left for America in 1900. Somewhere in an old album is a photograph of him from that time: his young, almost adolescent face, the bold pioneer's forehead and, overlying everything, some kind of shadow, or light, foreboding the defeats that were to come.

He left with a few coins in his pocket and a head full of crazy ideas. 'A socialist,' whispered the gossips. A 'crazy kid' who wouldn't listen, growled Grandfather, who locked the boy out of the house at night when he loitered too late in town.

It seems that during those years many small groups of people set out from all around the country for Alaska and California, some looking for gold, others chasing mirages. Shortly before the war, the American legation sent a document with the news that he had died in a small town in Texas where he had somehow become a plantation worker.

*

I gave Grandma the illustrated Bible bought on the train from Abraham Sulitzer, and now she's reading aloud to me and to Grandmother, who didn't get a school education.

It's a fairly ordinary Yiddish translation, I think; a popular edition, from its appearance, on poor paper, with cheap woodcuts. Grandma reads with a certain air of superiority. For her, Grandmother and I are both illiterate, since all my French and German books don't compensate for my ignorance of her Bible.

We began properly, in the beginning, with 'Let there be light'. I listen to Grandma and the story becomes new to me, its appeal diaristic rather than biblical. Grandma reads avidly, visibly curious, turning the pages nervously and immersed in the delivery, as if it were about people she knew, neighbours or close relatives.

Sometimes, at decisive passages, she stops briefly, shakes her head and makes a sound of amazement, regret or tribulation with her tongue against the roof of her mouth (tsk, tsk) as if wanting to tell Abraham, Esther, Sarah or Jacob that they're being foolish or imprudent.

There's nothing ceremonious in the way Grandma reads. The Patriarchs don't intimidate her. They, too, are hard-working men with wives and children, with troubles and sorrows. And if she, my grandmother, can place her experience at their disposal, as an elderly woman who has seen and lived through so much, why shouldn't she?

Who knows? – perhaps such-and-such a patriarch has a sick child who needs to be rubbed with aromatic vinegar, or somebody has hurt a finger and needs some healing herbs, or whatever else. Or some biblical wife may need some lemon salt to put in the dinner, she's out of it and the shop is far away . . . It happens – it happens in life – why not in the Bible? . . .

*

A vast, white, crystalline morning. The north wind raged through the night, through the streets, against the windows, against the rooftops.

Now, everything is shocked-still and transparent, as though under an immense glass sphere. If you shout, you can be heard from one end of the street to another, or perhaps further, as far as the Danube.

I finally made it to the docks. The mountains of snow that yesterday were surging up at us now lie defeated, like wild beasts, their muzzles laid upon their paws. Giant shaggy white lions, soft-maned, reclining.

There is only light, as if in the heart of a frozen sun. Something abstract in this steady, shining silence.

Only the Danube is rough and disturbed. Choppy, ashen – there is something agonized about it, arrested in its onward tumble. You would say it had frozen wave by wave, each wave struggling and suffering in defeat.

There is nothing of my lively, hurried Danube of March in it, my leisurely, regal Danube of autumn. It's different, utterly different, deeper, more tumultuous, more silent.

5

We spend the afternoons in the workshop, drawing and modelling. It's difficult, I have to admit. But it is work I could learn to love, unlike the standard morning classes, which are all as mediocre here as at the law and philosophy faculties. This is why I always return with pleasure to modelling clay in the workshop. Of course, what I'm making is absolutely worthless, and I wonder if I will ever manage to achieve anything in this world of earth, stone and cement.

As a mental exercise, though, I've never found anything more calming than this game of modelling clay. It's a docile, malleable material with its own odd character and sometimes between my fingers I find a shape I hadn't sought; a gracefully leaning oval, a rough face with terse broken lines or some other wonder drawn from the reluctant, indifferent material, which hides so many facets within itself.

And meanwhile, with my hands busy, my mind absorbed by the small phenomenon happening before my eyes, I have a feeling of freedom such as I doubt I've ever had before, even in the best days of the holidays.

It's a form of detachment from myself, as distinct as a physical sensation.

In the evening, when I hang my overalls on the hook and wash my hands, everything seems to me clear and orderly, as it is in a simple, well-managed household.

Were I of a slightly more lyrical temperament, I'd write a hymn to tools, a song of praise for work. Fortunately, though, I'm sensitive enough to the ridiculousness of my inner enthusiasm to be aware how immature and amateurish it is. I have something of the naivety of a first-year medical student, ready to discover a cure for cancer. A real architect would probably laugh heartily, were he to read what I write here.

*

It seems Blidaru's last few lectures, from Christmas until today, have been impressive. 'This is no longer political economy,' I've heard the specialists cry in the chancellery of the faculty. They may be right. From what I've managed to find out from the professor himself, and from what others have told me, it seems that, strictly speaking, his course about currency is no longer an economics course, but rather one about the philosophy of culture.

My study schedule doesn't allow me even an hour on Thursday and Saturday, when Ghiță Blidaru has his lectures. Anyway, he has vowed, if he catches me there, to just throw me out: 'You've no business being at my course. Stay here where you are, and work. Full stop.'

*

I see him only occasionally, evenings, at his house, but when I do see him we stay up late, talking. I haven't yet discovered a good technique for conversing with him. There's so much I'd like to say and it is only with difficulty I manage to speak. Sometimes, at home or on the way to his place, I make a plan, studiously, of the things I should say to him, but, once I'm there with him, it all falls apart, as though he's one of those people who makes the rules for everybody else, obliging you to submit to their temper and style as well as to their arguments. There is so much passion in this subtly constructed man, he hides so many storms with self-control and his rigorous thinking. He is the only man to whom I have ever felt it necessary to submit myself, but I do it with a sense of fulfilment and reintegration rather than of surrender.

*

I asked him a few days ago if he thought architecture condemned me to overly specific concerns and limited me to a field of entirely professional problems. And if I wouldn't be distracted, whatever my job, by what seems to me paramount and essential; to be connected with the ferment of my times, sensitive to it, to its preoccupations and its general thrust.

'No,' he replied, 'you can't talk in terms of limitations. Architecture, medicine, music and economics are all planets in the same solar system. Whatever we're involved in or working at individually, we reach our conclusions using guiding principles which are common to us all. The various truths and ideas about life in any period compose an organic unity, like members of a family.

'It's naive to think that a revolution which starts in one place, in one discipline, stops there. History is made from within rather than without, from the centre rather than the periphery. Crudely, we only pick up on the immediate, visible changes that impinge upon our lives. As a result we imagine that a revolution is first and foremost a political or economic upheaval. This is blissful naivety. A revolution can begin in physics, economics, astronomy, mathematics or anywhere else. It's enough for something to be changed in the structure of a single thought or human life, because from that moment virtually everything is going to be changed. Everything in this world is connected; there are no isolated facts or preoccupations. Everything participates in a cycle. Why would you wish architecture to be absent from this chain? Relax and do your work there: whether you wish it or not, we'll meet up eventually, you practising architecture, me in political economy, someone else doing anthropology, someone else again doing algebra. The vehicles vary: the road is the same.'

*

One evening recently, returning from Ghiță Blidaru's, I recalled how brutal my first conversation with him had been. Conversation! If you could call it that. I'd stopped him to complain about being thrown out of his course. How smartly he brushed me off! He didn't even want to look straight at me. And today, remembering, I shudder with shame. How I suffered then. I spoke to him about that day and, though I feared he would see this as some kind of impudent reproach, I couldn't refrain from asking:

'Don't you want to tell me what happened then, why you were so abrupt, so cutting?'

'I don't know, I can't remember. Maybe I was bored, or upset. I don't recall. But, to tell you the truth, I'm not sorry. I've never liked being too amiable with people, even with those I'm fond of. Particularly not with them. I tell myself, out of a hundred times you prod a person, perhaps twice you'll get their attention usefully. When I walk through the grass, I don't watch out for the blades of grass or beetles getting walked on. The earth doesn't care for such delicate attentions. Stamp on and flatten all you want – after you've passed by the roots will continue growing, if they're roots. When you walk on the soil, walk on the soil. When you walk among people, walk among people. A little blindly. It doesn't matter. You'll knock over a few things – the weak ones. But you'll stimulate the others. Leaping before you look is an essential exercise. I haven't spared myself and I'm not going to spare anyone else, particularly not if I'm fond of them.'

It's a tonic. Grit your teeth and carry on.

6

I realize, leafing through this notebook (it never occurred to me before to re-read it until yesterday, when, looking for *Les Liaisons dangereuses* to give to Marga, I came across it and opened it with a certain curiosity, as though it were an unfamiliar book) – that I've written nothing about her, about Marga Stern, for so long. This is rather strange because, of all the things that have happened to me recently, there is nothing I value more than having come to know her. (I don't know why I avoid saying 'love', which would be simpler and more exact, a hesitation which she herself has observed on a number of occasions, without reproaching me, but with a tinge of bitterness.)

I don't regard this omission as pure chance. With a little effort at recollection, I've discovered, re-reading my notebook, something even more curious. What I note is that most of the long gaps in the diary coincide with intense ('intense' is putting it too strongly) moments in our love. Whenever a break of several weeks occurs in my notes, I search for and find beneath the silence something concerning Marga.

I'm a 'difficult love' – according to her – and, fortunately, she manages to accept this difficulty.

I ask Marga to come, I ask her to leave, I call her several days in a row in order to avoid her for weeks later on. The game would be outrageous were there not between us a tacit pact of freedom and forgiveness. I'm grateful she can respect the rules of the game so lucidly. Then, there is a certain weariness in her, which prevents emotionalism. And something else. A slight smile of discouragement, which must be her revenge on me.

But here I am psychologizing – that's not what I intended.

*

The strange fact remains that, without exception, every good moment of our love has been marked here, in my diary, by a blank page.

There are days I love that girl with simplicity and an open heart and I feel how she makes me happy. I await her calmly and unhurriedly – a little indifferently perhaps, with the right amount of indifference this calm love requires – and when she comes, when I feel her nearby, leaning back against the terracotta stove, or tucked into the right corner of the divan, or leaning attentively over my shoulder, over the table I work at, all these details are all such great, natural joys.

Clearly Marga and my diary don't get along. There are far too many general ideas, too many 'problems' here.

I note I've picked up the detestable habit of stating categorical truths. Too often I use that plural formulation ('we' are this, 'we' are that, 'our' destiny, 'our' duty) and generalize a collective, confused experience in this 'we' that at other times I wouldn't allow myself to use without verifying it in the light of personal experience.

Marga, who takes pride in having no aptitude for abstractions, is for me – to use a pedantic term – 'reasserting her individuality'. (If she could read this, she'd be horrified. Forgiving as she is, I wouldn't be forgiven this.) I don't know, perhaps our love has its concrete, immediate 'problems', which simply derive from the meeting of our two individual selves. Nothing destroys general ideas and conclusions more radically than being in love, since love reduces everything down to your own sensibility, reinventing superstitions, certainties, and doubts and values, obliging you to live them, to test them, to re-create them. There is something profoundly *original* in every love, a principle of birth, of creating all things from the beginning.

No, I don't love Marga passionately, I'm well aware of that, as is she, but all it takes is for her to happen along for the 'big questions' to disappear and be replaced by the whole world of living, personal meanings. Small change, of course, yet so vital.

What I particularly love in her is her terrible fear of abstraction. If I happen inadvertently to mention one of my famous intellectual crises, this girl, usually so understanding, suddenly withdraws, discreetly but firmly, refusing not only to answer, but even to comprehend. She has a particular inclination for things, objects, particular facts and individual people.

Me, you, this book, this chair, that window. She alone in all my world – family, friends, acquaintances – did not consider my move from law to architecture an extravagance. When I told her, she responded, almost without surprise, 'Good for you.' Her awareness and interest in my new duties surprised me at first. She asks me to explain things exactly, wants details, looks and inquires. Once she made me take her to the workshop and she stayed there all afternoon, wandering freely between the tables, mingling with my classmates. Usually so uncommunicative, she asked questions, demanded technical details, picked up the modelling clay familiarly and tried to work it. If I'm busy at my drawing board when she calls to visit, she won't let me interrupt the work; she pulls up a chair, kneels on it, elbows on table, and watches with a seriousness that seems to me utterly childish. A true vocation.

There is certainly something lucid in her intelligence – and perhaps limited at the same time – something practical, and with a sense of proportion. I understand now why I was amazed by her reputation as a good pianist when I heard her playing for the first time, some time ago. Technically accomplished perhaps – I've no idea – but her musical style is odd, to say the least. Unfortunately, she was playing Chopin then, a nocturne, which she made unrecognizably straightforward, precise, well defined. Marga doesn't play, she follows the rules. Just by listening to her, I managed to understand for the first time what was meant by the 'construction of a piece of music'. I saw it drawn up, logically, phrase by phrase, movement by movement. (Maybe this is where her curiosity about architecture comes from.) This style probably involves numerous musical risks, and has certain advantages. It's a great pleasure to hear her playing Mozart; it's a tight, painstaking Mozart, like the cutting of an incredibly fine surgical saw.

*

How is Marga Stern able to relate naturally and calmly to things, and what is the source of her happy ability to shield herself from dreams

66

and illusions? I envy her for her happy, sane and easy-going practical spirit. I'm envious of her lack of imagination and her resistance to abstraction. I have the same kind of admiration for this sensible spirit as I would for a healthy body, secure in its strength and physical integrity.

Can it be that there is nothing Jewish in this beloved girl, not a single feature, not a shade, not a single turning inwards towards the broken layers of memory deposited there?

I foolishly asked her this, just like I'd ask her if by any chance she had a headache. She answered with a shrug.

'I don't know what you mean. I have my moments of melancholy, of course. When you're irritable, or when I love you too much or, well, when something bad happens to me, whatever that may be.'

The fact is, Marga is a woman before she is a Jew. And if the destiny of the race compels her towards insecurity and uncertain dreams, her destiny as a woman – which is more powerful – returns her to the earth and binds her to it, returns her to the laws of life, which are silent in her, in expectation of moving onwards, through childbearing. It's a physical calm, and it expresses itself daily through a powerful sense of practicality, a sense of preparedness and expectation.

I re-read what I wrote above and laugh. Dear girl! What is left of you, of your warm laughter, of your good unhurried kisses, of the arms you lazily wrap around my neck, what is left of you in this writing that complicates you, comments on you, changes you?

She has a receptive sensibility, is obedient and well behaved, and she struggles to suppress her tremors beneath the virginity she defends against both herself and me. I know her body, suffering in expectation, I know the line of her hips curving so lazily, with such melancholy, beneath her dress.

No, there are no big questions. It is the small certainties that concern her and are illuminated in her presence.

7

The lines written in recent days about Marga concerning what I ironically call 'big questions' are unutterably mediocre. If I had not once and for all decided to stop being foolish, I'd rip up the page. But keeping a diary would be too easy a job if you could modify it afterwards, correcting what was misconceived in the first instance. You can't correct without dissimulating. And that's not what I want.

But I was humiliated with the shame of it, cringing at the limitations of those thoughts, at their triteness and complacency, I was ashamed yesterday evening in the street when, turning a corner, I found myself in the middle of a revolution. I don't know exactly what had happened. There had been a local meeting of workers and in the end the police intervened. People didn't want to vacate the hall, or vacated it too slowly, or somebody shouted out some revolutionary nonsense and then the confrontation began. I arrived too late to see the fight in full swing – and I wouldn't have seen much anyway, as the struggle occurred inside, in the hall, and the exits were too few and too narrow for those packed inside to escape.

Now it was almost over. Most of them were being escorted away between bayonets, tattered and torn. Several were stretched out on the footpath, bleeding. There was one who was groaning terribly, his head under a frozen pipe that was thawing and dripping slowly. I felt as if something within myself had been crushed underfoot. It wasn't revolt or indignation, but a terrible sense of powerlessness in the face of pain, and I admit my first thought was that it was my tough luck to have been there, as I'd rather not have witnessed the unhappy scene, rather not have known it existed, seen it, heard it. But, once there, I couldn't pass it by, it wasn't possible, not because it's not in me to be cowardly, but because I had an acute feeling that I would never have forgiven myself, that I would have crossed a personal boundary, there in secret, and never been able to go back.

I felt the need to make a gesture of solidarity with those unfortunates, to shout – I don't know – 'Long live the revolution!' or 'Down with the bourgeoisie!' or 'We want higher wages!' or whatever it was I had to say in order to be beaten along with them, taken away with them – though, at the same time, I realized how laughable I was, how sentimental and philanthropic I was in my good intentions. I was utterly ridiculous there, with my little intellectual crisis, in the middle of the street, among people – the brawlers and the beaten – who amounted to something, had a cause, a calling. I felt alone, unarmed, useless, in a wave of life that was passing me by implacably, throwing me aside, and taking the others on forward with it.

I returned to my empty room, my drawing boards of no interest to me, my meaningless books. Tomorrow or the day after I will recover my foolish pride at being solitary. And will again be an intellectual, a pen pusher.

*

The joy of being at the heart of the crowd, like a tree in the sleeping greatness of the forest, the feeling of partaking and participating in the great chain of life, by which you are transcended and absorbed into the wider, inchoate physical current of the species . . .

This is something I have never known and never will. 'Me'. Everything I do, all I think, all I suffer is circumscribed: 'Me'. And I have the deplorable audacity to be proud of this infirmity, to consider the window from which I view the world as a 'vantage point' rather than a mere refuge. The audacity to believe that my solitude is a principle, when it is only an inability.

How poorly, how pathetically I confess this sin – and for all that it is no less real. I am a tree that has fled the forest. A tree with pride – a disease which does not kill violently, but attacks patiently from below, at the roots, at the very foundation of life.

Yesterday's events, which caught me unawares and left me baffled, demonstrate starkly the sad state of the class of people who call themselves intellectuals, to whom I belong. Strange perversion: to stand by the roadside watching those who pass and events, and from this drama – which excludes you, the spectator – to arrive at 'ideas', which you neatly record. To call this 'the conflict between thought and action' would be to be too kind to myself, as if we were talking about two separate, incompatible domains, each with its own validity. But this misrepresents the real problem – making it too abstract and easy on myself. The real problem is the intellectual's inaptitude for real life, methodically cultivated through reading, thinking and dialectic. It is deformity by stages, a systematic habituation, day by day, a slow atrophying of the reflexes and instincts, a step-by-step destruction of the natural vital power that allows us to pass untroubled through storms.

I don't believe any intellectual has ever done anything decisive in human history, when it was not a matter of culture but of actually saving the species. History should be re-examined from this perspective: I'd be surprised if I were mistaken. What can you do with such houseplants that wither in fresh air?

And the situation of the Jewish intellectual is certainly worse, as he stands at two removes from the active game of existence; firstly as an intellectual and secondly as a Jew.

I was reading in Şapsă Zwi's history, sold to me in December by Abraham Sulitzer, my friend from the train, that in 1646 tens of thousands of Jews were butchered in Poland and Russia, hundreds of villages and towns were wiped from the face of the earth, and while the towns were burning, while the spilled blood was pouring like lava from a still active volcano, in the synagogues, among flames and blood, they discoursed over Talmudic texts.

And the historian relates this terrible thing with pride, as a heroic fact, while it seems to me a sinister refusal to live, the undermining of the vital impulses, a shameful retreat from the law of nature.

*

I couldn't have bumped into Sami Winkler at a better moment. 'Just the man I need,' he said cheerfully. I'd recognized from afar his great square boxer's shoulders in the corner at the National, where he'd stopped to pass the time. I hadn't seen him since early December, on the day I went to the student dormitories and found him arguing with S. T. Haim, his ideological enemy.

I like Winkler's sturdy calm, the suggestion of physical strength, and the rough appearance which in fact obscures how much he has learned by applying himself methodically and painstakingly. Someone once pointed out to me a report in a foreign Zionist magazine which Winkler had submitted on behalf of the Romanian delegation at the annual Zionist congress in Basel: the subject did not interest me, but I noticed how much work he had put into it, his sense of order and great ability in organizing documentary material.

'A bureaucrat with a heart' is how S.T.H. dismisses Winkler. S.T.H. is too passionate and unfair. And in the end I think Winkler's worth lies not in what he is but in what he is not. He's not a lunatic, or a metaphysician, or crippled with doubt, or poisoned by complex intellectual crises. To not be all these things, and yet be a Jew – there's a challenge. I have the impression that Winkler is well up to it.

So, seeing him again, it occurred to me that he would have the answers to the questions troubling me lately – and though I have neither the appetite for nor practice in opening my heart, I talked about the events of recent days, of all my thoughts about the isolation of the Jew, and particularly of the Jewish intellectual, his isolation from the masses, and how poorly adapted he is for social reality and even life in general.

'You believe in Zionism and working to found a new country. Has your conscience never grappled with this sterile feeling of Jewish aloneness? Don't you feel this collective effort you're mixed up in is somehow contrary to the nature of the Jew, who is destined to live an interior life and to be unable to break the shackle that holds him back from the world?

'Forgive me, I realize what I'm saying is too abstract and pretentious, but follow me anyway. I'll try to be clearer. Look, I think that in an enterprise like this, which involves building a country, an absolutely epic adventure when you get down to it, what really matters are not the practicalities – industry, economics, finance, raw materials – but something else, something in the realm of psychology or metaphysics, if that doesn't alarm you. A bit of madness, a certain self-confidence, even a little recklessness. I wonder if we're bringing too many problems with us, to a place where you should go with your sleeves rolled up for work. I don't know, I'm not well informed and don't try to be, because I don't have much faith in figures, but without having thought deeply about Zionism, I believe it originates in an attempt to overcome our own futility. It's really a tragic stab at salvation rather than a natural return to the land.

'In recent days I've felt so ridiculous, having suddenly come face to face with life and these crowds, that when I think that there are young people like me who've put their books aside and gone to work with a pick-axe, in some terrible Palestinian colony, I ask myself if their departure is an act of heroism, as you probably believe, or just one of desperation.'

'I don't believe anything,' replied Winkler. 'I listen to you and see you don't understand. Too much psychologizing, and I've no time for psychologizing. I've never had these kinds of doubts, to be completely honest with you.

'I've always seen things clearly – I've always known what to do. I look at you, the way you get worked up, I look at S.T.H., how he chews things over, I look at lots of people and I just don't understand. You worry about rebuilding the country and I don't know how to respond. Maybe you're right, maybe not, I've no idea. To me, the matter is natural, healthy and straightforward. I have no doubt that it'll all work out, but I'm not in a hurry either. I work and wait.'

He stopped speaking, as though the discussion had come to an end, then, several beats later, added:

'Listen, if you want to find out more, come with me on Thursday evening, to Jabotinski's conference. He's a dissident Zionist, terribly at odds with the central leadership as a result of his violent actions. He's a strange sort, as you'll see for yourself. During the war, he organized a Jewish military legion to fight to take Jerusalem. Come and hear him, maybe he can clear things up for you.'

*

I listened to Jabotinski, and he didn't clear things up for me. But Winkler was right: he's a sort. He has a clipped, unemotional style of speech that is at the same time lively and lucid and reveals that he is a natural fighter. Not much in the way of gestures, few smiles or frowns. A certain roughness of bearing, a lack of expressiveness even, which may well be deliberate. Lots of facts and figures, but enclosed within a few simple – vehemently simple – ideas. I'm no expert on Zionist politics, but I think I understood the main thrust of Jabotinski's position regarding the movement's official leadership.

'The executive imagines,' he said, 'that Zionism can prevail through diplomacy. It starts with a legal fact: England's mandate to create a Jewish homeland in Palestine. This term "homeland" strikes me as vague and unengaging. I'd prefer them to clearly say "state". But, moving on. The central Zionist office thus believes that this legal document may provide a basis for its dealings with England, perhaps enabling it to gain land, to gain certain advantages and gradually achieve the movement's political and national objectives. The strategy is simple: the Jews behave themselves, and the English will be magnanimous.

'Well, this policy of haggling and hoping is for me the slow strangulation of the movement. Suicide. A national movement that hangs on a piece of paper is a recipe for death. We won't become strong through a diplomatic pact, but through an inner creative spirit. With Lord Balfour's letter or without, with a British mandate or without, it's all the one to Zionism. Without the desire to create, without strength of will, Zionism amounts to absolutely nothing.

'"But what is it you want to do?" ask the prudent Jews who've heard it whispered that I want to raise an army and start a war, or something to that effect. "Do you want to bring Great Britain to its knees? Do you want to destroy the English navy?

'"Do you want to fight against submarines, torpedoes and the admiralty's battleships?"

'These Jews of ours are pretty smart, as you can see for yourself. But I can be smart too when needs be and this is how I answer: I don't know what I want. I don't know and it doesn't bother me. I don't sit and wonder what will work out and what it will be like. I just feel that things aren't happening and the movement has to shift from international affairs to our own affairs. That we need purely spiritual strength rather than the backing of the force of law. That, in the end, the riskiest struggle for self-realization is a thousand times more productive, even when it fails, than the politest call for foreign goodwill, even when it succeeds.'

. . . And so on, for two hours. It was not a success. There were a lot of people, but they were disturbed, afraid even, of the speaker's boldness.

In the end, in the street, Winkler clapped my shoulder and said, 'Well?'

I didn't know what to say. The man interested me, but the issue remained just as clouded. As it happened, we bumped into S.T.H. in the hall, and the three of us went to a café on the boulevard to talk.

S.T.H. was relentless.

'A fascist, that's what he is. And don't ask me to consider him any less of a fascist because he's a Jew. The idea of a Palestinian Jewish state, created through an act of national will – what an absurdity! And at the same time, what savagery! Don't you see the machinations of the English in this whole business, a capitalist venture, which the massacred native Arabs and the Jewish proletariat of the colony will pay for, their very blood exploited in the name of the national ideal? Great Britain needs a right-hand man to guard the Suez Canal, so it's invented this myth of a "Jewish homeland". "Homeland" is too nice a word. No doubt some Quaker or Puritan came up with it. But millions of sentimental Jews have taken it at face value.

'I can practically hear that Jabotinski. "You don't make a country out of practicalities." Oh really? So what do you make it out of? Out of spirit? Perhaps with spirit, but before that comes the fact of geography, which you can't charm away with lyrical words, the way you can charm a roomful of kindly Jews. Land makes its own terrible demands: so many square kilometres of land, this many mountains, this much rain, this much drought. How are you going to colonize a land the size of three counties with 15–17 million people?

'And what will you do with the indigenous Arabs, who also have the right to a natural death, rather than an abrupt one by Zionist extermination? How will you bring to life an artificial conglomeration of people brought from every corner of the earth through a so-called national process, while ignoring the bloodiest problems of the proletariat, social class, falsified political economy? I'd like to know if this Mr Jabotinski has heard of Palestinian labour unrest, of a Palestinian proletariat, of Palestinian finance. And I'd like to know how he proposes to accommodate them.

'In fact, I don't need to know. Because I know without him telling me.

'I can almost hear him saying it: "The problem of social struggle is subordinate to the national imperative." Not even Mussolini talks that way. Not even German counter-revolutionaries. Not even Nicholas I, the Tsar of all Russians.

'Jewish national unity is an absurdity. I don't know any Jews: I know workers and the bourgeoisie. I don't know of a Palestinian national problem. I know about a practical economic problem involving Syria, Palestine and Mesopotamia, which is not any more interesting than the problems of Cuba, Indochina and Eastern Rumelia. The rest is a myth, an idyll, a chimera.'

S.T.H. is an incurable Marxist. It's gone beyond a system of political thought and is now a complete inability to understand life in any other terms. Anything that's not expressible in figures is for him not real. For every fact there is a document, every proof a counterproof, and beyond that everything else – as he puts it with terrible finality – is an idyll . . .

I was afraid Winkler would be provoked and feel compelled to make counter-arguments. I don't know if he'd have lost the battle –

polemicists like S.T.H. put up a stiff fight – but I know we would have spent a wasted evening. Winkler would have produced a set of figures, demonstrating the viability of a Jewish Palestinian state, and S.T.H. would have produced another set of figures to demonstrate the exact opposite.

Again I observe that Winkler, despite his obtuse exterior, can sense nuances when he has to and size up a situation. He replied to S.T.H. by shifting the plane of the argument.

'I'm not going to argue with you about matters of Palestinian geography and economics, though I could do so. Nor will I attempt to show you that your arguments about the Arabs and the Jewish proletariat carry no weight. I don't deny their reality, but there's a hierarchy of realities which you refuse to recognize. So between two equally valid arguments, one may cancel the other, because it has another meaning, is of another order. So let's leave it.

'The question for me isn't whether Jews can create a Palestinian state, but whether they can do anything but. Understand? The chances of the enterprise succeeding matter less than the fact that it is so pressing. If we don't do this, we die. If we do – according to you – we still die. I don't know. Maybe we will, maybe we won't. And for this "maybe" it's worth making the journey. Don't ask a nation on the road to creating a country to count its money, take out an insurance policy and make a hotel reservation. In the end, to be honest with you, I find this whole argument pointless. I'm a soldier, a bricklayer, a miner. I listen and work. The rest is an idyll – if I may quote you.'

'No you may not. You reason like a girl. Why do you love me? "I just do." Why don't you love me any more? "I just don't." Admit it, your argument isn't any better. You explain yourself with "just because". Why are you a Zionist? "Just because."'

I wanted to interject here, though the lightning flashing in S.T.H.'s eyes made it risky.

'I'll ask Winkler to allow me to reply for him. I just want to tell you, dear S.T.H., that this "just because" you laugh at is still a decisive reply. To be a Zionist "just because" means to be a Zionist naturally, by destiny, it's like being white, or blond, or dark, a Zionist

because it's raining or snowing, because the sun's rising or setting
. . . I think this is the point at which the Zionist drama begins. In any
case, this is where my doubts begin. Because I don't think Jews are
ready to live such a collective life directly and naturally. I regret saying it – though it's not the first time the idea has occurred to me. I
have the feeling that the Zionist movement is an expression of
despair: a revolt against destiny. A tragic effort to move towards simplicity, land, peace. Intellectuals who want to escape their solitude.
And I believe, ultimately, that the Zionist project contains this tragic
seed while we hurry on, hoping we might be able to forget about it
. . . But won't it rise to the surface some day? For me, this is the only
question.'

'No,' Winkler replied, sure of himself.

S.T.H. was quiet for a while, and just looked from one of us to the
other, with a certain compassion. Then he burst out with it.

'Let's go, we're wasting the evening. It's impossible to talk to you.
Myths, superstition, poetry . . . Do you pair reason about anything?
On what basis? You sing. A couple of tenors, that's what you are.
Puccini, Giacomo Puccini – our master. Waiter, the bill.'

*

I don't think Winkler is trying to convert me to Zionism. But he has
time for me, because I intrigue him a little. With his believer's calm,
my psychological doubts about Zionism throw him off much more
than S.T.H.'s political objections.

He sought me out yesterday evening to invite me to a meeting.

'Come on,' he said. 'You'll meet a Palestinian. A pioneer, Berl
Wolf.

'Really, until now we've just been talking like in books, about
ideas, impressions, arguments. But this is a living man, flesh and
blood. You have to meet him. I told him about you and said I'd bring
you.'

Indeed, I went and, I don't know why, on the way I was very unsettled
. . . I had cold feet. I had asked Winkler for a few details about this

Berl Wolf, whom I was going to meet and find out about. A fabulous tale, in short. At age fourteen, he flees on his own from Russia in the early days of the Revolution, a docker in a southern port several months later, stuck in Kiel in 1918 when the sailors mutiny, studies for a year at an English college, crosses the Atlantic, spends some time in the United States, where he's a successful scandal journalist, and one day drops everything and leaves for Palestine, as a labourer in a colony. He's there for a year, working from dawn till dusk with pick and spade . . . One morning, at the hour when they set off for the fields, there's an Arab attack. He takes a bullet in the right arm, near the shoulder, breaking the bone. Crippled, there is nothing he can do on the plantation. He goes to the office of the Zionist executive and says: 'I want to continue working, use me somehow, give me a task.' So they sent him to Europe as a propagandist.

Climbing the stairs, I was sorry I'd come. If Winkler hadn't been with me, I might have turned back on reaching the doorstep. 'Who knows what's waiting for me.' A long conversation with an agitated prophet, another series of arguments, another string of misunderstandings, another S.T.H., a Zionist this time and much more intolerant than the first one, because this one would speak, without wanting to, in the name of his sacrifice, with the silent prestige of an arm lost in battle. I felt already humiliated by any victory possible over him through argument.

And what am I anyway? A machine for arguing? What will this man say to me? What will I say to him? Who will arbitrate between his truth and mine? What is the point of all this wasted time, all this hot air? What's the point, if you end up back against the same dead-end questions, with that same stubborn sadness? An argument, a hundred arguments, a million – to hell with them all.

We went in. A big, empty room with a few wooden benches and – on the walls – a few photographs, Palestinian scenes probably. Some twenty girls and boys of between fourteen and sixteen years old were sitting around an older boy, listening to a story. They were speaking fluent Hebrew, which surprised me at first (I hadn't known it could be spoken easily, colloquially) and then made me feel awkward. I understood nothing and felt like an uninvited guest.

However, the older boy, the one telling the story, made a welcoming gesture and, as we approached the group, I realized with surprise that this child, this adolescent, had to be our man, the Palestinian missionary. While he gestured expansively with his left arm as he narrated, almost singing, his right sleeve was empty to the shoulder, tight against his body and tucked into his pocket.

In amazement, I ran over everything Winkler had told me about him on the way, watched again as if seeing brief cinematic images of his flight from Russia, the prison in Kiel, the crossing of the Atlantic, refuge in Haifa, the years of work in the colony, and I asked myself where this man with the cheeks of a child kept his scars and memories hidden . . .

When he had finished his story, he approached me and Winkler, extending his undamaged left hand and asked in clumsy French if we didn't mind waiting half an hour until he had finished with the children.

'In the meantime, join the circle.'

I hung back. The game seemed rather silly to me, but hesitating seemed even sillier, intimidated as I was before the kids.

'What the hell, I'm not that old,' I told myself, and two young pupils made space for me.

Our Palestinian friend, always in the centre of the group, was now teaching us a Yemeni song. He would say a verse and the kids had to repeat it after him, first speaking it out loud, then singing it together. I kept quiet at first, but he stopped the whole choir after the first few words.

'That's no good: everybody has to sing along.'

I blushed, feeling myself singled out, but kept quiet. He insisted again, in a good-tempered, comradely way.

'Somebody here doesn't want to sing. It seems he's annoyed with us – what other explanation can there be for not wanting to sing? Let's all ask him to sing, then I'm sure he will.'

Anything but that. I'll do what they want, sing if they want, do cartwheels, tumble, roll head-over-heels if I have to, just don't all stare at me like that, like a bad student caught copying and put in the corner in front of the whole class. So I sang.

S.T.H. should have been there to see me. He would have roared with laughter. Recalling it, I feel rather embarrassed – wrongly in fact and fussily – for – why should I be ashamed to say it? – it was a pleasant hour, an hour of holiday, in which I was conscious of doing a thousand silly irresistible things, things more powerful than 'my critical spirit', more powerful than my fear of being ridiculous.

In the middle of the room, with a lock of hair falling over his forehead (as he conducted us by nodding to the beat), with a wide smile lighting his adolescent face, our man managed to get us playing in the end. By the time we were leaving, I'd forgotten that we'd gone there to debate ideas. He came up to me and shook my hand again.

'I don't have anything else to tell you. I wanted you to sing and you sang. That's all there is to it.'

And that really is all there is to it. Can you sing? You're saved.

Well, I for one can't sing. I am discreet, have a critical disposition, a sense of the ridiculous, self-control, and other tragic nonsense of that kind, and possess the supreme folly of self-regard. Yes, indeed, at precisely the moment you hide behind your own penmanship, writing what you think is a confession and a severe internal reckoning, somebody within creeps up and claps you on the back and decorates you with the order of merit, first class. I write here plainly and in good faith that I'm an unfortunate fool and meanwhile a voice secretly consoles me. 'You're a martyr,' it says, 'the hero of your own destiny, the guardian of the purest values of human dignity.'

The duplicity of humility and pride, which frustrates all my sincerity ... There's no cause that I haven't undermined, no revolt against myself that I haven't annulled with a small hidden reserve, with a prearranged excuse.

And still I believe, I want to believe, I am convinced that my inability to sing is an infirmity, not a mark of nobility. I believe this inability to join the crowd – any crowd –to cast myself into the throng, to forget myself and lose myself there, is a sad failure, a sad defeat.

If I could only not be proud of this. If I could achieve only that ...

8

I hadn't seen Abraham Sulitzer, my old Ahasverus, since that meeting on the train in the Christmas holidays. And now, our paths cross. It's extraordinary how opportunely people enter and leave my circle, as if directed by an argument that calls them closer or pushes them away, depending on whether they are required or not. Life has this kind of aptness, which is not allowed in literature. Were I a man of letters, I think the hardest thing would be to mask the unbelievable twists of reality, which show such daring and initiative . . . (But what is this thought doing here? I'll tell it to Walter. He, as a critic and newspaperman, could at least put it in an article.)

It turns out that Abraham Sulitzer is my neighbour. He lives a hundred metres away, to the left, in an alley that opens on to my street. But because he heads out for work at seven in the morning and I closer to nine, an age has passed without us intersecting. Yesterday, though, I had to get to the train station at dawn (a package sent home through Lulu) and on the way back I turned a corner and bumped into my friend Abraham.

'I saw you last week at Jabotinski's conference and wanted to call out to you, but thought better of it. Who knows? I thought, maybe he's forgotten me. A bookseller he met once on a train . . . But I wanted to ask if you'd read Şapsă Zwi's history. It's a book I was fond of.'

I reassured him somewhat, telling him that it had interested me greatly. But I'm sure my reply did not please him. (What was 'It interested me' supposed to mean? A book either knocks you down or raises you up. Otherwise, why pay money for it?) Abraham Sulitzer certainly thinks this way, but doesn't say it out loud. He just smiles, full of reticence and eager amiability. (Well? Didn't you like it? Let's say, as you do, that you found it interesting. Well? Aren't you entitled to? Perhaps I can do something for you . . .)

We separated quickly – we were both in a hurry – but he invited me to visit him some evening – an invitation I accepted with pleasure.

*

Books, books, everywhere books. I've seen people talking to their cats, their dogs . . . Abraham Sulitzer talks to his books.

'Come down here to Papa, third in line. Easy, now, don't wreck the whole row. Who'll put you back in place if you do? You? The hell you will. It's always me. And who does Roza shout at? Also at poor me!'

Mr Sulitzer exaggerates. Roza, his wife, doesn't shout: at most she grumbles.

'Lord,' she complains to me, in that same lilting Jewish-Moldovan as his, 'I have brothers too, and brothers-in-law, who are salesmen. One sells bobbins, another sells boots. And? They spend the day at the shop, and shut up shop in the evening – and that's the end of it. Does anybody take their bobbins home to sit and talk to them?

'It's a curse, life with this husband of mine. I'm so embarrassed when neighbours call by to borrow a little tea or salt when they run out, and come across a fully grown man, talking to himself, to the walls, to the books. Now, tell me if you think that isn't pure madness.'

I avoid a straight reply, so as not to add to conflict in the Sulitzer household, but my friend Abraham, at his table, besieged by books, shy and wise, smiles at me from behind his glasses, from behind the covers of a book opened wide – a smile of complicity ('Let her talk, that's how she is; women are like that; she'll get over it'), the smile of a child who has upset a jam-jar and awaits his punishment.

I look at this kindly old man, who loves books with a passion, like an addiction. I look at this patient philosopher, terrorized by the nagging of a terrible wife, against whom he has no defence but a hidden smile, and I suddenly remember Monsieur Bergeret.

How well Abraham Sulitzer resembles him in this moment, surrounded by books. Abraham Sulitzer and Anatole France. A Yiddish-speaking Anatole France. What a blasphemer I am!

He shows me an entire library, full of surprises. A Yiddish translation of Cervantes. Molière, Shakespeare. And, nearer to us, Galsworthy, Dostoyevsky, Turgenev, Thomas Hardy. I'm amazed, he is triumphant. With every volume he places in my hands, he has a kind of smile of false modesty, like a host proud of the vintage wine he has served you, without announcing its quality, precisely in order to test you. However often I exclaim in surprise at a new discovery, he buries himself deeper between two covers, with an attempt at indifference which only half-hides his pleasure. And, when his triumph is decisive (a Jewish edition of Dante, printed magnificently on parchment, with tiny letters, as if engraved in wood), he can take it no longer and explodes almost furiously, struggling with I know not whom.

'Beautiful? Beautiful you say? Beautiful like a puppy? Beautiful like a tie? No, sir, it's not beautiful: it's earth-shaking.'

His eyes burn – frowning for the first time. Roza, a little frightened, unsure what is happening, says nothing. Me, I feel embarrassed somehow. (I don't like you, Abraham Sulitzer; I thought you were a serious sceptic, not an amateur, subject to tantrums.)

But he calms down quickly and becomes tolerant again. Now, with a little courage, perhaps my life may not even be in danger if I said – to test him – that I didn't like a particular edition which inflames him with feeling. I don't think he'd kill me; he'd settle for throwing me out.

The truth is that I am not in the mood for joking either and the revelations of his library open for me a world I never guessed existed. A culture in dialect? European culture in dialect. Why? For whom?

I ask Abraham Sulitzer and his reply this time is no longer excited or furious. It is sad.

'I thought you'd ask. I'm surprised it took you so long. When it gets down to it, you're no wiser than some street kid who runs after Jews with caftans, when one wanders along, shouting "Oy vey" and "Achychy azoy". Dialect! Broken German! A ghetto language: that's what Yiddish is to you. If I told you it was a language, neither a beautiful or ugly one, but a living one, through which people have suffered and sung for hundreds of years, if I told you that it's a language containing everything in the world which has been pondered, you'd look at me, well, just as you're doing now. Dialect indeed! It's a living language, with nerves and blood, with its own troubles, its own beauty. With its own homeland, which is the ghetto – the whole world, in other words. It makes me laugh when I hear those Zionists talking Hebrew picked up from books. Is that what we need? Hebrew? With dictionaries, grammar and philology, or whatever they call it? God help them . . . Turning their backs on a healthy language to go searching in a tomb for a defunct one. God forgive me, I speak Hebrew myself after a fashion, having picked it up in my old age, but – what can I say? – to me it's cold, harsh and empty somehow, like wandering through a long, long deserted stone hallway, without a single person or plant or window. How do you say "It hurts", "I'm burning up" or "I miss you" in this language? And if you say it, does it do any good? Say "It hurts" in Yiddish – and you sense the pain. There's blood there, it's warm, it's alive . . .'

'I don't know either of them well,' I replied. 'I wonder, though, to what degree you're right, but – and I hope you don't mind me saying this – I don't think you're entirely right. Yiddish is still a dialect – and that's a serious problem. It's a deformed language, derived from the corruption of another. Isn't that a humiliating origin? I find it hard to believe that from the degeneration of one language you can create another.'

'But that's where your Zionists get it wrong. It's not a case of a language that's degenerated. It's a case of another language altogether.

'Yiddish is only ridiculous in the mouths of rich Jews with a *Fräulein* to take care of the kids who think that by speaking bad Yiddish they're speaking good German. But real Yiddish, the straight Yiddish of a Jew without a *Fräulein*, is a living, breathing language.

Millions of Jews speak it, millions live through it. For these millions are printed these books you see, for these millions Yiddish is written, translations are made into Yiddish, and Jewish theatre is performed. It's a complete world, a complete people, with its own elite, without diplomas or universities. This elite wants to be informed, wants to know, wants to reflect.

'There are Yiddish novelists, poets, critics and essayists. If you had any idea of the great beauties encompassed by this dialect-culture – which you ignorantly despise – you'd probably have many pangs of remorse. Not to mention the folklore of the ghetto – all in Yiddish – a still-living, creative folk-culture, with its roots deep in the periphery, with anonymous singers, unknown humourists, with heroes, with legends, with myths. And doubly alive. Once through the immediate presence of the life of the ghetto, and then through the more distant mystery of the life of the synagogue. The edgy, gritty urban realism of the ghetto and the mysticism of the synagogue unite in this folk-culture of the Jewish neighbourhood and together add up to something which, if you have an ear and a heart, is worth living and dying for.'

'Dying, especially,' I interjected, 'because living through it is rather difficult. I can't really see those millions of Yiddish speakers. And I don't really see the Jewish ghetto either. But I do see a multitude of Jews passing definitively into the culture of the countries in which they live: French Jews, German Jews, American Jews and Romanian Jews. A hundred years ago they spoke in dialect. Today they've forgotten it. Tomorrow, their children won't even remember that it once existed. And to such a precarious thing – however beautiful it may be – you want to bind a culture?'

'Have you forgotten that, luckily, there are still anti-Semites? And, thank God, that there are still pogroms from time to time? However much you're assimilated in a hundred years, you'll be set back ten times as much by a single day's pogrom. And then the poor ghetto will be ready to take you back in.'

'Why a ghetto and not a Palestinian colony? You speak about the ghetto with so much passion, as though it were a place of exile, and with so much love about dialect, as if it were not a borrowed language. If it's a matter of returning to ourselves, why don't we return to where we first started, the place we left two thousand years ago? It's not easy, either way. But if it's going to be hard, it might as well be for once and for all.'

'Two thousand years? Do you think Zionism has something of those two thousand years in it? Do you think that these boys of Jabotinski's who wear boots and salute each other like soldiers, who ride bicycles on Saturday and can say "Give me a cigarette" or "Let's go to a football match" in Hebrew – do you think these boys have anything in common with those two thousand years of our blood? Two thousand years through flames, through disasters, through wandering come to us through the history of the ghetto. It's a history lived under lamplight. "We want sunshine," they shout. Good luck to them – and let them become footballers. They'll get plenty of sunshine then. But this lamp by which I've read so many hundreds of years, this lamp is Judaism – not their sunlight.'

'You're old, Mr Sulitzer. That's why you talk like that.'

'I'm not old! I'm a Jew – that's what I am.'

*

I was slightly mistaken. Abraham Sulitzer is a Monsieur Bergeret only as a husband to Madame Roza. As an intellectual, however, in his relationship with ideas, he becomes dogmatic and overbearing. In defending the ghetto, he is no less intolerant than Winkler defending Zionism or S.T. Haim cursing about both. Extremism is their common vice.

I visited him on a couple of evenings but avoided arguing. He reads beautifully and I asked him to read to me from his favourite books. Several good hours of reading from Sholem Aleichem. A wonderful fellow and probably untranslatable. What sad humour, what lucid laughter, what a fine, acute critical sense, all enveloped in a melancholy of misery, of terror . . .

9

Grandma has died. Ten hours after a heart attack. Summoned by telegram, I arrived in time to hold her living hands in mine: those small, thin, bony hands that haven't rested in seventy years; even in sleep they signalled restlessness.

She died slowly, fighting until the end, suffering terribly and completely conscious until the final moment, her eyes open, searching. The merciless lucidity of the dying! A slight glaze to the eyes, but aware in the final struggle, not allowing a single gesture, sign or shadow to escape her attention.

Why such resistance? Death comes, let it come. Receive it.

I would have wanted this old woman of ours to understand the end with simplicity and to smile in friendship, with acceptance. I would have wanted her to remember the Bible she read to me, the patriarch-friends, their harmonious wives, I would have liked her to remember the candles lit on Friday night, the white headscarf she wore when among the brass candlesticks, the bread she kneaded with her hands all her life, all these simple things, all these gentle joys, and to pass away in their homely glow.

Why such resistance? Why so much questioning? She seemed to cling to every minute, struggling with each one.

It reminded me of Grandfather's agony, which was even more terrible, as in addition to physical suffering it was a quarrel with God and destiny, a final protest, a cry.

But she, Grandma, looking like a child disguised as a grandmother, should have died differently, more calmly, more easily . . .

*

How badly we die! We haven't even learned to do that from the centuries of death we've passed through. We live badly, but we die even more badly, in despair, struggling. We miss our last chance to make peace and be saved. The sad Jewish death of people who, not living among the trees and the beasts, haven't been able to learn the beauty of indifference in death, its simple dignity. The greatest Jewish sin – perhaps.

. . . And the terribleness of Jewish mourning. The vigil from the night before the burial, the tired, unbelieving shaking of heads of the women keeping vigil, the lament of the Kaddish.

A single beautiful thing: the white death shroud. There could be something regal in this return to the earth, a good, generous solemn fact. But we mutilate it with our despair, which is suffocating. We call ourselves sceptics, but we don't deserve such praise. I've seen how they cry at a Jewish funeral, and I know nothing more unrestrained, more awful. To cling so stubbornly to this life, to renounce all else so as not to give it up, to choke it with your desperate love, to believe yourself lost when you have lost it – such a terrible inability to rise above it.

Whoever has ever leaned against a tree, who has ever thought with melancholy of his loneliness, can't fail to meet death without a feeling of being a bit above it, and smiling at it nonchalantly and indulgently, with friendliness, with gentle farewell, with a certain sensual thrill.

Our grieving is visceral, tyrannical, uncomprehending. And, more seriously, it is lacking in love. Of the many trivial aspects of the Jewish sensibility, this unrestrained mourning is the most unworthy. I think, however, that it is something we have accustomed ourselves to do here, in the ghetto. Death in the Bible is a glorious event.

Mama's pain saddens me. It irritates me, in fact, as I'd like her to be accepting rather than resigned. There were moments when we almost quarrelled. 'She was my mother and I want to mourn her,' she snapped, defending her right to grieve. (I sometimes have the mean impression that her mourning is a new form of indulgence and that she deliberately seeks it.)

Of course, I'm unfair. I know how much love wounds, without forgetting Grandma's death. But that's exactly what I don't want to forgive – this love which has greater rights than death. This love that struggles to tie down and preserve a shade that has passed on. Such rights don't and can't exist.

And there's something else that disturbs me. I feel that my personal freedom is affected. I can't accept that someday, when my turn to die comes around, I will leave in my wake such wild, desperate, pointless suffering. I don't want to be loved so unrestrainedly.

If I were asked one day to give up my life for something – for a revolution, for love, for whatever nonsense – the idea that Mama would suffer for me the way she's suffering now horrifies me. Does she have any right to suffer in this way? Doesn't this trespass on matters which are mine to deal with? Isn't this an obstacle to me fulfilling my destiny? Isn't it a terrible moral pressure? She loves too unfairly, too oppressively, to the point at which it becomes suffocating and undignified. There is too much devotion in the Jewish family, too many gushing emotions, too many sacrifices made. Terrible advantage taken of good children and mothers prepared to sacrifice themselves. There is no reticence, no coolness. This leads inevitably towards a sense of obligation. I envy the cool and dignified reserve of the peasant: a formal farewell and off they go into the world. And when death comes, it comes like a relative.

The only person at home not shaken by Grandma's death is Grandmother. At ninety years of age, there she is outliving the other grandparents, who were so much younger and more passionate to live than she. 'God doesn't choose. Today it was her, tomorrow it will be my turn.' I think living and dying is all the one to her. Grandmother is of father's tribe, a people that dies late, in old age, at a hundred years old, placidly, without regrets. Their deaths are simple and good. But my mother's branch of the family has a completely different way of dying, and this was how Grandma passed away. They die by burning up swiftly, with short agonies, in which you feel the last shudder of pointless struggle. Their health is tenuous, nervous, maintained through unflagging effort and hard-won daily victories over a weary body. It's more than an intellectual resistance, a continual act of will. One day, the inner arch that holds them suspended in tension suddenly collapses. It's a Jewish death.

Father's side of the family haven't known it, and I think this is something of a family rule, as there are no examples there of any grandparent or great-grandparent who has passed away before they were in their nineties. Their blood is strong, not thinned by Talmudism or poisoned by the lights of lamps and late evenings in synagogues. They lived by a river, among boats, among grain. Grandma looked down on them, when in their company. Their excess of good health probably struck her as a sign of vulgarity.

*

Several times this morning I went down to the port, to see the new tugs that have started to arrive. The light is cold and lively, washed by wind and rain. It smells of wet willow bark, the young shoots emerging from under the freshly melted snow. In the distance, the blue Măcin Mountains, their peaks still white.

From time to time, the call of a boat's siren, its adolescent pitch like the whinnying of a foal.

Let us forget, old man. Let us forget what needs be forgotten: look, the season is turning.

10

Labouring in the workshop gets harder every day. This spring is unbearably beautiful. It bursts forth violently, as if in revenge for the five months of winter and the eighty days of snow it has tolerated. I continue to endure the morning classes, awaiting the reward of the noon bell of freedom. The streets seem wider, the houses white, the women glowing. There's a sense of nakedness everywhere.

But on returning to the workshop everything goes dark, the season is blotted out. The modelling clay is sticky and strong-smelling, the air has the chill of a damp cellar. We work sullenly, irritably, unproductively. For four hours I worried away at a ball of clay and got absolutely nowhere. Towards evening Marga came by and took me out for a stroll, which made up for everything, and we walked long and far, towards Băneasa. We watched planes practising taking off and landing. Marga, who had never seen a plane up close, enjoyed it immensely, as though watching some miraculous spectacle.

She ran through the fields after the shadows of the planes, the wide shadow of a big bird, flying low, several metres above the ground, and let out a cry of victory whenever she managed to step on the tail of one of these fleeting shadows with the toe of her shoe.

Then, tired, she fell into my arms, flushed and breathless, her hair blowing loose in the gentle evening breeze – unable to laugh as much as she wanted, but happy. Exuberantly, noisily happy.

The evening fell slowly, like a fluttering flag, and we turned back towards the city, tired after so much fresh air.

'Come and sleep with me, Marga.'

I said this to her so simply that she knew I was not joking. She let go of my hand. Not brusquely, but decisively. She is a virtuous girl, after all – and there's nothing anybody can do about that.

Her moral resistance is more powerful than the most miraculous April dusk.

'Moral resistance' is overstating it. Really, it's something more than a virtue: it's an inability to cede. Somewhere in the mind of that sensual, loving girl is a voice that asks, 'And, after that, what will become of you?' That's called foresight, and is also called mediocrity.

I don't doubt either her sense of shame or her passion. But they are both equally modest. She doesn't have enough of a sense of shame to resist embraces. Or sufficient passion to surrender to them completely. There is always a final line of caution, marking where the effusion must cease.

I've watched people playing roulette, contorted with suffering – but those who threw themselves into the game, losing everything, money, honour and life, didn't seem as abject as the frightened players who trembled for every chip, made endless calculations every five minutes and bowed out the moment they'd lost a 'reasonable' amount. I think mediocrity in vice is the most dishonourable kind of mediocrity.

There is something of this fearful moderation in Marga's way of hesitating. And the feeling that, even in our closest moments of understanding, she has taken, as they say, 'all the necessary measures' discourages me.

I know that from this point on any spontaneous action is out of the question.

I'd like to be a vulgar king of the slums, a charming rake, who could seduce his love and be indifferent thereafter. Marga's excuses would be of the highest order and yet insufficient. Then the issue would not be me and what I can give in exchange, but what she can light-heartedly give away, with a total lack of precaution. In love you're only worth as much as you can afford to lose.

*

I'm tired of myself, fed up with her. We're splitting up. She's a good girl and will make an excellent wife. She's part of a race of wives.

I can't recall: is there a female beloved, a lover, in the Bible? Seems there are only mothers, sisters and wives. It's very nice, but stifling somehow.

I think from here, from this slow slipping into too many attachments, comes the Jew's taste for solitude, a nostalgia for being on your own, like a stone. I envy the supreme insensibility of objects, their extreme indifference.

PART THREE

I

I walked back to the site from the station, after accompanying the master, who was taking the train to Braşov.

'Who'd ever think they've been working here five years,' he said to me on the way, at the corner by the river Ursu, from where you still see, among the tops of the oil derricks, some of the tops of the roofs of our buildings. It was an offhand comment and I didn't sense he was looking for a sentimental reply from me. He's not the kind.

'Five years, indeed,' I agreed.

At the station, awaiting the train, we again went over the work schedule for the coming week. I gave him some documents to sign and tried to reopen the discussion about the Rice villa, hoping to catch him in a more conciliatory mood in the moment of departure.

'We might at least wait a few days, until old Ralph gets back.'

'No, not an hour's delay. Work will continue as planned. Understood? You'll answer for any delay and I'll brook no excuses. The work will continue, even if it rains. Tell Dronţu that.'

Then, because he'd spoken rather harshly, he took my arm and suddenly lowered his voice:

'That's how we work. If Rice doesn't like it, he can demolish it. But all the same, that's how we work.'

We separated, agreeing.

The day was still bright and I felt the need to wander about on my own. I told the driver to go on ahead and to tell Dronţu I'd be late for dinner.

Five years! I'd never given them thought, never counted them. The master's reflections came back to me anew. Five years. I added them up – exactly five.

I can still recall that rainy day in March; the master, old Rice, Dronțu and I getting out of the automobile in the middle of Uioara, surrounded by frightened children and spied on by the entire village, holed up in their houses behind windows and curtains. Rice hadn't anticipated entering a completely hostile area. All we had to go on was a vague notion from the papers about the conflict between Rice Ltd, Mining Surveyors, and the peasants who were the previous owners of the concession. In any case, I knew nothing about the extent of the conflict. Possibly not even Rice had any idea how serious things were, as he had signed a whole string of cheques and was under the impression that this had resolved everything. This bony American would never lose the awe-inspiring attitude of a man who could say, 'I can pay!' wherever he went, at any moment, to anyone.

That first walk of ours on the site was a sombre affair – Rice, calm, hands in pockets, the master with a silence that was at the same time interrogatory, Dronțu curious, looking in bafflement at the deserted little street, crossed only by an occasional panicked chicken, a sign at least that the place wasn't utterly dead.

'Hello!' shouted Dronțu randomly, in case anyone could hear.

Nobody replied and we wandered on in that ringing silence, far past the edge of the village, from where you could see the scaffolding of the first test wells some three kilometres away.

Despite our strange reception, the fine rain in our faces and that muddy washed-out road, the landscape was beautiful. Immense chunks of black earth had recently been cut from the flank of the hillside. Great boulders and the trunks of giant trees had been tossed about together as though in the wake of a giant plough.

A cold, gusty wind blew, the sharp smell of damp vegetation stronger than that of burning oil and coal.

From the derricks came the beating of hammers and the high, almost musical, whine of a saw. The sounds were distinct in the thawing March air.

The master looked around 360 degrees, taking in his domain,

and I immediately understood that the project interested him. He made several sketches on the spot, took some photographs (I'm still amazed today at the speed with which he took in the relevant features of a site), noted some figures, gathered all the papers and prints in an attaché case and said briefly, in conclusion: 'We'll see.'

On the way back, in the automobile, I asked Rice to tell me something about the people who lived in Uioara.

'Never seen them,' he confessed. 'They run away from me and I'm not crazy about them either. I paid for the land to the last penny, as evaluated by the surveys. What more do they want? They're stubborn and stupid.'

'It must be because of the plums,' interjected Marin Dronțu.

'What plums?'

'The plum trees. Didn't you see them? They're white from top to bottom. No idea what the hell fell on them: cigarette ashes, coal dust – no idea what it could be.'

'It's drilling mud,' Rice informed us. 'What we used for test-drilling. Last autumn I took a first sounding from Hole A 19.'

'But couldn't the plum trees have been protected?' exclaimed Dronțu, rather to our surprise.

'Nonsense, sir. It's clear you don't know the oil business. There are inevitable risks. And they're usually minimal. And what's a plum tree at the end of the day?'

'Well, this is the source of your quarrel with the people of Uioara. You don't know what a plum tree is.'

I've recalled this comment of Dronțu's many times, since there would have been no conflict in the area, no litigation, if it hadn't been for those damned trees, which he, having come straight from the land, had seen from the first with his peasant's eye.

'This thing with the plum trees is serious,' he tells me still, when at the derricks we come across somebody from Old Uioara and he looks straight at us, scowling, tugging his cap down over his ears to make sure we notice he's not greeting us.

Rice understands nothing. 'These people are crazy,' he shouts.

'Completely crazy,' he goes on, 'but you have to deal with their madness.'

I still laugh today when I remember old Ralph's face in April five years ago, in his office in Piaţa Rosetti, when the master put the preliminary proposals before him.

To perform a new evaluation of the concession area and to distribute supplementary compensation. The village of Uioara will be moved from its present location to one several kilometres to the right, to the valley of the river Ursu, its new location. Conservation of all orchards beyond this point and the regeneration of those previously harmed by drilling mud and oil, and avoiding any future harm.

The present village of Uioara is being bought from the peasants who are its beneficiaries and will be at the disposal of the company for the construction of any buildings necessary in future: refineries, storage facilities, offices, housing for engineers and officials, roads to the wells and derricks. The village of Uioara is simply erased from its present location on the map and rebuilt in the valley of the river Ursu, so that nothing stands in the way between the wells and Company headquarters.

'Absurd,' shouted Ralph Rice. 'Absurd,' echoed all the mining engineers.

The master's plan was indeed a grave matter. The risks were clearly great, and it was arguable whether it would succeed.

Nevertheless, Rice argued it. I'll never forget the hours of fighting in the old man's office, where the master, stimulated by coffee and cigarettes, argued until three or four in the morning night after night, using sketches, diagrams and figures, Rice listening to him, furious and sombre, pacing from one corner of the office to the other, exclaiming from time to time or beating his fist on the desk when he felt he couldn't argue back. It was impassioned and exhausting.

The general meeting of technicians was indignant that an architect, a layman, had the nerve to stick his nose in business he did not understand.

'Your job is to take care of the construction side of the business.

To build a refinery, an office block and a number of homes. That's all. What's the hurry with oil, drilling mud and wells?'

'I don't care about your wells. Whether you're extracting petrol, vegetable oil or whey, it's all the same to me. However, I can't build using scraps. I need a site and I need space. And furthermore, I can't build an industrial complex in a village of viticulturists. And I can't build to the right of the village, because I'm not so mad as to leave a belt of peasants between the complex and the wells whom you'll fumigate or poison a year or ten from now, or else their plum trees, and who will one day get fed up with the smoke and set fire to you too, along with the wells and the whole petrol game.'

. . . The argument would go on until dawn without a conclusion, and with both combatants exhausted.

Every point of the plan was buried and resurrected ten times. Everything old Ralph acquiesced to would be retracted the next day, when he'd got his strength back. One day, when the matter seemed further from resolution than ever, he went along with everything, signed everything, surrendered completely. At the beginning of May, I turned the first sod. That was five years ago . . .

How hard it was and yet how simple! What I love most about architecture is its progressive simplification of an idea, how the dream takes shape. For all the precision of the original plans, there's something nebulous about the beginning of any construction project, as the precision is technical and abstract, and the concrete feeling of realizing it comes only later, after life has begun cooperating with your work. In these five years of work all I can recognize is the outline of the master's plans. The rest has come through surprises, through encountering opposition, through accidents.

'*The village of Uioara will be moved several kilometres to the right, to the valley of the river Ursu.*' It was easy to say. And to do, up to a certain point. But we had to contend with unforeseen opposition, and were obliged to take account of superstitions and hidden forces which never figured in any plan. Nor is New Uioara exactly the village the master designed, a transplantation of the old community of viticulturists, held at arm's length from Rice's enterprises. And nor has Old Uioara been completely replaced by industrial buildings. There were some old maniacs who wouldn't give up their old homes for anything and stupidly stayed on with their plum trees, battling waves of crude oil and drilling mud, and beyond in New Uioara some of the disoriented young men decided they'd had enough of tending vines and headed down into the valley, towards the wells, to become oil workers. This two-way traffic has changed the whole region, sweeping through old communities and precipitating changes in the structure of society. All this was too complex to have foreseen.

There is less litigation than before, but there is still enough. Rice keeps paying and they keep suing. There are some local adversaries who won't give up while they're still breathing.

From time to time a window or two gets smashed at the refinery or the offices. Where do these stones fall from? Who throws them? Why? As usual, the investigation makes little progress. It's more prudent that way. Twenty years from now, everything will be forgotten completely.

Meanwhile, we build. The refinery was finished nearly two years ago. I'm astounded today to think that I participated in its construction. The offices have gone well enough, the houses incomparably better. I think by next summer we'll have finished everything. We've kept moving our cabin and building site outwards, always towards the edge of this little town, which has gone up before us. Five years! I can't believe how it's flown.

*

There's been a switch of night-shifts at the oil wells. From here, on the porch of the cabin, the lamps of those returning to the village are clearly visible. It hasn't rained for about two weeks and the night is perfectly clear. Towards Ploieşti, the sky is phosphorescent. It must have been a terribly hot day there. The newspapers talk of 40 degrees in Bucharest.

How strange the chirping of the crickets seems, here, among

factory smokestacks, oil wells, water tanks and factory walls!

Occasionally a locust will leap from among the stones and disappear somewhere. We haven't managed to wipe out the flora and fauna of the area. The grass grows furiously wherever there's a scrap of soil. A few days ago, Marin Dronțu was astonished to glimpse a squirrel on top of the house. (But where did it come from? Where?)

The persistence of the natural world, of centuries of vegetation. This too will pass . . . Nothing remains unchanged when Ralph T. Rice descends upon it . . .

The nights here are long, calm and congenial. I can't bear to go to bed. I read a little, stroll a bit, and spend a long time stretched out on the deckchair 'with the stars' as Dronțu calls it, ironically. There was talk of going this evening to the home of a young couple, the Duntons, to play music on the gramophone. They've received some new records from England. But I feel so lazy.

I think Dronțu has a romantic assignment in Uioara. A fresh conquest. 'Some of these girls, pal, they're like roses.'

'You'll be the terror of the women, Marin.'

'Well, yeah, why not? Do I have the energy? You bet I do.'

Twice a week he escapes to the city to buy powders and perfumes for the 'girls and wives'. He has a special love for rouge and tobacco-scent. All New Uioara smells of bad cologne.

It would be easy to establish by smell the houses where our Marin has passed through and made a conquest.

> Green leaf of the beanstalk
> You're a miserable little weed

I hear him singing inside in his room, and his happiness is infectious. In several minutes he'll come out 'prepared', with a stiff collar, a red tie and a walking stick in hand, and he'll say to me again, before leaving:

'I wouldn't put myself out for that Marjorie you're all swooning over, wouldn't put myself out, though I could sweep her away. In three days, the game would be played out. I'd have her wrapped around my little finger. But I don't like her, sir, I don't like her, she's pale and kitten-eyed. Call yourselves men? Tulips, the lot of you.'

I needed time to learn to know and love Marin. At first, I couldn't for the life of me understand what he was doing in the master's office. I don't think he's achieved much as an architect. A decent sort, scoring just enough marks to graduate, he was doubtlessly a useful office worker. He is less use in the workshop, disliking calculations and drawing boards, rather better on site, where he sees and does everything. Anyhow, I was more than a little surprised to find him in the office of the most refined man I know.

Mircea Vieru is a Cartesian lost in Bucharest.

Marin Dronțu is a seminarian lost in architecture. A seminarian in his mode of thought, in his superstitions, in his stubbornness. 'Salt of the earth', as they say, flatteringly – a compliment that Mircea Vieru would detest, he being composed of a thousand nuances and not at all straightforward.

But Marin happily accepts such a description. And Marin (from whom I've learned to call Vieru 'master', though it was hard at first to call him anything other than 'sir') loves him with devotion, like a subject. 'He's a Lord,' he told me once, with utter respect, speaking of the master, and his use of this word endeared him to me because I understood that if Vieru is in fact a lord then Dronțu is, in turn, a peasant rather than the urbanite he strives to be, with his offhand manner, his vulgar sense of humour and his three-tone ties.

Later, when I heard from others the story of the chapel which he erected in his village in Gorj with money scrimped daily, in poverty, when I heard the proud inscription he engraved there in stone, I thought there was after all something to him that outbalanced his vocation as a successful Lothario with 'the ladies', as he called them, proud of his conquests.

'This chapel has been erected by Marin Dronțu, son of Nicolae Dronțu, who was born in this village, as were his own father and grandfather before him and all his forefathers.'

Having become a townsman, Marin Dronțu retains an ancestral contempt for those with pretensions. I think this is the source of his deliberate, affected vulgarity. He wants to be seen to be mocking 'frills and fripperies' – an expression that definitively dismisses all that can't be put plainly and in three words. Sometimes he wears me out with his insistence on recommending himself with: 'I'm a peasant'. This kind of exaggeration is another form of affectation. For Dronțu, speaking correctly is a sign of pretentiousness. Bad grammar and using a certain vocabulary is almost a duty with him, a way of stressing that he still has his hand on the plough and is laughing at all our sensitivities. 'The apples ain't bad, the girls ain't ugly, the wine ain't neither.' When he catches himself speaking correctly, by accident, he immediately reverts to form. Rudeness is his personal form of elegance, lightly illustrated with a smile to tell you that he could behave differently if he wanted, but he'd rather not.

To all this, you can add his extraordinary bad taste, his unparalleled sartorial eccentricity. If one evening he wears a black coat, he's sure to put on yellow boots. If his tie is blue, his handkerchief will certainly be red. If he wears a raincoat, he's sure to choose a melon-coloured hat. It's an inventive and vigorous bad taste. I think it's a sign of health and self-assurance. Marin Dronțu doesn't have doubts, doesn't question himself, doesn't look for secrets. In Bucharest he has numerous 'lovers', one or two in every neighbourhood, he takes them to the cinema, buys them peanuts and gives them red carnations and Flora cream on their birthdays. Here, he sleeps with girls and women from Uioara. If he happens to suffer disappointment in love, he sings one of his songs from Gorj, and it passes.

He went to church on Sunday, in the village, and sang hymns. He has a warm voice, like that of a big child. He sings seriously, with all his heart, imbuing the song with solemnity. Leaving, I clasped his hand and told him how beautifully he had sung. He blushed and, for the first time, I saw him embarrassed in the face of praise.

*

In Câmpina, at the railway station, awaiting the courier which the master had announced by telephone from Brașov, I caught sight of Marga and her husband through the train window. She's still beautiful, which makes me happy about the past – but looks set to put on weight, which makes me happy about the future.

The way she responded to my greeting, with the same attentive tilt of the head which I knew from before, reminded me suddenly that I had loved this girl and it struck me as unusually comic that now we were such strangers, separated by the glass of a train window, like a barrier between two worlds.

The courier arrived on the following train. I swore terribly at him. He had found it necessary to talk politics with the stationmaster for two hours.

*

Marjorie Dunton came by the oilfield in the morning. I was covered with dust, my hands dirty, my hair messed up, and I didn't want to go down. She greeted me from below.

'I was waiting for you last night with new records. You're a deserter.'

'Sorry, I had work to do. If you'll have me, I'll come this evening.'

'Can't this evening. We're going to the Nicholsons'. Phill has promised a game of bridge. Come along yourself.'

She was dressed in white. Marin Dronţu is right: white doesn't suit her. She's incredibly blonde – the white-blonde of corn straw. Light colours make her inexpressive. In the sun her eyes, which are green, turn violet, her cheeks lose the contour which usually shadows them towards the corners of her lips and the line of her neck no longer reveals that fine familiar curve.

I watched her for a long time as she went away, jumping carelessly from one stone to another, between rubble and plaster.

I've often wondered what kind of a life Marjorie Dunton leads. She doesn't love her husband, and he doesn't love her. This at least is clear between them. They have common interests which make their partnership pleasant: music, skiing, swimming. They also have their individual preferences. He likes bridge and she likes novels.

Enough for a marriage between two such intelligent people. Still,

I find it hard to believe you can get by on so little. At least Phill has the refinery laboratory, where he can continue his work and perform experiments. But what has Marjorie got?

Young Dogany suffers in vain. I don't think Marjorie will ever love him. I don't think she'll ever love anyone. I say that with a certain sadness, but a certain pleasure too, as I wonder if I wouldn't suffer knowing her to be in someone else's arms. I can't explain it, because I've never expected anything beyond the fact that we get on well together.

Three years ago, when the Duntons came here, Marjorie intimidated me. I was afraid of what might happen. I had so much work to do, and God knows I didn't need romantic complications. Things resolved themselves naturally. Marjorie is excellent company.

Back then we were reading Emily Brontë's *Wuthering Heights*. I remember speaking animatedly about the book, about its passion, about the hallucinatory poetry of its heroes. She knew the book, but didn't like it.

'I don't like overwrought books,' she said. 'If you're interested in the Brontë sisters, I recommend Charlotte. She's simpler, "homelier", calmer.'

She lent me *Shirley*, Charlotte Brontë's novel, which I loved straight away, on first reading. It was relaxing, clear, with a certain juvenile naivety, through which I tried to see Marjorie Dunton. I congratulated her on her discrimination, which later I saw reconfirmed many times in literature and music.

I asked her once if she'd ever thought of writing. She laughed. 'What a notion!' Still, when I get a letter from her in Bucharest in winter, I'm amazed at the liveliness with which she imbues little happenings, the images she evokes, how she can lightly, negligently, drop a confession between the lines.

*

I'd been working all day and, tired as I was, hadn't expected I'd stay so late at the Nicholsons'. These people have managed to create here, in Prahova, in Uioara, real society life.

It's probably their national character. At first their insistence on keeping up society manners here in the back of beyond struck me as somehow comic. Marjorie dresses fancifully only in the morning. She is a passionate adherent of evening dress. The men always come to dinner in black coats. I tried to rebel in favour of short-sleeved shirts with open collars, but had to accept defeat.

Once, concerning this matter, Eva Nicholson said something silly and over-excited to me:

'You're wrong to laugh at this. It's not frivolous. It's something more serious, it's a matter of dignity; no, it's a matter of salvation. If, because we're on our own, because nobody sees us, we conceded a little of what you consider society manners, and a little more tomorrow, we'd wake up one morning living in the most terrible promiscuity. It would be unbearable. Without black tie and evening gown, nobody would have any real privacy. Privacy is such a fragile thing and it's worth making sacrifices for.'

Though I don't entirely follow Mrs Nicholson's reasoning, I have to admit that their strict dress code evenings are relaxed and welcoming. I have a sense of freedom, well-being, of simple elegance.

Marjorie played Déodat de Séverac on the piano, the Debussy-ist she recently discovered. It's amusing to watch young Pierre Dogany listening as he leans against the corner of the piano, visibly sad and happy. His strange head has both Semitic and Mongolian features. He really is handsome, this boy, and deeply appealing in his unrequited love for Marjorie. Marjorie looks at him directly, loyally, as if to say: 'It's nothing, Pierre, it'll pass, you'll see.' At the end of September he has to return to Budapest to sit exams, and the prospect is already weighing on him.

We left late, together, and walked to the Duntons'. Then he walked a bit with me, towards the cabin. He recited some verses by Endre Ady but wouldn't translate them for me. His voice trembled and I could feel how furious that made him.

Entering my room, I probably woke Dronțu who, from beyond, struggling out of sleep, couldn't keep from shouting out to me once again:

'See how you waste your nights? That Marjorie's going to wear

you out. And not one of you is up to the job. You call yourselves
men . . .'

*

What a surprise, meeting S.T. Haim in the casino in Sinaia. A pipe
on the construction site had burst, right in my work area, and I suddenly found myself with a few free hours. I didn't feel like conversation or reading, and, as Hacker was leaving with the Ford for Predeal,
where he has a sick daughter, I asked him to drop me off in Sinaia.

Same old S.T.H. Blond, kinky-haired, short, with extraordinarily
intelligent eyes, alive to everything, the flash of a smile or the beat
of a pulse; his agitated hands twitching with the impatience to
express too much. 'He has too many gestures and only two hands,'
Winkler used to say.

He had completely disappeared for the past few years. I can't have
caught sight of him more than a couple of times, from afar, in the
street. He went abroad, travelled extensively, had a few love affairs,
made some good business decisions. Now he's working with some
very profitable foreign engineering firms. His doctoral thesis in
mathematics caused a bit of a stir in the university, but that was
three or four years ago and I don't think he cares much for maths
these days.

'I'm like those Jewish girls who play Beethoven and Schubert
with feeling, then one day get married, stop playing the piano, forget
about music, get fat and have children.'

I felt he was telling me this in anticipation of my question, but I
don't actually believe anything he says. In fact, he's unjust with himself. Money, no matter how rich he may be, has had no effect on his
air of being a free man, ready to lose everything and start from
scratch. He has that rather childlike and distracted air that people
with an interior life retain in wealth; a sign that wealth, even if they
aren't indifferent to it, is certainly not indispensable to their identity.
Off-handedness is the humour of elegance, and I don't know a true
intellectual whose elegance does not involve this kind of humour.
S.T.H. certainly has it. His silk shirts, his flannel suits from London,

his fine bulky shoes, the delicately patterned tie – not only is he not intimidated by any of this, but he treats it all with bonhomie, as if they're amusing trifles.

We strolled through the gaming rooms and through the park, very happy to be seeing one another again. S.T.H. knows about the work going on at Uioara and seems well informed.

'Very interesting, everything Vieru's attempted there. You're working for us. You're making this entire region proletarian. In fact, you're doing something even more serious: you're dissolving the antagonism between the peasants and the proletariat. Another superstition that's disappearing. No sir, you can't have rural reaction in the middle of fighting for the revolution. I don't recognize the peasantry. I recognize workers and property owners. What work they do and what they own makes no difference. In the factory or in the field, the problem of class remains the same.'

I didn't attempt a reply, but smiled at finding him, despite the years, just as attached to his Marxist rhetoric. I commented, lightly, that things weren't that simple, that if he were in Uioara he'd see that the process was deeper and more complex, that I didn't believe the antagonism between workers and peasants was a superstition and that in any case, we were a long way from having dissolved it, so he had nothing to congratulate us for. I would like to have talked to him about 'the plum-tree issue', which I had so often been forced to reflect on since settling in Uioara, but that certainly would have infuriated him and I wasn't in the mood for an argument. I was very much enjoying strolling with him and I didn't want to spoil my enjoyment. We moved on to other subjects – books, women – and I was happy to see how sensitive and open the fellow was when you get him off Marxism and dialectics. I asked him to visit me some day at the oilfield, and he said he wasn't sure he could, as he wasn't alone in Sinaia. This probably meant a woman, but I didn't ask for details. Judging from his reluctance to speak, it was probably an affair of the heart. But he clearly felt the need to explain himself, as he burst out, with a certain weariness in his voice:

'Books, love affairs, money, they're all substitutes. I'd be bored without them. I'm waiting for something else entirely ... But the right moment is yet to come. We're in a stupid year, a year of prosperity. I'm waiting for the crisis. That's when everything will fall, be overturned. There's too much money around now, too much excess, too much optimism. We'll see what happens in 1930, in 1931. Things will come to a head one way or another. Until then, I'm going to rest. I'm neither sentimental nor a martyr. I'm not going to get sent to Jilava Prison for poetry. The moment that counts is the moment of spasm. Six years ago, when we met, was one of those, but it passed and I missed it. It'll be back some day, and I won't miss it again.'

Evening fell. The sun bathed the big windows of the casino with a violent glow. It was clear we were both thinking of the same thing, the meaning of that red blaze, as we suddenly looked up at one another.

'I think you're wrong. And if you're not wrong, that's even worse.'

The park was full of beautiful women, full of white dresses. We parted as friends.

General ideas are S.T.H.'s vocation. I lost the habit for them long ago. When was the last time I had a discussion involving arguments, issues and principles?

One might say I'm becoming coarsened. But life is so simple now, so clear.

I remembered my blue notebook from 1923. Where could it be? At home, perhaps, in some drawer or box. I'm going to look for it someday, though I think it'll be embarrassing to re-read it. Lord, what folly must be written there ... But perhaps not entirely my fault. S.T.H. is right: it was a moment of crisis. I was expecting signs in the street – and there was nothing in the street but confusion, the fog of stupidity, intoxication. So I took refuge in intellectual problems, which cast no light, but gave me consolation. It was a simple game and also gave me a certain illusion of personal superiority. I reduced everything to the drama of being a Jew, which is perhaps a constant reality, but not such an overwhelming one that it should cancel or even supersede strictly personal dramas and comedies. I was, I believe, two steps away from fanaticism. Interrupting my diary was a good thing to have done. Writing only fed my fever. From the day I tossed that notebook aside and let the days pass of their own accord, without commenting, without escapism, things settled down bit by bit and became simpler, calmer.

*

On Thursday, old Ralph returned from abroad and went straight to the oilfield from the train station. It was clear he had an intuition. He made a terrible scene, sowing panic for a kilometre around.

I later heard that at the wells and in the offices everyone was trembling with apprehension. 'The boss is furious' went the news, in a chain of whispers. I was lucky that Marin Dronţu was there too, so I was able to keep quiet without my silence appearing insolent. The old fellow wouldn't stop. What? Whose villa? His own villa? He, the master's? He, who's spending a fortune? His own personal villa, just the way he wants it? Just as he ordered it? How could we? On what basis? How dare he? This messing about has to stop! Enough of this nonsense! Enough! Really enough! He'll take measures! He'll demolish the lot! Rebuild the lot!

I let him talk, knowing he'd tire – and that's what happened. For two days he didn't come around here. I saw him at the wells and he mumbled a reply to my greeting. Next week, when the master comes, there'll be a burst of indignation, and then it'll pass.

*

This evening, a reception in honour of old Ralph T. Rice. A gala reception in Uioara, in Prahova! So many dinner jackets and long silk dresses – almost unreal in this place of oil and plum trees. Of all the master has built there, I like the club most. There's something both solemn and cordial about it. It's British and local in equal measure. The ballroom and the billiard room are linear and sober; the verandas and reading rooms have the air of small interior gardens.

Almost every evening, before dinner, I meet there with Phillip Dunton to play a game of chess.

I'm not going to Rice's reception. I'm still *en froid* after Thursday's scene, and then I don't have the required dinner jacket. I'm happy to stay at the cabin and listen to records borrowed from Marjorie. I'd have liked to convince Dronțu not to go either, but there was no way.

'What? Me, afraid of an American, three Germans and five Englishwomen? You tell me I've no dinner jacket? Don't you worry, sir, I know all about being elegant.'

He powdered and perfumed himself and very carefully constructed a triumphant look: a bright blue suit, a coffee-coloured pullover, a stiff collar, a polka-dot bow-tie and white spats. For a moment I wondered if Marin was not a comedian, engaged in gratuitous outrages against convention. Seen this way, his entry in the club would be a master-stroke.

Dear fellow! He left happy, twirling his gnarled walking stick, and I envied him his iron constitution, his absolute imperviousness.

*

I worked flat out all day. The master is coming the day after tomorrow and I want everything to be in order. Marin Dronțu arrived very late at the oilfield, tired after a sleepless night and, on arriving, told me there was something he wanted to talk to me about.

'At lunch, Marin! I've no time now.'

But I stayed and ate lunch at the site, quickly, as I'd convinced everybody to take a break of only half an hour, and Marin was unable to talk to me. I knew it had to be very serious, judging by his worried air. Whatever job he had at hand, I found him always at my side, fretting over some secret he wished to unburden himself of.

'Marin, go to bed! You must be sick.'

He stayed until late in the evening, when the third shift sounded, down at the oil wells. As I too was very tired, we went straight to the cabin, to eat what we could find.

'Well,' he finally said with a deep sigh, 'I'll tell you one thing, I'll do anything, but I don't touch my friends' women. Anything but that.'

I didn't understand a thing and waited for him to go on.

'Look, this is what happened: last night I'd had a couple of drinks and I went out on to the veranda to cool down. I found your Marjorie out there. Her husband was playing cards. "Let's take a walk," I said. "Certainly," says she. So off we went. When we passed by her house, she said, "Come in, I'm thirsty, I want to drink a glass of water." I went in and, in the dark, I tried to kiss her, and she didn't object. In the end we went to bed and she told me not to ruffle her dress. Then we went back to the club, and her husband was still playing cards.'

Marin Dronțu has gone quiet and is looking at me, awaiting a response, a sign. For a few moments I say nothing either, not knowing what to do. There are so many things to be done . . .

My first thought is to stand up, run down to the Duntons' villa and ask Marjorie. Ridiculous. When it comes to women, Marin Dronțu never lies.

But I should inquire further, get him to tell me everything, right down to the details. I should stand up and pace about the cabin, I should rush over to young Dogany, I should tell Dronțu what a pig he is.

I raised my head.

'Bravo, Marin. And is that all you've been fretting about for an entire day? You slept with her, so good for you.'

'You mean, you're not angry?'

'Why should I be? What's it to me? Is she family? My wife? Lover? It's between the two of you. Come on, let's eat now.'

I drank a bottle of wine and Marin sang a few sentimental songs.

'What the hell, they're all the same, the lot of them. Women.'

That's my consolation.

*

The work goes on. The master's visit has put things in order. But his interview with Rice went worse than I expected.

I'd counted on a five-minute argument. It lasted an hour. The master left the director's office, slamming the door, and went straight to the oilfield, where he remained with us until evening, running from one corner to the other, scrutinizing everything. I could feel his bad humour, and everybody worked in silence, with their heads down. It was like a tacit act of solidarity with him. I think he understood that.

Old Ralph turned up, too, around four o'clock with a long-faced look of consternation. He hovered around Vieru, not knowing how to begin speaking again, but Vieru was determined not to lighten his penance. In the end, the old fellow had to bite the bullet: he took it all back, apologized in a roundabout way and vowed not to meddle any more.

That night the master slept here with us, in the cabin. We stayed up late talking, drinking wine and smoking, all three of us. You could hear brief rumblings from afar, which then echoed down the whole valley, as if every sound were broken into thousands of tiny splinters. It's a well that's been gushing for about two days at Romanian Star. Like the breathing of a caged animal, somewhere in the night.

*

Pierre Dogany came by the cabin yesterday evening to see me. I was surprised, as he'd never done this before.

Poor boy! He senses something has happened but doesn't know exactly what, and doesn't have the courage to imagine.

If I could be sure his suffering contained enough freedom of spirit, I'd tell him and, with a little intelligence, he would be consoled.

We went together to the Star well to see how it was working. There were a lot of flares, like some strange torchlight procession. Human shadows grew immense around us, into the distance, upon the hillsides.

He spoke of his approaching departure, and tried to seem indifferent.

'Why are you really going? Do you think the university in Budapest is better than the one in Bucharest?'

'I don't know if it's better. But it's my university.'

'I thought you were a Jew.'

'I'm Hungarian. A Jew, of course, but also a Hungarian. My father opted for Romania. His business. He was born in Satu Mare, he wants to die in Satu Mare. He votes, pays his dues, reads the Bucharest newspapers. None of that interests me. It's not part of me, I don't understand it. I grew up with Endre Ady. I'm sticking with him. I'd feel stifled if I stayed here, in this atmosphere, with these people. And if it weren't for my parents, who I have to see in the holidays, and especially if there wasn't something else –' he fell quiet, hesitating – 'I think I'd stay there for good. You have to understand: it's my memories, my language, my culture.'

'A culture that, from what I've heard, doesn't embrace you with the same enthusiasm with which you embrace it.'

'I foresaw that objection. And I'm surprised you haven't reminded me that Budapest University has a *numerus clausus*. Of course it's not pleasant. It's humiliating at times. But when you really love something, you love the good and the bad together. This will pass too, some day. You'd do the same in my place.'

We headed home, on the Ursu road. There was still a light on at the Duntons', and Dogany suddenly fell quiet. He took his leave brusquely, with a quick goodbye. For a moment, I wanted to call after him. I'm not sure what I wanted to say to him. Something to make him feel less alone.

*

Marjorie came by the oilfield today. She was wearing a green knitted dress and a white scarf.

I was terribly busy, but took care to talk with her for a long time so that she wouldn't think I was annoyed. She had leaned back against some support beams, arms hanging loosely at her sides, legs slightly bent, the soft shape of her knees protruding against her dress. She has fine, long bones. She spoke with great animation and seriousness, but I couldn't understand what it was about. I tried to follow her or at least to seem focused, but my thoughts were elsewhere. Marin Dronțu approached us, but she continued speaking to me, completely unchanged, completely unsurprised, showing no awkwardness. He coughed a couple of times, shifted his weight from foot to foot, then went away, shrugging his shoulders in boredom.

'She's just showing off,' he said to me later.

*

I wasn't expecting the professor's visit, and the telegram he sent me to announce his arrival was a real surprise.

'At last, he's given in,' I said to myself. I'd asked him so often to come to Uioara, and he refused vehemently each time.

'What you're doing there is barbarous, criminal. It's the most artificial thing that's been done in Romania since 1848.'

Since I began work at the Rice concession, much opposition has subsided. Ghiță Blidaru's opposition alone has remained firm. Vieru doesn't say anything, but I think that deep down this disapproval hurts him, and is all the harder for him to deal with as it's purely intellectual in nature. If 'Professor Ghiță' – as he calls him – were an engineer, I don't think Vieru would care less about his objections. One set of figures can always be countered by others. But the professor's hostility to the Uioara project does not concern technical or economic issues. He's thinking of 'the problem of the plum trees', a perspective he would readily recognize as being at the very core of his thinking. '*Whenever the struggle is waged between life and an abstraction, I will be on the side of life, and against abstraction.*'

The master despairs utterly before this unassailable position, as it transcribes the issue to a level and a scale of values with which he has no connection.

'What drives me mad about Professor Ghiță is metaphysics. In a matter involving so many facts and practicalities – money, stones, oil, drainage work and water supply – he comes along with moral problems. I'm thinking in terms of practicalities, he in terms of metaphysics.'

'Practicalities, practicalities!' replies the professor contemptuously. 'There's only one thing it makes any practical sense to talk about: man.'

The argument has been going on for over five years, ever since Rice started work. Ghiță Blidaru has pointedly refused to visit us in Uioara, and thus refused to set eyes on what he considers always to be a 'deliberate crime'.

'At last, he's giving in,' I said to myself, hastily, receiving the telegram. It was premature of me. Far from giving in, he has decided to criticize our work publicly.

His course this year will deal with the Romanian economy and its European deformations. The opening lecture will focus specifically on the two Uioaras, Old and New, as the starting point for the entire course. That's why he's here: to get some first-hand information.

He wouldn't let me accompany him on his walk through the village. He assumes I'm in league with Vieru.

'Stay at the oilfield and do your job. I'll wander around on my own.'

In the evening he came to my workplace to get me. I was in boots, overalls and a short-sleeved collarless shirt. It seems I've turned terribly dark in the sun over the last few weeks.

'You resemble a stonemason,' he said to me. 'It makes me happy to look at you.'

Like a stonemason . . . I don't know about that. But I do feel free, at peace, ready to take things as they come, to await their unfolding with acceptance, to behold them without fear, to lose them without despair. I think of the big personal problems I used to have and I don't understand them. I don't understand them, and good riddance.

Life is easy. Life is terribly easy.

*

It rained two days in a row and the road from the cabin to Old Uioara is full of mud. I made a mighty fire in the stove and spent both evenings reading until past midnight. It smells of autumn – and we're only in September. It brightened a little this morning and I thought the weather was picking up, but then it began pouring again, even more heavily.

At five, I received a visit that took me aback. Marjorie Dunton, in a raincoat, bareheaded, wet and trembling and noisy. (I hadn't seen her in recent days. Except for once, last Wednesday I think, on the way to Prahova. She was with Dronţu, whom I just greeted in passing as he seemed terribly embarrassed.)

'I've come to get you out of your lair.'

I found for her a dry blanket, slippers, a dressing gown and settled her by the fire so she could dry her hair, which, being so wet, was no longer blonde.

I made tea and had her drink it with lots of cognac.

So, we talked about this and that . . . I told her that in three or four days I would be leaving for Bucharest.

'I know. You left around this time last year too.'

I like the direct way she speaks, without pauses, without pushiness, rather boyishly.

Later, Marin came in from the oilfield, not at all surprised at finding her with me. We walked her home together and, several times, where there was too much mud, I carried her over, swinging her and singing 'Rock-a-bye Baby'.

She sang, triumphantly twirling the beret I'd given her to cover her head.

It's a long way to Tipperary
It's a long way to go . . .

2

The November issue of *Der Querschnitt* features a long essay on Mircea Vieru's work, with photographs, scale models and reproductions. A special section on the Uioara project.

So, success. Definitive, incontrovertible success, from beyond the horizons of Bucharest. Who would have said, years ago, that it would come so soon?

When the professor took me the first time to Vieru's house, I found him at the lowest point of his career. He was close to giving up the fight. If Ralph T. Rice hadn't appeared from nowhere, Vieru would have been a broken man. I still don't know today how he managed to put up with so much.

I couldn't open a newspaper without finding a piece of news, an act of treachery, a farce. Everywhere, in the gossip columns, the society pages, in humorous magazines, in caricatures, the 'affair of the day', everywhere Mircea Vieru, only Mircea Vieru, every day Mircea Vieru. Every gaffe was attributed to him, every piece of nonsense was spoken by him, every joke was on him. In the summer, in the Cărăbuş review theatre, Tănase, with a trowel in one hand and a brick in the other, recited a couplet explaining the whole 'affair'. Everybody laughed terribly, and I remember I found it amusing myself at the time. I later learned that Vieru had made a point of not leaving Bucharest that summer, so that it couldn't be said of him that he was trying not to be seen. What cruel moments he must have lived through, he who is so proud, so sensitive to the smallest detail, such a child when it comes to slights and revenge.

It was mostly out of curiosity that I accepted when the professor offered to recommend me to Vieru for a place in his workshop. A second-year student, I didn't have high hopes of any great personal success with an architectural firm; I lacked even a basic grasp of what was going on with which to orient myself. But the man interested me; he had initiated so many attacks, got involved in so many struggles, and aroused such opposition. Everyone was against him: the press, his peers, the school, officialdom, ministries, all Bucharest, all Romania, the whole world.

'You're going to meet the most detested person on the face of the planet,' said the professor, climbing the stairs ahead of me, to the office.

The most detested person on the face of the planet! Blond, blue-green eyes, a bright, open smile, a modest bearing, with unexpected flashes of pride, nervous hands, a deep, even voice, never raised, though often giving an impression of vehemence, by emphasis, phrasing, pauses . . . The abominable Mircea Vieru looked something between a schoolboy and an amateur botanist. Only later, getting to know him, did I realize that his forcefulness, of which they make so much, is not imaginary. On the contrary, it is very sharp and penetrating. It is an intellectual force, an objective force in the world of values and ideas, which has nothing to do with his personal goodness and limitless generosity. Vieru is forceful as only the good can be, disinterestedly, passionately, freely. I now understand well that poison vortex in 1923, which he had to rise above at all costs.

When, immediately following the war, Mircea Vieru came up with some rather insolent notions in his works on architecture and town planning, he seemed more amusing than anything. 'That damned Vieru,' would think his fellow architects, with a mixture of vague admiration and disbelief.

'*Architecture isn't a private matter between a man with money and a man with a diploma. Architecture is a matter of communal life. Any liberties can be taken, but the liberty of bad taste may not. A badly conceived house is a disturbance of the peace.*'

'That damned Vieru!'

But when Mircea Vieru went from general ideas and opinions to the nitty-gritty of individual cases, naming names and involving people and projects, things took another turn. Toes were stepped on – and that's a serious matter.

For some three years, this man did nothing but denounce. A building over a certain size couldn't be built without him putting it on trial publicly and in writing. In detail, with photographs, figures, names, following the entire process step by step, checking, challenging, attacking. He no longer took any interest in his own projects. What excited him now about architecture were its fashions, errors, clichés and pointless attempts at innovation. He had stopped being an architect and had become a pamphleteer. How many competitions were disrupted by one of his inopportune interventions, how many contract-winners were endangered by him, how many artistic collaborations fell apart as a result of his lack of tact! They still laughed, here and there, at his audacity, at his extraordinary polemical verve, but it was nervous laughter. Because no one knew what was coming next from this blond, edgy, intolerant little man who spent the little money he had printing magazines of art and criticism, which he wrote, corrected and administered alone, exhausted by work but relentlessly passionate.

His pamphlet *Academic Bombast and Revolutionary Bombast* caused complete bafflement. Everyone had known Vieru as a modernist. Now nobody knew what he was any more. Anything was possible and there was no way to protect yourself. Vieru disposed of your peace, your freedom, your private arrangements. For three straight years he was the artistic police, spreading panic, sowing enmities that would bide their time, awaiting their moment. The moment wasn't long in coming. Vieru's first misstep gave the signal. And it truly was imprudent of him to accept at that moment a project in the Engineers' Park. They gave him sole responsibility for building an entire neighbourhood. Admittedly, the enterprise was dizzyingly attractive for a man who had dreamed of nothing his whole life but building something grand, extensive, new, from scratch, his alone to direct and plan. But had he been more prudent, he would have known the moment was not propitious. A man in the midst of such hostility would not be granted the peace needed to create. A prickly Vieru would be put up with as long as he was poor. How could you hurt him? By attacking his intelligence? His passion for dispute? Lucky enough to possess nothing, how could he be condemned for compromising, for being afraid, for being cautious? But a Vieru engaged in something big, a Vieru on the path to realizing a grand project, went from being dangerous to being vulnerable. Very vulnerable. The day the ex-pamphleteer stepped on the site, his fate was sealed: there were old scores to settle and slights to be avenged.

And what a show it was! And not just the newspaper articles, the coffee-shop talk and the anonymous letters to the consortium that had hired Vieru. He could have defeated all that alone, he who knew about writing, arguing and declaiming. But there were neighbourhood meetings too, protesting against 'the disfiguring of our Capital by irresponsibly ceding the construction of an entire neighbourhood to a pretentious bungler'.

And then there were questions raised in Parliament, telegrams to the Minister for the Arts, 'spontaneous' demonstrations in front of City Hall, mass walkouts of workers . . .

I remember well those enormous placards hanging from a cart pulled down Calea Victoriei by a donkey who became popular very quickly.

Citizens of Bucharest! Will you tolerate a newcomer's risky experiments in your city, in the capital of a united Romania? Will you permit the sacrifice of the most picturesque corner of the citadel of Bucur?

I didn't know the master during that period, and I would have been indifferent to the whole story if I hadn't had an instinctual glimmer of sympathy for the man who had drawn such unanimous enmity. I followed the affair in the papers and was very distressed to one day read that *'good sense triumphs at last, architect Mircea Vieru's contract has been revoked and work at the Engineers' Park has halted, to general satisfaction'*.

I met him several months later, in autumn.

It was an empty office. His friends had one by one deserted him, no clients appeared, the summer had passed without any work and winter was coming with no projects in store. Vieru was writing a pamphlet to 'set the record straight' about the sad affair of the revoked contract. He wrote at night to give us an overwrought read in the morning, complete with gestures and outbursts. He was at war with the universe: with the government, with Parliament, with City Hall, with the Liberal Party, with the Romanian people. When he found a strident phrase, he perked up: 'I'll show them.' It was hard to say what he was going to demonstrate, or to whom.

One man alone remained always by his side, sharing his fury and suffering his disappointments: Marin Dronțu. He carried a stick and had obtained a permit for a gun. What he really wanted was to shoot one of the 'thugs' who wrote in the papers against his master, and if he didn't do it, it was only because it was hard to know where to start. But there were some suspicious fights at night, resulting in some bloodied heads, and I wouldn't be surprised if Dronțu had a hand in them. And today, when I ask him, he smiles mysteriously. 'I don't know, I didn't see anything.'

There were also days when Vieru caved in, when his fever subsided, when he lost his appetite for the fight, when he trudged through the workshop, when it all looked empty, senseless, worthless, when he despaired of the drawing boards, when he was tired of arguing, when nobody mattered to him, whether friend or foe.

'One day we'll shut up shop,' he said with indifference, worn out, after ten cups of coffee and hundreds of cigarettes, smoked nervously down to the filter.

Sometimes Ghiță Blidaru would come by and his breezy presence would shake the master from his apathy. They always found something to fight about, as there were no facts or ideas which these two men, who had known each other so long, could agree on. The arrival of the professor was always invigorating. When he had left, the desire for work would return, as would the courage to curse fate and to have faith in it.

'Just you wait, I'll show them.'

And so he did. In spring, Rice turned up out of the blue. True, he didn't look like a gift from heaven, but he had plenty of money and a pinch of craziness, which was exactly what he needed to get along with Vieru. And now, nearly six years later, *Der Querschnitt* is presenting in Berlin the work of the great architect of Uioara in Prahova.

Last night I stayed up late talking with Marin Dronțu, drinking a glass of wine and recalling all that had happened.

'Where are they, the ones who cursed him, where are they? I'll eat them alive!'

I think what draws me most to the master is his wounded pride. I myself had so many personal humiliations to overcome that I find the company of this man, who has been struck at from every direction, stimulating. He had bursts of mania and disgust, turning vengefully on everything, like a flame, like a blade. I preserve an old sense of obligation, an inevitable sympathy, for the isolated or beaten individual. The only pain which I understand directly and instinctively, without needing it explained, is the pain of discouragement.

I too had breathed the diffuse poison of hostility, I too knew what it was like to have someone swear at you over their shoulder, or to land a punch without a word, or to slam a door in your face.

I'd known all these things, day after day, breathing the same adversity, bearing down on you from all around, anonymously, stubbornly, without beginning or end. Today, recalling it, this drama looks puerile and overdone to me. But back then, along with the experience of my first lamentable years of university, it was a burden I suffered. Anybody I met could have been an enemy, every hand held out could have been about to strike you.

Even Blidaru I approached with apprehension. The uproar at the university, the street fights and the tension of that year of confrontation maintained my consciousness of the sin of being a Jew like an ever-raw wound. I turned this feeling into an obsession, a mania, and now I understand that my perturbation was excessive, and it must have been deadly tedious to anybody not involved. The naivety of those with something to hide – a crime, a disgrace, a drama – is that they imagine they are under suspicion. In reality, there's a strong dose of indifference in the world, enough that you can go off and die and nobody will notice. In the case of Jews, their mistake is that they observe too much and thereby believe themselves to be under scrutiny. Back then, I felt interrogated by every glance cast my way. I felt hounded. I felt the urgent, comic need to denounce myself: I'm a Jew. I was sure that if I didn't I'd sink into compromise, that I'd slide into a series of lies, that I'd sully the part of me that longed for truth. More than once I envied the simple life of the ghetto Jew, wearing his yellow patch. A humiliating idea perhaps, but comfortable and clear-cut, because they had finally put an end to the horrible comedy of uttering their own name like a denunciation.

I've never had a conversation with someone without wondering apprehensively whether they know I'm a Jew and, if so, whether they'll forgive me or not. This was a real problem to me, and caused me an absurd degree of suffering and awkwardness. So, I had resolved long ago to renounce all equivocation and to clarify the matter from the outset, confessing everything brusquely and readily, which must often have seemed the mark of aggressive pride, when in fact it was only wounded pride.

I tried behaving this way with Vieru, right from the first day, to explain myself concerning this issue, but he quickly cut me short.

'My dear fellow, it doesn't concern me. It's a personal matter and I beg you to keep it to yourself. Do you want me to tell you if I'm an anti-Semite? I don't know. I'm not familiar with the matter, it doesn't interest me, never could. But I'll say one thing: any general judgement about a category of people gives me the shudders. I'm not a mystic. I have a horror of generalizations. I can only judge specific cases, individual people, detail by detail.'

I thought he was trying to be nice. Later though, getting to know him, I realized how sincere his opening declaration was. It wasn't directed at me personally, but reflected his convictions. I subsequently found this to be true not only in Vieru's attitude to anti-Semitism – in the end a minor matter for him – but in his attitude as an artist, a critic and an architect.

I think it was in the first year of the Uioara project that someone turned up one fine day to ask his opinion for a feature in *The Universe* about 'the national character'. I cut out his reply and still have it today.

There is doubtless such a thing as a 'national character'. In art, it is the lowest common denominator. The more specific the character, the more commonplace it is. That is why creation always requires overcoming such a character.

An artist, if he is anything, is an individual. But to be an individual means embodying your own truths, suffering your own experiences, and inventing your own style. But these things can only occur by renouncing facility, and the most unfortunate facility comes from these so-called national characters, formed by the sedimentation of collective mediocrity, which lies there ready-made. National character is by definition that which remains in a culture after you have removed the personal effort involved in thinking, the personal experience of life and the triumph of individual creation. That's all.

Two weeks of abuse, polemics and revulsion ensued, to which Vieru did not respond. But from Berlin, where he was delivering a paper at the Institute of Current Affairs, Professor Ghiţă sent him a blunt telegram:

Read your views in *The Universe*. You're a wretched fool.

To which he replied:

Wretched fool, perhaps. But not of the common kind. My style's my own.

3

Yesterday, the professor's opening lecture. The atmosphere of an important happening, with a note of festivity and tension in the air, as in an arena where, from one moment to the next, something decisive will be thrashed out. The banging of the desktops, voices calling out from one end of the hall to the other, people noisily taking leave of one another, familiar faces, unfamiliar faces – all mixed together confusedly, humming with curiosity and impatience.

Vieru, on his own in the back row, irritated, was drumming his fingers on the bench. I was afraid he'd be recognized, which would have caused a rather tiresome commotion during a lecture that would discuss him enough as it was.

Marin Dronțu was absent. 'I'm not coming. It makes me sick. Look, I admit I can't be objective when it comes to the master. I'm not a critic and I don't know about that sort of thing. I love the master and believe in his destiny. So what do you expect me to gain from Ghiță Blidaru's lecture? Whatever he says, whether he's right or not, it'll just make me bitter. And I don't want to be bitter.'

Basically the professor's lecture – though he advertised it as vehement – was not vehement. It was clear that it was merely the threshold of an entire system of explanations and categorization going well beyond the particular case of Uioara.

I transcribe here from the notes I managed to jot in haste.

Let's be clear: the issue here is not the value of the architect Vieru's project in Uioara. Perhaps it shows the mark of genius. What is questionable, however, is its significance in relation to the Romanian spirit and, for this lecture, to the Romanian economy. My question is whether a person has the right to exercise genius when this goes against the needs of the land on which he lives. Further: if someone, as an individual, may interfere in the latent process of the collective life-force, modifying it, imposing upon it an alien, though perhaps superior, project. In fact, the claim to superiority becomes entirely spurious when two differing structures are involved. A shower of rain isn't superior to a drainpipe, nor a drainpipe superior to a fork. You cannot establish a scale of values between differing phenomena. The crime of an idiot tiger aspiring to be a paramecium would not be less than the crime of a genius paramecium dreaming of being a tiger. A betrayal, a degradation, is involved in both cases, and you won't find it written anywhere that, from the point of view of life, the degradation of a paramecium is less tragic than that of a tiger.

At Uioara, in five years, a daring man has replaced a settlement of viti-culturists with an industrial complex. Based on what calculation? For the sake of the prejudice that values a smokestack above a grapevine. Well, this is a monstrous judgement. Neither a smokestack nor a grapevine, taken alone, mean anything. They only become meaningful when brought into a family, a structure. Outside of this structure, they remain discrete, dead abstractions. The abstraction of a smokestack in Uioara and the no less abstract grapevine in Manchester.

This blindness to the laws specific to life, this blindness to the ways spe-cific to living, is a perversion of those historical roots which must be traced all the way back through the nineteenth century, to the roots of the French revolution and, further, to the roots of reform. Our lectures over the past years have sketched the general framework of the problem. I propose this year that we study several particular aspects of the Romanian economy, deformed by the revolutionaries of 1848 and liberalism to the point of smothering the most elementary local features.

It was a beautiful lecture, and Vieru had to admit it. We took a walk together afterwards.

'Decidedly, I'm never going to see eye to eye with Professor Ghiţă. He's a seminarian, a theologian. A man who's happy when he can be subject to something, whatever it may be. With a thousand Moldovans and a thousand Muntenians like him, I'm not surprised that for centuries this place has been dominated by whoever imposed their will: Turks, Russians, Phanariote Greeks. His whole life consists of subjugations. "Subject to the demands of life,'" as he'd say. Subjugation to everything above and beyond you. For my part, the day I start to believe that by the very fact of being a man I'm condemned to be circumscribed in this way, I'll shoot myself. If I'm not free, then I'm nothing. Free to think, free to ascribe values or fix hierarchies. The world can be understood through critical discrimination or through rigorous examination. And, conversely, it can go permanently dark if we give up on thinking and take refuge in mystical intuitions.'

Ghiță Blidaru and Mircea Vieru are divided by a whole history, an entire worldview. Were it not for the picturesque aspect of each, Vieru with his blond faun-like head, Ghiță Blidaru like a wintry wolf, were it not for their colourful and contrasting lives, with their passions, struggles and loves, what fine characters in a Platonic dialogue those two would make, these two ideological poles! 'The drama of modern Romanian history', as portrayed by two heroes. Utterly schematic, but representative nonetheless.

To put it crudely, Romanian culture has remained stuck with the same intellectual problems which arose when the first railroad was built in 1860. With the problem of identifying with the west or the east, with Europe or the Balkans, with urban culture or the spirit of the countryside. The issues have always remained the same.

The poet Vasile Alecsandri formulates them with naivety, Ghiță Blidaru and Mircea Vieru formulate them with a critical spirit. Yet the rural type and the urban type are the only categories that remain permanently valid in Romanian culture. I believe you can always easily distinguish the devotees of one or the other of these two orientations, anywhere, in Romanian literature, in politics, in music, in journalism . . . The choice is clear for Vieru. He's the urban type par excellence. One of those Europeans who have been shaped by Cartesianism, the bourgeois revolution and civic culture, a new nation on this continent, and one that transcends any national borders.

'I believe in the identity of man. I believe in permanent, universal values. I believe in the dignity of intelligence.'

I'm convinced these three short sentences sum up the basis of Vieru's thinking. I once asked him if the war, from which he returned with two poorly mended wounds, had not turned his intellectual certitudes upside down.

'Rather the contrary. I fought seriously, because I like to take everything I do seriously. But I always knew what it was all worth. After I was wounded the second time, I woke up one night in a field hospital, dumped on a stretcher in a corner, beside a German corporal, also wounded, who couldn't have been more than nineteen and who told me he was waiting for the war to end so he could go to Paris, to work on his thesis about the connections between Goethe and Stendhal. We talked about this all night and helped each other to reconstruct a map of Beyle's pilgrimage through Europe between 1812 and 1840. The next morning we were going to go our separate ways for good, me to one hospital, he to another, and perhaps both to our graves – but, in the meantime, that night, our most urgent problem was that one. In two years of war, that meeting was the finest thing that happened.'

*

I can see the master living just as easily in accordance with such principles, such simple laws. What I find hard to understand is not Ghiță Blidaru's thinking and his life, but how the two mesh. They seem so contradictory to me!

This man, who has passed through libraries, through universities, through metropolises, strives to remain a ploughman in his thinking. 'That's all I am,' he tells me. Perhaps that's true. But in the same evening I listened to Bach's second Brandenburg Concerto on his gramophone and, for the treason to be complete, good old Couperin's *Les Folies françoises*. He has a fine understanding of art, down to the slightest nuances and the finest shades. And then there's that Brueghel, the only painting in his study. What is it doing in the house of a ploughman from Vâlcea, who never tires of reminding me what he is?

So Ghiță Blidaru inhabits an environment his thinking rejects, lives by values he denies, enjoys victories that he disputes.

'Europe is a fiction,' he's been saying in his university course for six years, while never ceasing for a moment to love the spirit of this fiction. Brueghel belongs to this fiction, and Bach, and certainly Couperin.

Nevertheless, having passed through and loved them all, Ghiţă Blidaru inevitably returns to his grapevine, in the name of which he was lecturing the other day at the university.

The miracle by which this man manages to think, effortlessly, unaffectedly, like a peasant, is not something I can comprehend. His vision of life seems to open towards as much sky and earth as is visible between the handles of the plough. He requires no more than that. He believes in natural laws which are made and unmade from on high, he believes in hierarchies which no one has the right to challenge, and in the limitless dominion of the land over man. 'You are what your land makes you, no more.'

For me – tired of having believed excessively in my right to assert myself against life, as though shouting 'Stay still!' – this notion of ease, of submission, of renunciation, was a lesson in modesty and the beginning of peace.

But I wonder why his own pride, which I reckon to be immense, does not revolt. Or how his desire for adventure doesn't protest, or how his instinct for vehemence, struggle and wandering does not assert itself, and how these passions are tamed. Is it because his intelligence has set the example by sacrificing itself?

Because this intelligence, which is fiery enough to start a revolution, seems determined to bury the passions in ashes, to die one day with the simplicity of mind of a peasant who has never left behind the sickle blade with which he has cut grass for seventy years out of eighty.

4

I came across Phillip Dunton at the company offices in Piața Rosetti. He'd delivered some reports for Rice and was hurrying to catch the two o'clock train back. We stopped on the stairs to shake hands.

'And how's Marjorie doing?'

'She reads and sits by the stove. It's terribly cold in Uioara. It was freezing, like in mid-winter. But didn't you see Marjorie here last week? She was at Ghiță Blidaru's opening lecture too. She came specially: said she couldn't miss it. It was about Uioara, wasn't it?'

I didn't manage to answer. He had only five minutes to catch the train. He shouted from the bottom of the stairs:

'Come to Uioara some Sunday. It would make Marjorie happy.'

So, she was here last week. At another time she would have burst into the workshop in the morning and shouted from the doorway: 'I'm kidnapping you. You're mine until 22.17.'

. . . And that stupid lie about the opening lecture, which she didn't even attend. It's not your style, Marjorie, to lie.

And I would have bet that in adultery you would have remained straightforward and without cowardice.

Now I understand Dronțu's sensitivity, his inability to bear Professor Ghiță's lecture for fear of it being too rough on the master.

Today, in the office, I said to Marin in passing:

'Phillip Dunton was here yesterday. We met at the office.'

For a good few seconds dear old Marin kept his thoughts to himself: to hear or not to hear what I was saying? He opted for deafness.

'Who took my set square?' he suddenly bellowed. 'Yesterday I left it here, and now it's gone. Maybe we're haunted. It's unbelievable. You can't work in this place.'

The louder he bellowed, the falser the outburst sounded to him. Not knowing how to end it, he shouted even louder.

Then he suddenly went quiet, frowning and sombre. He muttered from time to time, shrugged his shoulders, swore by all the saints.

He caught up with me in the street after work.

'Why don't we go get a brandy?'

'Sure.'

'Come on, then.'

And, later, on the way, apropos of nothing. 'To hell with women. I'm telling you, there's no end to the trouble they bring.'

*

A long, despairing letter from young Dogany. Things are not going at all well in Budapest. The university has been closed again, there have been major disturbances, street battles, arrests. He himself received a pretty bad blow to the head.

'Everything would be fine and I'd put up with it all, if at least I could manage to stay. On Thursday I have to present my papers at the secretariat of the faculty for another review. Will I be allowed to stay? Will I be expelled? My father threatens to cut off my allowance if I don't return to Satu Mare. But I can't, I simply can't. What can I do there, in a country that's not mine? But is Hungary my country? Yes, absolutely, whatever my father says and however much you might laugh. Only one man could understand me, if he were alive today: Endre Ady. I'd write to him and I'm sure he'd understand me.'

I wrote back:

Dear Pierre Dogany, stay where you are. It'll pass, you'll see. Six years ago I went through what you're going through now. It has passed, and one day I'll forget. They beat you up? It's nothing. They'll beat you up ten times, then they'll get tired of it. Do I laugh at you? Yes, I admit I laugh and your Hungarian fervour strikes me as comic. That doesn't mean I don't understand you. In your place, I'd do the same thing. In your place I did do the same thing.

Today, everything has settled down calmly and nicely. Sometimes I recall my past despairs and I don't understand them. They seem embarrassingly childish.

Force yourself not to suffer. Don't allow yourself to indulge your suffering. There's a great voluptuousness in persecution and feeling yourself wronged is probably one of the proudest of private pleasures. Be vigilant and don't indulge such pride. Try to take whatever comes with a certain good humour. Think how ridiculous we would be if we were alarmed at every shower of rain that soaked us. Believe me, what's happening to you now, however sad it may be, is no more than a shower.

*

I've tried to remember where I know Arnold Max from but it just won't come to me. I no longer have any idea of the place or the circumstances of our first meeting.

I've so often promised myself to limit my relations with people, but I'm incapable of controlling myself. The ease with which various acquaintances manage to crowd around me is intolerable. At first they're neither hot nor cold nor black nor white, but eventually, without me realizing it, I become subject to suffocating demands.

One evening I sat and thought of my connections with various people, and was alarmed to realize how many of my friends are superfluous and uninteresting. You just find yourself surrounded by the dramas and farces that pop up in the wake of your indifference and one day make their demands on you. Why? How? When? It's too late to figure it out and, in any case, too late to put it right.

You'd need to be cruelly vigilant at every moment, to pinch the shoots of all those attempts at cordiality that will eventually make you their victim. I dream of a life reduced to a few carefully chosen relationships, perhaps three or four, and only those I find strictly necessary and which serve my personal needs. The rest held at a distance, in the well-guarded zone of brief greetings in the street, from where no effusions, confessions and emotionalism can reach you. The first concession, the first weakness, is fatal.

Take Arnold Max, for example. Yesterday he spoiled my whole afternoon, dragging me up and down streets, in order to tell me of his endless problems in art and life.

'Interesting fellow.' But I, for one, am not a novelist and to hell with all these 'interesting' fellows, I've no use for them.

Another of those fevered types. He's thirty-three but looks twenty-two, small, slight, with a face like that of a frightened badger, his raincoat flapping in the wind, pockets stuffed with pieces of paper (laundry receipts, verses, beginnings of poems, love letters, modernist manifestos). I'm curious what logic underlies the association of the ideas he articulates in conversation.

'Greetings ... Lucky I met you, come on Thursday evening to Costaridi's, everyone will be there ... You know, I've discovered a great novelist; the greatest of them all, he's fabulous ... Leon Trotsky. The episode of the dead person in Finland from *Mein Leben* is Dostoyevsky, pure Dostoyevsky ... That imbecile Costaridi was telling me about that Moréas of his again ... I can no longer breathe with the number of windbags that have sprung up in this generation. Listen, about Moréas ... I'll say it loud and clear: Tardieu's dead. There's a scheme involving Herriot and then there'll be a social revolution ... Stănescu told me once that his socks cost 600 lei a pair.'

He talks a tremendous amount, with a strange, nervous volubility, in which you hear a dozen thoughts, ideas and memories muttering at once. Each thought remains uncompleted. He trails them behind him like so much torn paper, snagged on random words or images.

I have the impression that he speaks from a fear of silence, from a fear of finding himself alone.

'What do you think about when you're alone?'

'What do you mean, alone?'

'Just now, for example, before you bumped into me. You were walking along the street, no? And there was no one with you. Therefore, you were alone. So, what were you thinking about?'

He stops dead for a moment, trying to remember.

'Wait a minute ... What was I thinking about ... I don't know ...'

Arnold Max, the-man-whom-nothing-happens-to. He doesn't love, he doesn't go to the theatre, doesn't go out, isn't interested in people or books. There's no woman in his life, no friends. Nothing. A desert haunted by moods, by problems.

He's always writing, adding things, erasing. I wonder if he's ever calmly and patiently listened to his own verses. He doesn't have the time. He has to be writing them. His life is plunged in them, immersed in them, besieged by them. Suddenly, in mid-sentence, he pulls a piece of paper or a visiting card from some pocket, from which he reads for half an hour, with a kind of fury or enthusiasm to devour it all, poem and paper. It's all the same to him whether you listen or not. He reads on with a certain cold illumination, ready to brave an ocean of indifference. Most of all his own indifference, which is greater than his passion for poetry, half-simulated in order to give some sense to the terrible void in which he lives and from which he flees.

It's the poetry of a man who's lonely, troubled, drunk on unexpected bursts of pure melody, and it is painfully simple for such a complicated man. Out of all his writings, I like the 'Five Tales for a Small Voice'. The rest is tiresome and obscure. He has talent, I know. Everybody agrees. But I want a life without poisonings, fireworks and problems. A life of 'good day', 'good evening', 'the bread is white', 'stone is hard', 'the poplar is tall'.

*

I glimpsed Majorie Dunton in a tram. I don't think she saw me. And she was also here last Thursday. (Hacker from accounting brought her by motor car and I heard it from his mouth.) 'Give her my regards, if you're heading back together this evening.' 'No,' Hacker replied, 'I'm going back alone. Mrs Dunton is spending the night in Bucharest.'

On Friday, in the workshop, I dropped it on Dronțu. 'Did you sleep well last night, Marin?'

Stupid question.

*

Sami Winkler called by to see me at the workshop, to ask me for a letter of recommendation for Ralph T. Rice.

'Are you looking to be a miner?'

'It's not for me. It's for some boys we're training for going to Palestine. And they need a couple of months' experience in a refinery. I thought you might be able to smooth the way in the head office. Unpaid work, you understand.'

I brought Winkler round to Piața Rosetti and introduced him to old Ralph. I think he's going to do it.

'I hope you don't mind, Winkler, and excuse me for asking. Did you complete your thesis?'

'I abandoned it a long time ago. It no longer interests me. I'll stay another two or three years, then I'm leaving. I'll be a farmer in some colony.'

'Why a farmer? Don't they need doctors over there?'

'Doctors perhaps, but not diplomas. I'll be working the land somewhere, in a colony, and when a doctor's needed I'll act as a doctor. I still know how to do a bandage.'

Winkler means what he says. For the last four years he's worked from spring to autumn on a farm in Bessarabia organized by Zionists to train pioneers.

'I'm not boasting, but I can plough very well.'

He says this simply, without giving himself airs, almost with indifference, as if it was the most natural thing in the world.

'Explain to me, please, why you're leaving. In 1923 it would have been understandable. But today, now that things have settled down?

I've the impression that everything has changed over the last five years. It's safer, there's more goodwill, more understanding. You can breathe, you can talk with people.'

'Perhaps. But I'm leaving, not running away. I'm not leaving because it's bad here and there it's good, but simply because I can't live anywhere in the world but there. I'm a Zionist, not a deserter. Listen, in 1923, in the middle of anti-Semitic unrest, Zionism was at its apogee, while today, when everything is calm and prosperous, Zionism finds itself in crisis. But I prefer this Zionism in crisis, because it's made up of determined people, while the Zionism of 1923 was made up of frightened people.'

*

Evening at Costaridi's. Long arguments about angst, contemporary neurosis, Gide, the war generation, Berdyaev . . . I'm amazed at the verve with which people can discuss angst while drinking a coffee. In 1923, in my green notebook period, I would probably have argued passionately. These days I experience a very specific discomfort in dealing with any broad problem, whether it's angst or destiny or crisis . . . It's the abuse of language that puts me off.

Look at Radu Şiriu, broad-shouldered, fit, pink and plump, declaring, with no sense of the ridiculous, as if in a Russian novel:

'I know nothing, I don't understand anything: I'm experiencing a crisis.'

How does he manage not to choke on the poor taste of such a declaration? 'It's trivial,' I remark to those around me.

'Yes, trivial,' says Ştefan D. Pârlea, picking up the remark from the other corner. 'Yes, it's in poor taste. So what? Is that what we need? To be delicate, spiritual, sceptical? A culture based on good manners – it disgusts me. Don't feel any pain, because it's in poor taste. Don't scream, because of what the neighbours will say? Don't live, it isn't polite. Dear people, enough of this stupidity. We've had ten generations of sceptics who've checked themselves in the mirror all the time, with the excuse that they have a critical spirit. I want us to say, to hell with all these proprieties and let's live. Stormily, without good taste, unrestrainedly and unfastidiously, but with a personal voice, with authentic feelings.'

Pârlea looks straight at me, with barely controlled violence. He polishes his glasses nervously, in order to see me better, his eyes shooting lightning that has been long gathering there to smite me. Beautiful forehead: proud, high, challenging, lit by his flashing eyes, which his short-sightedness makes that bit more intense. I'm attached to this adversity as to a friendship. I can't explain it, I can't understand it, but from the first day I sensed in this person an unshakable resolve. And, in a world of easy-going attachments, it's no small thing to spontaneously earn serious enmity. A raw, healthy human enmity you can really count on.

And more, he's the only person for whom these vague expressions – crisis, angst, authenticity – have vital meaning. His essay in *The Thought* – 'An Invocation for the Barbarians to Invade as soon as Possible' – showed for the first time the possibility of a spiritual position from which one could say with a measure of justification: 'We, the young, who have come of age since the war.' Pârlea's cast of mind is too lyrical for my taste, while to him I must seem too sceptical. I would like only to make him understand that it's not possible to be desperate and to hold debates at the Foundation on desperation, or to be anxious and to discuss angst. I'd like to tell him that these things, if they are real, are emotions, and that emotions are for living, not for chatting about. There is some demon of oratory in Pârlea's nature which impels him towards speechifying, a thing I am altogether incapable of, since all my quarrels are with myself. To argue until two in the morning at Mişu Costaridi's about 'angst' and then go home to bed is the height of comedy. Unfortunately Pârlea has no sense of humour.

S.T. Haim (a good friend of Pârlea's – since when?) added his own Marxist spiel:

'An "anxious generation" . . . How amusing you are, friends. The key to your problem lies elsewhere. You're a generation of proletarians without class consciousness. There are fewer jobs, the scholarships are miserable, all the places are taken. You've been left out and so, for the sake of something to do, you engage in metaphysics. One day you'll see that the bourgeois democratic state no longer accommodates you – and then you'll join the revolution. That'll blow your angst away, you'll see.'

5

Only yesterday evening, leaving the office, I remembered it was 10 December. I was with Marin Dronțu, heading down towards Calea Victoriei. It was snowing sumptuously, with immense flakes, like a New Year's Eve, and there was a real festive bustle in the street, the good-natured hum of a cheerful Sunday. At Capșa's, on the corner, our way was blocked by a procession of students coming down from University Square.

'What could this be?' mused Dronțu. 'Tenth of December,' we remembered simultaneously, laughing. I have to admit there was a celebratory air to the whole demonstration, the light-hearted rambunctious mood of the start of the holidays. We stopped along with everyone else at the roadside to watch the march.

'Down with the Yids! Down with the Yids!'

The shout passed from column to column, syllable by syllable, in a long, winding chain of sound. It was beautiful: I ask myself if that's a ridiculous thing to say, but it really was beautiful. A crowd of young men – most of them certainly first-year students. Tremendous high spirits, an atmosphere of schoolyard fun. Nothing serious.

We remembered our first 10 December, Dronțu with enthusiasm, me with a trace of bitterness.

'The blows I dealt that day,' he testifies.

'Perhaps you were the one who struck me.'

'Perhaps. Where did it happen?'

'In the main lecture hall in Law.'

'No, I wasn't there. Us architecture students went to the college of medicine, because we didn't have enough Jews in with us.'

He is moved, almost. It would be unfair of me not to understand:

these are his memories of his younger days. They're mine too – though they're less cheerful. In any case, it would be grotesque of me to want to get indignant about these dead and buried matters. It's not serious or aggressive any more. These 'Down with the Yids' of today are almost innocent, almost likable.

We strolled until late, relating innumerable tales of those times. Marin boasted of his deeds.

'Back then I had a cudgel you wouldn't believe. The Jews scarpered at the sight of me. I'd become famous at the faculty of medicine. 'Dronțu from architecture.' Who hadn't heard of me? I'm surprised you hadn't heard of me . . . I was wild!'

Isn't it strange that I find myself good friends today with the unhappy heroes from the notebook of 1923?

I couldn't say exactly how the successive truces which have brought us together were made. In any case, in our first year of university we were thrown into opposite corners, while today we find ourselves together in the same place. It's no small matter.

A new page has been turned, and new questions arise. The uproar at the university was fine and well, but insufficient. You can't build a life out of that kind of thing. Not even for those engaged in 'a struggle to claim their rights'. Nor for us, whose struggle concerned 'internal problems'.

I realize, as though in the wake of a storm, that the same winds buffeted us both and that we were being wrecked in the same sinking vessel. It's easy to cry 'Hooligans', and very convenient. It's almost as simple as 'Down with the Yids'. Is that all there was to our little drama?

Back then I guessed there was something else to it. Now I'm sure of it. But it's got nothing to do with a natural bandit like Marin Dronțu. It concerns Pârlea. Marin Dronțu flailing about with his cudgel is irrelevant. He's just a demonstrator. Pârlea is a more serious case and, with him in mind, I wonder if it is always easier to be a hooligan than a victim. I have no doubt that Pârlea has suffered greatly through the path he has taken. His political nihilism, his innocent revolts and his formidable imprecations perhaps show puerility of thought, but what is interesting is not their quality, but his sincerity in living them, the passion he submits them to. It goes without saying, when someone is beating your head with a stick, it's all the same to you whether he's a bandit or a hero, and I won't get so precious about it as to declare I'd prefer to be killed by an ideological revolver than by an illiterate one.

Though I can see my personal situation as being just as bad either way, I can still allow myself to reflect a little on my aggressor. Well, in the case of Ştefan Pârlea, I don't envy him at all. Student unrest was for me perhaps a tragedy, but it was for him too. I provoked him one evening into speaking about his role in the movement. He replied with deliberate harshness.

'I'm not sorry about what happened. I'm sorry about how it ended: in indifference, in forgetting . . . Smashing windows is fine. Any act of violence is good. "Down with the Yids" is idiotic, agreed! But what does it matter? The point is to shake the country up a bit. Begin with the Jews – if there's no other way. But finish higher up, with a general conflagration, with an all-consuming earthquake. That was our ambition back then, our real aspiration. But I for one have not finished. I'll suffocate if nothing new happens.'

Perhaps Ştefan Pârlea is being poetic, with his symbols and myths, but in fact this tumult is for him a form of political thought. Who can guarantee that S.T. Haim's ideas and calculations are closer to the truth than Ştefan Pârlea's visions? What I find refreshing in this fellow is his total incapacity for schematic thought. His thinking is a flash-flood that demolishes, overturns and embraces, without method or criteria, according to the rhythms of his frenetic outbursts. I can trace in his habitual vocabulary a number of terms that he has never properly clarified, either in writing or speech, but which have some magical significance for him. He'd probably find it difficult to say exactly what is meant by the 'barbarian invasion' he calls for, or by 'the seeds of fire' he says lie latent in each of us, and which we need to blow into mighty blazes. It's all so vague and inconsistent as to sometimes seem ridiculous . . . Yet Ştefan Pârlea passes from words to action with utter commitment. His departure from the university, for example, which came as an immense relief to everyone as, with a little patience, he would have been a lecturer within a few years, was not permitted to be a mere departure.

'The only thing I can do for the university is burn it down,' is what he is said to have written to the dean in an explanatory letter.

Even if this was what he really wrote, I still don't see what the fuss was about. The recklessness of youth. A poor person has to compensate internally for poverty by slamming a few doors. Otherwise he'll never learn to open life's big doors. Pârlea's abandonment of university was certainly a piece of nonsense, but I tell myself it was a healthy one. Or could have been.

But it turned out otherwise. And other pieces of foolishness followed, some were harder to explain than others. I confess that his escapade at Records is beyond me. Sub-archivist at the Ministry of Records? Perhaps. Perhaps, though, it's stupid to accept such a low-ranking, badly paid and menial job when you could have been a professor or the editor of a big magazine. And, once finding yourself there, to continue experimenting with self-mutilation seems like childish play-acting.

In September he was listed for promotion; he would have received a higher salary and have been moved to the central office. He turned it down. He just returned the difference in money to the cashier, saying he wouldn't accept a penny over 3,300 lei. 'He's crazy,' they said at the ministry three days later, where the news passed from office to office, from person to person. The General Secretary called him to his office, in order to take a look at 'the man who turns down money'.

'Are you in your right mind, good man?'

'I believe so,' replied Pârlea, without further explanation.

But he erupted that evening, among us, when I reproached him for performing experiments *'pour épater les bourgeois'*.

'You turned down 1,200 lei in exchange for the chance to astound a ministry of 600 people. That's 2 lei per person. Never has a reputation been bought so cheaply.'

'You're fools. What did you want me to do? To receive an extra 1,000 lei today, another 1,000 next year? To be sub-archivist today, next year head archivist, main archivist, general archivist? Is that why I escaped from where I escaped from? Don't you see that any job you accept from this state implies complicity? That every success in this culture is a betrayal? I want to demolish. I want to burn down. And to do this I have to keep my hands free. I don't want to have anything to cling to, anything to lose, anything to protect. Nothing to hold me back on the day everything gets fed to the grinder. You accept a lectureship with the idea of working, and one day find that the 15,000 lei they give you are indispensable, that along with them you've created needs, imposed obligations on yourself. The habits you acquire end up choking you, paralysing you. You become prudent, cowardly, grow old. The great perfidy of the order we live in is that it makes us its unconscious servants. And it buys us cheaply, by stealth. You know, I look at you and it scares me. Scares me. You've all got your own little affairs, your own little things going on, your own little arrangements. Your wasted years disgust me. I wish you'd get pot bellies faster, that your hair would hurry up and fall out, once and for all. The great conflagration is coming without you, it doesn't need you, it doesn't burn in your hearts . . .'

What I find interesting about Pârlea's problem is that its origin lies in the movement of 1923. What remains from those years is not only the bloodied heads, the careers that were made and a steady engagement with anti-Semitism, but also a revolutionary spirit, a seed of a sincere rebellion against the world in which we live. This seed of revolution couldn't be seen from our unfortunate dormitory in Văcărești, but my unhappy memories are perhaps not the only testimony capable of shedding light on those years. Certainly no one is going to blame me for this, as you can't expect exercises in moral objectivity or a dissertation on higher reasoning from someone who gets beaten perhaps twice a week, on average. Being persecuted is not just a physical trial. It is one that affects you intellectually. The reality of it slowly deforms you and attacks, above all, your sense of proportion. Now is not the moment to reproach myself for being slow to understand my assailants. That would be a belated and grotesque excess of objectivity. But I'm glad that times have changed in such a way that I can meditate in peace on the justifications for the beatings. The role of martyr has never sat entirely well with me, though I recognize in myself enough of a tendency towards this peculiarly Jewish occupation.

Pârlea represents the opposing side. For a long time I could see and understand nothing of it, owing to the endless coils of barbed wire strewn between us. It's so comfortable and consoling to regard your adversaries as bad and stupid, to the point that, in my lamentable desperation back then, it was the sole crutch available, the last remaining bit of pride. That was a long time ago. More than the relatively few years that have passed. The clouded waters have cleared where the trouble was superficial and become yet more stirred up where the trouble ran deep. People have made their choices, opinions have hardened, foolishness has found the company of foolishness, truths have become more marked. Everything is more ordered. Perhaps the time has come to write the history of the anti-Semitic movement. By which I mean 'the human comedy' of people and what they thought rather than the dry facts of actual history, which I am familiar with and which have nothing new to tell. I'm convinced that once I excluded the imbeciles, the professional troublemakers, the agitators, the scattering of layabouts and dimwits, and after identifying in turn brutality, stupidity and scheming, there would still be something that would be a real drama. And that's when Ştefan D. Pârlea would appear.

6

Ghiță Blidaru's course has become something of an 'official matter'. Last Saturday a deputy from the biggest party asked the government at question time if it was going to tolerate the university becoming a centre of political unrest.

'The authority of the state must not be disturbed, Minister, from behind the mask of general theories.' (The evening papers reproduced this phrase as a headline.)

In fact, nothing serious happened. There were just some lectures about the liberal economic legislation of 1924. Very calm lectures in style, very violent in their stances and conclusions. Starting with the mining law of Vintilă Brătianu, Blidaru has analysed Romanian liberalism. The party is alarmed, the government bored. Vintilă Brătianu must have made a fuss at the last council. 'He must desist, gentlemen. He must desist.'

Blidaru did not desist at all. For next week he has announced an inquiry into the stabilization plan and credit mechanism that's being prepared. What's peculiar about this whole struggle is that while the newspapers are censored and all opposition excluded, an economics professor can openly attack anything he wants and there's no way to stop him.

Professor Ghiță's situation is excellent. He teaches his course, follows his schedule, and nothing else. However, his lectures have become the last refuge for anti-liberalism. The whole public crowds in. Blidaru, unaffected, converses with his students. He has been discreetly offered several foreign posts: the presidency of an economic delegation in Paris or, should he wish, a small delegation in a neighbouring state. He's refused them all. 'We'll see, later, in the summer break. For now, I have my lectures to finish.'

I have trouble understanding his passion for politics. He has no personal ambition to satisfy, no fights to win. He's certainly no warrior. He is an idler of genius. Rather than marching forward to meet life, he sits still and lets it come to him.

If I've learned anything from Ghiță Blidaru, it is exactly this lack of aggression in dealing with life. His laziness is that of a plant, of a tree. Life grows and decays, storms come and go, death waits somewhere, in the shadows – all harmonious. I believe nothing will ever surprise Blidaru or shake his composure. Not because he is sure of himself, but because he is sure of the earth he walks upon and the sky he finds himself beneath.

'Worries? Where do you find worries in this world full of certainties? Shouldn't the simple fact that the sun rises and sets be enough to reassure us?'

If he had been a carpenter, a stonemason, a boatman on the Danube, a ploughman in Vâlcea, his thinking would be no different to what it is today. He is the only man I know whom I feel that fate can do nothing to harm, because he accepts fate, submitting happily to whatever it brings.

With his formidable laziness, his deliberate lack of initiative ('I have nothing to do with life, life has everything to do with me'), Blidaru is ready to waste every big opportunity, to miss every decisive rendezvous which good or bad fortune arranges. He will always find a book to open in the final hour, a woman to love. For him, nothing is urgent. He has told me so countless times. Every joy has its season, and every pain. Let's await the passing of the seasons. It's useless to hurry, because you can't arrive too soon for winter, which comes to meet you. There is an autumn for every hope, a springtime for each despair. In this race you can never come too early or late: you always come on time, whether you wish to or not.

*

I don't know how many persistent pains, hidden deaths or unanswered questions Ghiţă Blidaru faces with equanimity. But I can guess. He has made countless renunciations in the fields of intelligence, pride, victory and excitement. Each one of us is barricaded within himself, and most of us seek to strengthen our barricades, to make our inner defences impermeable, while he cooperates with life to knock them down, surrendering before the fight, already beaten. Beaten? No. At most, he has conquered his own self.

7

I've been to Uioara to see how things are going. Rice bores us time and again about every accident with a heater, a lift or lighting. The master wanted a first-hand report.

I'd have liked to have stayed in the cabin where it's not cold at all once a good fire gets going. But the Duntons wouldn't hear of it. Marjorie was waiting for me at the station with Eva Nicholson.

'I'm glad you came,' she said. Then, in the sleigh, she was quiet the whole time. Eva was asking me about everything and though I answered in a lively enough fashion, I had the impression that Marjorie was paying no attention. She was extraordinarily serious, in her blue ski-suit that gives her that impossibly adolescent air. At the corner of Ursu, she asked the sleigh-driver to stop, and nodded her head to indicate the snow-laden oil wells in the distance.

'Look how desolate it is.'

To me, the landscape looked peaceful rather than desolate.

In the afternoon I worked at the refinery and took a walk to the oil wells, to see what could be done to put old Ralph's mind at rest. His alarm was unnecessary. The inevitable trivialities.

In the evening, I spent a long time talking with Marjorie.

Her serious smile, her temples illuminated with blonde hair, her lively young hands were the same as ever, but she was listening as if someone had told her to behave herself. What I still like most about this girl is how she moves, her bearing, the way she leans against a wall, the rather lazy way she sits in an armchair, the sudden way she rises as if frightened. There's an odd mix of awkwardness and sureness in all her movements, in the way she speaks, in her attention as she listens to you, in her loyal laughter.

She talked about the books she's been reading, played several pieces for me on the piano, gave me a short theoretical lesson on skiing and put me in the role of judge between her and Phillip, to decide who can get down from Uioara to the Ursu Corner fastest.

'Tomorrow morning we'll have a race,' I proposed.

'No, tomorrow morning we have other plans for you. It's a surprise.'

The surprise was a walk to the cabin. I found it all tidy and clean, as if I'd never left. On the brick chimney, two framed pictures: Marin Dronțu and myself. Between them, a small photograph in which I could just make out Marjorie from last summer, in sandals and a tennis dress.

'Who put these pictures here?'

'I did. Sometimes I come to the cabin to read. I don't know, I find it more beautiful here. As if I weren't alone. I have someone from the refinery to get a fire going in the stove and then I come and spend an hour or two. Look there, in the cupboard, there's tea, rum and sugar. You can't imagine how I like doing the housekeeping here, where you two stayed. And look what lovely expressions you have, you and Dronțu, in the photos.'

She laughs. She goes up to the chimney and curls an arm around the post on the right, as though around a man's neck.

It's hot, the water for the tea snoozing in the teapot, a dry oak log crackling in the fire. The windows are white with snow and it gives me the feeling that we are far away, in a mountain refuge, overtaken by an avalanche that has cut off our route of return. For a moment, I wonder if I'm going to get up and walk over to Marjorie and take her in my arms and kiss her. We look at each other for a long time, like in a children's game where you have to try not to be the one to blink first. I close my eyes and my questions receive no answer: yes? no? yes? no?

PART FOUR

PART FOUR

I

A long night with Maurice Buret at the Coupole. All humanity parading before our 1.25-franc glasses of beer. Smiles, shouts of surprise, short familiar scenes, loves, betrayals, dramas . . . The spectacle became slowly more drunken, with the imperceptible passage of time.

The Coupole isn't a café, it's a continent, and Maurice isn't an onlooker, he's an explorer. He observes it all, down to the finest detail, understands the show, organizes it. He's keenly perceptive. Among an apparently ordinary group, his eye discovers every possible passion. From the smallest clues under the indifferent light of the electric globe-lamps, a bare hint is enough for him to penetrate the private life of a café patron, or comedies or disasters hidden behind an expressionless smile. An adulteress, an unhappy lover, a young first-time pederast, an Anglo-Saxon blonde, still chaste and dazzled by the lights of Paris, a youthful adventurer, a grey-haired cynic, a dark-haired femme fatale looking for her ethereal other half . . .

Anybody might be a hero, every gesture the beginning of a drama. From our table, Maurice patiently watches the film unspool and notes decisive moments. Nothing in this immense hall, nobody in this agitated throng, escapes his vigilance. The spectacle is complex, but ordered. A smile from the third table to the left of the pillar may not reach its target, but it won't be lost on Maurice, who will follow its trajectory and discover, in the far corner, the one for whom it was intended.

Maurice knows the geography of the Coupole because he has constructed it. A veteran drinker of 1.25-franc glasses of beer, he has also bought an observation post from where he deciphers nightly the mysteries of the quarter and its inhabitants. For Maurice, this population is divisible into couples, families and social groups, to the point where from one table to the next, from booth to booth, from the first floor to the ground floor to the street, there is an entire chain of networks and connections, giving unity, order and logic to a world spinning dizzyingly with colours, lights and voices.

Any adventures that have gone on here, Maurice has known about. Some only guessed at, others given away by an exclamation or a pallor, others, in the end, tracked down methodically from day to day, from happening to happening. This fellow has one great passion, which he has cultivated: curiosity.

(Curiosity also led him into medicine, as I don't know what could have made him a doctor except his taste for provoking and hearing confessions.)

Observing gives him far greater pleasure than living does. Nothing that happens to him personally interests him except as an extra experience. He doesn't require his own life to be more than just another spectacle, similar to that vast Coupole through which people come and go, in a vain race that is only redeemed by the secret pleasure of watching and comprehending.

Of the several Maurice Burets I know (as this man has enough raw material for four or five successful characters), the most interesting is the Maurice Buret of the Coupole, with his ruffled grey conventional clothing, a hat that's neither new nor old, dress spats of an unremarkable sort. He has the drab appearance of any passerby, lost in the crowd, neither handsome nor ugly, with nothing rough, insolent or seductive in his aspect, giving him the right to always stroll through life without anybody turning their head when he passes, a man among a thousand, a hundred thousand, settled in front of a glass, past which a curtain is being raised to reveal a theatre of accidental heroes, playing before this watchful and faithless witness.

'See that brooding brunette over by the mirror?' he asked me about two weeks ago. 'What a goose she looks. I'd be surprised if she didn't hate men and love women. Either she's waiting for a lover or seeking one. Now look what a dramatic face she's making.'

A couple of evenings ago, Maurice completed his 'dossier' of observations.

'The brooding brunette is definitely looking for a match. How about the blonde on the right? No, not the one at the big table. Look closer, the second, the third, yes, the third on the right. Pretty, isn't she? They smiled at each other a couple of times this evening. You know, they wouldn't make a bad couple.'

The study continued over the following evenings. The small blonde became known by Maurice – I don't know why – as 'blonde Aline', while the exchange of smiles and invitations between the two tables progressed visibly. I doubted the outcome, however. The 'moody brunette' was on her own and there was no difficulty there, but 'Aline' was always with a large party of young men and women.

'You're wrong, Maurice. You invent novels everywhere. You have the soul of a detective.'

'I could be wrong. I still maintain they're a potential couple, and there's a chance they'll get together.'

For a few days I didn't make it to the Coupole. (I was working at the time on some plans for the master and sent them on to Bucharest. It really seems that in summer work might start at Le Havre for Rice Operations. It's not final, but it is likely.) So for a while I didn't make it to Montparnasse. Last night, entering the Coupole, the first thing I noticed, not without a genuine jolt, was the two girls – 'moody brunette' and 'blonde Aline' – talking on their own at a table, the former sombre and passionate, the latter submissive, and clearly excited.

Maurice, in his usual seat, savoured his victory with modesty, but not without a vague smile of triumph. I think he felt a kind of paternal sentiment, an authorial pride concerning the romantic couple, which he had predicted from the earliest hints.

'You're happy, and proud of yourself!'

'"Happy" is putting it too strongly. I'm pleased my findings have been confirmed. Success in the laboratory, if you will.'

I've no desire for psychological studies. And, if I had, the example of Maurice Buret would cure me once and for all.

The only unmistakable quality I can recognize in people is indifference, which constitutes for me the height of civility as well as a guarantee of security and peace. I've never despaired about the so-called tragedy of one person never being able to know another or the thought that two people can spend a lifetime together without one ever knowing what is really going on deep in the soul of the other. Far from being painful to me, the thought of the impenetrable solitude our nature destines us to cheers me up. It satisfies in me an old nostalgia for a healthy, reliable and certain ignorance, the only durable thing in a world where truth is provisional and uncertain. To honestly not know is a first step towards salvation. I say this without irony, with a grain of exaggeration at most, precisely to disapprove more strongly of Maurice's psychological experiments.

*

Ça fait toujours une petite expérience, says Maurice Buret of his most recent success at the Coupole. Experiences, always experiences, only experiences. Life's only merit for this fellow is that it is observable. He always has with him an invisible register, in which he carefully notes a multitude of systematic conclusions. Each person has his file, every feeling has its chapter. He calls this exercise *du jardinage*, 'tending the garden', and he is well equipped.

'You're a Cartesian, my dear Maurice, one of the most unfortunate cases.'

'Oh? I didn't know that. I read Descartes at school, but I've forgotten him.'

I read him a few lines from *Discours de la Méthode*. He listens attentively.

'Indeed, that does fit me. But Descartes isn't my master. Too abstract. Anecdotes are what interests me, and only truths conveyable through anecdotes. I'm not a philosopher. I'm just curious. At most – and I'm saying this just to please you – at most I'm a psychologist.'

I see him occasionally. He may be missing for two or three weeks, then turn up one morning, out of nowhere, with a vast harvest of events, discoveries and sensations. He operates on a number of fronts, which are not allowed to mingle. He lives among a number of groups of people which he does not mix, maintains several friendships which he carefully keeps separate from one another, and cultivates a number of well-guarded love affairs.

'You see, my good friend, life would be impossible if it weren't organized properly. I have only one bed and there are a thousand beautiful women, I have only one telephone number and there are a thousand interesting conversations. Much discretion is required in order to make the correct choice, to move ahead quickly and with little risk.'

Without doubt, Maurice Buret has enough love affairs for three lives. He lives all three at once and keeps close tabs on them. Firstly there's his very serious life at the university, the laboratory and the clinic.

In the two years since passing his internship exams, he has published a number of authoritative papers. So there is Maurice Buret the 'young savant', who is sober, stern and reserved. In this role, he has a 'complex' love affair with a young 'passionate, dark' nurse whom he went to bed with for the first time enthusiastically, after a long technical discussion about gold salts.

And then there's the second Maurice Buret, the easy-going man about town, a Parisian Maurice, well-read, intelligent and gallant, well received in diplomatic circles and very successful in the great salons. In this second role he has other and more varied love affairs, from the adulterous to the innocent, from the heart-breaking to the frivolous.

Then, finally, comes Maurice Buret the moralist, the director of the previous two, observer and cynic, reader of books, judge of people, seeker of interesting psychological cases. It's the version I first knew and the one I prefer. Does this continual shuttling between different mind-sets not tire him out? Judging from his excellent health, it seems not.

'Maurice, you're a master.'

'Let's not exaggerate. All games are complicated when you're not familiar with them, and very simple when you are. I know the game

– that's all. I always know what I want and I know where to find it. Do I need a cynical love affair? The dark Christine can always be found between five and seven at the laboratory. But perhaps I need a sentimental interlude? Fair Alice Vignac can be contacted through the operator at 14-99. I need frenzied conversation with metaphysical exhortations? Robert Grévy is at his editor's desk every night from twelve to two. I'm interested in social issues? Bertrand is always well informed. I finally want to give all these stories a certain order, to classify them, to taste them, to judge them. You're here and suit my requirements perfectly.'

'But what you're saying is monstrous. Where are you among all these experiences? Which one is you? The cynic? The sentimentalist? The sceptic? I fear you're nothing. You live by being reflected in others. You're something very artificial: you're the *raisonneur* of the comedy.'

'I don't dislike the role and I accept it – minus the compassion you extend to me. I take delight in my way of life It consists in asking of each person precisely what he's able to give you. Think of any emotional scene you know and you'll see that it arises from an inappropriate demand being made. My whole philosophy can be reduced to one precept, which I warmly recommend to you: "There's no point riding a calf in the hope it'll become a stallion."'

*

But the most wonderful thing about Maurice Buret isn't his passion for analysing people, it's his lack of a moral sensibility. More still, it's his feeling for vice, his curiosity about the twisted. He's a healthy, orderly fellow with a strong sense for what's appropriate, a sense of balance inherited from his provincial bourgeois family. He's a Breton, from a nation of merchants and sailors.

That doesn't prevent him looking for, and provoking when needs be, various 'scandalous acts'. For two months he was in love with Germaine Audoux. To my amazement, as it was one of his longest love affairs, and nothing explains such constancy to a girl who is perhaps not ugly but is certainly no beauty. I discovered the secret one day when Maurice had wound up the chapter with Germaine with all the necessary details: she was addicted to ether.

'You've no idea how instructive it is. At the clinic I've only come across cases of severe intoxication, and in the manuals only generalizations. Without Germaine, ether would have been something abstract. With Germaine, it's a drama.'

I'd like to burst out with: 'But what are you, a machine for recording dramas? A detective? A psychological secret agent? A dabbler in souls?' But I stop myself in time. The one feeling Maurice is incapable of is indignation.

He's probably the most intelligent man I've ever known, because that's all there is to him. Nothing else: neither moral nor immoral, neither good nor bad. Intelligence for him takes the place of sensitivity. There are emotions and nuances that he can't help but feel. He understands them. He doesn't have instincts, he doesn't have reflexes: he orients himself through awareness. I wonder what he would do if caught up in a great passion, one that devastates him, consumes him and overwhelms him ... Ridiculous! There's no chance of such a person having to face this kind of passion. Maurice would be up to imposing order on a cyclone.

Wherever he goes, he finds out how to orient himself. In a crowd of people or in a symphony, in a landscape or in a book, his first concern is to establish north and south. Then, knowing the route back, he allows himself to get adventurous. (*S'égarer est un plaisir délicieux, à condition que la route de Paris ne soit pas éloignée.*)

*

At the moment, Maurice is taking care of the Robert Grévy–Jacques Bertrand business. 'A must-be couple', he's engraved in his imaginary notebook under the heading 'Robert', the day he introduced him to Jacques.

'But Bertrand isn't homosexual,' I object, scandalized.

'He will be. He has what it takes.'

'And Robert Grévy?'

'Used to be. Filled with nostalgia.'

Robert Grévy is married. His wife, Suzanne, who knows certain things about his past, doesn't let him out of her sight. She's a fiery, watchful wife.

'As long as Suzanne's around, there's nothing doing,' observes Buret, summing it up. Then he decides: 'Suzanne needs to take a little trip.'

Tuesday, lunch with the Grévys.

'Why are you looking at me that way, Maurice?' asks Suzanne, surprised.

'What way?'

'I don't know; worried, perhaps.'

'Oh, it's nothing. I thought you'd coughed.'

'Yes, I had something stuck in my throat.'

'Just as well it was nothing. It seemed suspicious.'

'Suspicious?'

'What are you getting alarmed about? It was imprudent of me to say anything. You won't give me any peace now. Now I'm sure you think you have tuberculosis.'

'No Maurice – but, anyhow, if you say . . .'

'Know what? How about you pop into the hospital tomorrow and we'll do an X-ray. To put your mind at rest.'

Three days later, Suzanne leaves for Savoy, advised to spend a month in the sun on a deck-chair. Of course, the X-ray showed two or three lesions.

Maurice Buret gives a modest laugh.

Is he a corrupter? No. He has nothing in common with Gide, neither vice nor proselytizing nor disquiet. No, particularly not disquiet. People – whether they fall or are saved – matter little to Buret.

'I trouble myself only to vary as much as I can the psychological vistas open to me. I have the impression Robert and Jacques would be a very good combination. So I'll try to facilitate bringing them together, to smooth the road, to clarify their own vocation. It's a small effort, behind the scenes.'

I listen to Maurice and make a serious effort not to be scandalized. I should understand once and for all that this man has no moral scruples and therefore should be accepted in his totality. Or rejected in his totality, which I find even harder.

His spiritual patron (if the term 'spiritual' can be applied to him) isn't Gide, but Laclos, and the moral atmosphere he lives in closely resembles that of *Les Liaisons dangereuses*, which is libertine rather than perverse, because it is not vice that dominates, but the intellectual appetite for always coming up with amusing games.

*

Only after an absence of several weeks (one of those mysterious trips, from which he returns with surprising personal reports), do I realize what Buret's friendship means to me. He brings with him the daring sense that everything is possible in life, that all women are for the conquering, all doors to be opened. Something odd: though I know him to be cautious, methodical and reflective in everything he does, he still gives the impression of living spontaneously.

'You even simulate spontaneity, my dear Maurice.'

'I don't simulate: I organize. I organize my spontaneity. You take me for a cynic, but I'm an enthusiast. It's just that my enthusiasm is systematic.'

An hour of conversation with him is a personal lesson in clarity. A term must be found for every nuance, a corrective for every misunderstanding. 'Everything can be defined,' he stubbornly believes, and does not forgive a single ill-chosen word or ill-defined distinction. I've never heard him pass a vague judgement on anything, be it a woman or a piece of music or a painting. He will always tell me exactly what he likes or doesn't, strictly maintaining the distinction between one nuance and another.

In his company, life becomes clear-cut, correctly proportioned, the horizons visible.

2

The offices of Ralph T. Rice in Boulevard Haussmann are barely a
modest agency compared to the head offices in Piaţa Rosetti in
Bucharest. A few rooms, some desks, a small archive in the process
of being organized. I don't know exactly what old Ralph wants to set
up here: a simple sales office or a public company. It's up to him to
decide whether or not we get working on the Le Havre project. (I'd
prefer Dieppe, however, which seems to me more suitable for com-
merce, and from the construction standpoint is immeasurably more
open and spacious. I've sent a number of plans to the master, who'll
decide.) He may in the end do nothing. It's not the moment for
heavy investment in a business that, even if all goes well, won't turn
a profit for several years at least. At the end of 1929, when Rice
Enterprises Inc. began to realize old Ralph's age-old plan of estab-
lishing a French division, the project seemed feasible. Today, in 1931,
it's risky at best, and perhaps even foolhardy. Petrol is suffering a
crisis matched only by agriculture. Rice is a daring businessman, but
not one to play the stock markets.

The master has never really taken seriously what we in the office
term 'the French expedition', though he still would have liked to be
able to build here and had no reason to discourage Rice. Also, he was
happy to give both Dronţu and I the chance to go abroad for a year.
We drew straws and I was first.

'Good: you go this year, next year Dronţu.'

It's been about a year now. I waited for Marin to take my place,
but he hasn't come. He sent me a letter exactly four lines long, the
first I've received since his wedding.

'I can't come. Married man, too tied up. Good luck over there. I miss you, pal, and wish I could see you. Marjorie sends her regards. She'll write to you one of these days.'

She'll write to you one of these days. No, Marjorie won't write. I know it, and so does Marin.

So, one more year.

*

At the office on Boulevard Haussmann, I sometimes run into Pierre Dogany. He's doing a doctorate in public and company law here. He struggled as much as he could in Budapest and left when he saw it wasn't working out. Though he intends to return there as soon as he's completed his thesis. He's determined to be a Hungarian whatever it costs, whatever it takes. His excess of zeal bores me. I sense he regrets that letter he sent me two years ago in Bucharest. He doesn't forgive me for remembering so well his disillusionment with being Hungarian. He wishes he'd never complained to me of having to put up with being persecuted, oppressed and hounded, and having the very fact of being a Hungarian questioned. This relentless devotion seems excessive to me.

He invited me to the university last week, to hear a paper at Lapradelle's seminar on international law. He spoke about the legal side of the affairs of those who opted for Romania and, as Lapardelle was legal adviser to the Hungarians at The Hague, the whole meeting was an indictment of the Romanian side of the argument. I felt bad and though I lacked the hard information, dates, figures, I felt the need for a counter-argument. To my delight, it was made by a Romanian student in the hall who, once Dogany had finished his lecture, took the lectern and spoke from there for a full half-hour, his eyes flashing at times with a passion such as has probably never been seen in that cold lecture hall.

I went up to him on the way out to introduce myself.

He introduced himself to me as Saul Berger. I was almost repelled by the facile symbolism of this, too obvious to ignore, and too melo-dramatic for my taste: two Jews fighting each other for nothing more than abstract victories. Destiny, inevitable destiny.

*

Blidaru asks me in his last letter when I plan to return home. He has reserved a site in Snagov through the teachers' association and he'd like me to build him a house there.

I replied *par avion*.

'I don't know when I'll be back, but when I am it'll be I who builds the house. Wait, professor. You'll have to. It's too great a pleasure for me to miss.'

3

Maurice Buret returned yesterday from Normandy, where he had, at Oizy-sur-Glaive, a 25-day sojourn. He's happy with the harvest he's brought back, so happy that he's renounced the usual modest smile with which he usually excuses his victories. He had two successes in Oizy, both of them beauties, and he now animatedly but methodically recounts them to me, in numbered chapters.

1) Doctor Sibier.
2) Register of income.

1) Doctor Sibier is the medic he was substituting for.

He went on holiday to the south of France and then asked Paris for an intern to substitute for him.

As chance would have it, they sent Buret.

'From the outset,' recounts Maurice, 'I knew he was no ordinary fellow. He had two paintings in his house, a Braque and a Marie Laurencin, which in Oizy isn't just an act of courage, it's a provocation. A Parisian, thirty-six years old, intelligent – what's this man doing there, in that provincial backwater, in a town of 8,000 people, alone, without connections, without memories, without hopes? I asked the driver, I asked the nurse, I asked various patients who came along. Nobody could explain it to me. So I had to take up various means of private investigation and I opened the lower drawers of his bureau. He hadn't left me the keys, but I managed well enough with a knife. I found a stack of letters of no great interest, a few ordinary photos and, finally, an intimate diary. Some 600 pages. I read it all over two nights. Well, it's extraordinary. I tell you,

ex-tra-ord-in-ar-y, and I mean it. You're going to read it too, and
you'll see.'

'How, did you bring the notebooks?'

'Ah, no. What am I, a brigand? I just read them, and transcribed
the essential passages. Anyway, I had nothing much to do in the evenings. I transcribed them, then put them back in the drawer. Two
days before the return of the doctor, I called a locksmith from the
town to repair the damage. Nothing suspicious at all, everything in
order.

2) 'Doctor Sibier returned to Oizy on the evening of the 10th, and
I had to leave at dawn the following day. I handed over the register
of takings in which the consultations and money received were
recorded. I counted out eighteen notes of 1,000 and a few notes of a
hundred. I counted out eighteen, though there were only seventeen.
A thousand remained in my wallet. Don't ask me why. It amused me
to do it, apart from the fact that 1,000 francs is 1,000 francs.'

'He could find you out.'

'"Find me out"! Ugly expression. He could observe a small error
in calculation, you mean. Possibly, but he hasn't observed it.'

'He might yet.'

'Obviously. I expect a letter from him today or tomorrow.'

'And what are you going to do?'

'I don't know. Depends on the letter.'

Indeed, Doctor Sibier's letter arrived.

It seems to me you have made a small error in your calculations. I'm
not certain and, believe me, I dislike bothering you for such a minor
matter, but I can't account for a thousand francs. Is it possible that
we've missed something or, conversely, noted the same figure twice?

Maurice replied immediately. He doesn't know if there was an error,
but, if there was then he is responsible and ready therefore to immediately send on the missing sum. 'Whether it is 1,000 or 10,000 francs,
it would not be too much to retain a trust which is more valuable to
me than anything.'

Eighteen hours later, he received a reply by telegram.

> Don't send anything. It was not a question of you for a moment. A
> thousand apologies.

'Look, this is what's called solid good manners,' concluded Buret,
waving the doctor's telegram.

Though I am aware of the total moral vacuum in which he lives, I've
once again sought explanations. Maurice isn't just some debauchee,
and nor is he impulsive. He proceeds with utter calm and takes complete responsibility for his actions. It's awkward to talk of 'conscience', but I'm interested in how this fellow's head works and his
system of reflection and self-examination, that private space where
we each one of us judges, absolves or condemns ourselves.

'Oh, my conscience works excellently. Like a good lung, like a
good stomach. My conscience can handle the most serious crises.
It's because I don't fool myself and I don't make a moral problem
out of a practical one. Ever played football? I have. You'll be familiar
with the general principle at any rate: getting the ball in the back of
your opponent's net. The main thing is not to touch the ball with
your hands. Perfect. If you want to play football, you have to submit
to this rule. If you don't accept the rule, don't play. Simple. But it's
one thing to accept a rule and it's another thing to *believe* in it.
Whether or not you touch the ball is *in itself* unimportant and meaningless. It only acquires sense in the context of the game. But a moralist who takes up football won't delay in pronouncing on the
transcendental nature of handling the ball. Well, I don't go in for
that kind of thing. You see, the notion of "sin" is for me an abstraction. There's no such thing as "sin". There's only such a thing as
"tactlessness".'

*

I've been in Buret's home but twice, back when he lived with his
mother, in their apartments in the Rue Vouillet. On both occasions,

I felt I was inconveniencing him. He closed doors carefully after himself and led me hurriedly through the corridor, towards his room. At one point, through a half-open door, I caught sight of a lady and greeted her awkwardly, not knowing if I should introduce myself. 'It's nothing, a friend,' he told her casually, in passing – and carried on by.

He talks of so many things with me but has never mentioned his family. This is a private area and out of bounds. Abundant conversations about women, books, friends. But nothing about what lies beyond, that is deep, constant and enduring in the spirit of his family, who have long been settled in Paris, yet remain Bretons. For all his apparent cordiality, his terrible discretion, his passion for conversations and 'cases', Buret is still a private, self-possessed and reserved individual. I've never caught him in a moment of depression or joy that has caused him to speak imprudently, or even freely and without reserve. What is called 'the need to open oneself up' is completely foreign to him. He doesn't experience outpourings of emotion. At most he has considered sympathies. Somewhere, in his private life, a censor checks every word, suspects every impulse, cools every enthusiasm. A ring of steel protects his strictly personal secrets from attack.

Last week, out of the blue, he said to me: 'I've moved. I live on my own now. I've decided, with Mama's agreement, for us to live apart.'

I was taken aback. Less by the news itself than the fact that he was sharing it with me.

'Why?'

(I had asked out of politeness, for the sake of a response, not believing he'd give me the reason. I've no particular talent for extracting confessions. But, to my surprise, he responded in some detail.)

'I don't know how it happened. For some time I've felt it's no longer right. There's a silent pressure that exerts itself, more upon my thoughts than upon my personal affairs. Anybody who says they're free in their parents' house is fooling themselves.

'You know, I think I could live easily enough with Father. He's a cold person and that doesn't bother me. I don't think I've ever spoken more than five words to him at a time. I'm indifferent to him. We don't love each other. But with Mama it's endlessly difficult. We love each other, and that's intolerable. I'm good at dealing with adversity, but I can't stand strong affections. Adversity forces me to define myself. Love, on the other hand, is indulgent, ready with sentimental transactions, ready with false amenability. Love in families, in particular, where the bonds are old, durable and invisible. I explained all this to Mother. I don't know if she understood, but she accepted it anyway. We've concluded a treaty of mutual understanding: we'll see each other twice a week.'

Maurice Buret, without his physical presence, his modest and attentive smile, without the intelligence that enables him to simulate sensitivity and emotion, would be a horrible character. Clarity, order . . . Is that enough to make a person? God knows how long I've stumbled after such order, how many shadows I've wrestled with for such clarity. But isn't this kind of victory too sterile, too arid?

I take my revenge by transcribing Descartes:

... ne recevoir jamais aucune chose pour vraie que je ne la connusse évidemment être telle, c'est-à-dire éviter soigneusement la précipitation et la prévention et . . . ne comprendre rien de plus en mes jugements que ce qui se présenterait si clairement et si distinctement à mon esprit que je n'eusse aucune occasion de la mettre en doute.

What a miserly rule.

4

In Boulevard Haussmann, at the Rice offices, I was met by an extraordinary character: Phillip Dunton. I had to embrace him. He was unprepared for such a show of feeling and was rather taken aback, standing there with his pipe in his mouth.

'Forgive me, Phill, it's just I'm so glad to see you ...'

He's straight in from Romania and his arrival has somehow awoken in me a thousand images of over there – of people, streets, newspapers, cafés, the whole thing, everything that slowly faded away here, where I've been subject to so many new impressions. Phillip Dunton is a meticulous, slow-talking fellow (a habit I'd say he has picked up from chess, where you need a quarter-hour to consider each move). I bombarded him with questions and he didn't know which to answer first.

He's going to spend a few days here until old Ralph turns up, as he soon must.

He doesn't really know what he'll do after that. He's certainly not going back to Uioara, where there's no longer any work for him. He's going to try to get a year's leave from Rice Enterprises so he can go to America to complete some laboratory experiments and personal observations. Possibly to publish there the study which he completed a draft of in Uioara. When the year's up he'll go to any place Rice sends him. Anywhere: but he'd prefer Russia.

We lunched together, me impatient to hear him talk, he as calm and relaxed as I remember him. I could hardly restrain myself from asking about Marjorie, but I feared opening a well-guarded wound. My fears were unfounded. He spoke about Marjorie when he remembered her, effortlessly and without embarrassment. He considers what has happened to be straightforward. They've separated as good friends. He attended her civil marriage ceremony and she, three weeks later, saw him to the station.

'It never for a moment occurred to me that I might have trouble with Marjorie. She truly is intelligent and, really, that's what allowed us to stay married so many years. We couldn't have asked for more. I knew she'd leave one day and for a long period the only question for me was with whom it would be. When we met at Uioara, I thought you might be the one. I watched you with a fair degree of interest and – please believe me – a fair degree of sympathy. I don't know why, but nothing happened. Then, when Pierre Dogany appeared, I thought it would be him. I confess, it didn't cross my mind once that it could be Marin Dronţu. I laughed when I realized: it seemed grotesque. Now, though, with the passage of time, I see it was a piece of luck. Poor Pierre Dogany has the great disadvantage of being in love with Marjorie, but what she needs is to love, not to be loved. And she loves Dronţu. You should have seen her leaving the Town Hall on his arm: she was radiant.

'She's a good partner. I don't think I'll ever forget her and I wouldn't swear that I won't ever go back to Romania to see her and talk of all that's passed.'

*

Old Ralph T. Rice came for a couple of days and brought the master's response to my report. In theory, my viewpoint has been accepted. If work starts, it will be in Dieppe. The advantages of the site are obvious, and there are no commercial disadvantages over Le Havre. But will work start? Hard to say. The Crash has given him a bad fright. What scares him even more than the Crash is the mood in Romania.

'You've only been away a year,' he said, 'but if you went back now there's much you'd no longer recognize. Something's going on over there. Something's brewing.'

A final decision on the fate of the French project won't be taken until later, towards autumn, when I hope the situation will be clearer.

But the decision to scale back the project from what was originally planned seems already to have been taken. Possibly a network of small sales and distribution points will be set up throughout France and an attempt made to promote Rice petrol and oil in the motoring world. Modest enough, compared to what we once wanted to do.

I tried to get a clearer idea of why the old man – usually so calm and strong-willed – is alarmed. I inquired at length, but he was unable to tell me much. Not even Phillip Dunton, so nonchalant and sceptical about 'serious events', knew very much.

It seems Uioara has experienced some trouble over the past year: a number of small strikes, not serious in themselves but recurrent, as well as tussles between workers and management and a series of negotiations about wages. Along with the eternal outbursts from the people of Uioara concerning their eternal plum trees whenever a new well is sunk and yet another wave of drilling mud is misdirected. But Ralph Rice isn't the kind of man to be rattled by such trifles. There must be something else lurking in the background. I'm going to write to the master to ask.

I sense that European matters are hard to judge from Paris. I note with surprise, and not for the first time since arriving here, that Paris is a poor vantage point for viewing the continent. There are too many certainties here, too many habits of thought for the view from Paris not to be distorted. An 'instability factor' should be worked into any problems we solve on the banks of the Seine. Security provides a poor environment for reflection.

5

I went to see some Chagall paintings in the Rue de La Boétie. What tumult! The flowers are white, dreamlike, and beneath them, in shadow, the weary heads of the lovers – with pale brows and long hands and smoky gazes – detach themselves. Everything – the colours, the sky, the trees – is washed in light other than daylight, in shadows that are not those of the night. Where do these strange plants and petrified trees come from? The sun is diffuse, as if smothered beneath the burden of several superimposed oceans.

From what mountain does this hay cart descend, blue like a retouched photograph, unreal and solemn? The season is weary, with remembered light, with fields from dreams, with windows that open inwards. The grass is a brutal green in places, with an excess of colour and a straining at life that betrays a desperate nostalgia for the sun.

The timidity of the Jew before open country. His awkwardness in the face of plants, his reserve before animals! Of all the forms of loneliness, this is the hardest. It's so hard to get close to a tree in a simple manner when you've never lived close to one.

Chagall loves grass, hay, trees, but doesn't know how to love them. There's too much fervour in his love and then too much sadness. These are arrested impulses, enthusiasms without the courage to go all the way, shouts that get tripped up over a smile. Humour? Perhaps. But, more, the inability to escape or renounce yourself, to go tumbling among stones and weeds, to shut up shop and pull down the evening shutters on your personal problems and step fully into the sunlight, without memories or nostalgia.

*

The synagogue of my childhood had small windows with blue and red frames. That's the source of the light in Marc Chagall's paintings. I remember well those two bronze lions that sat guard on each side of the tablets of Moses. In Chagall's drawings I come across them again. It's a new kind of fauna, passed first through gold and bronze, through fabrics, ornamented by an entire folk-memory. Chagall has his roots in this old synagogue tradition. He's a Talmudist who has had his fill of abstractions, a Hasid who has set off for the countryside, where he will turn his worried eyes on the lazy gait of oxen, where he will smell the damp earth, follow the skittish flight of sparrows, but will not forget, will not manage to forget, the eternally nodding reader in the synagogue, leaning over the open books.

*

I've returned to the rue de La Boétie with Maurice Buret. He's a good judge of painting, but he doesn't like Chagall. When he stood before the paintings, I could feel the hostility of a man who has only ever permitted himself carefully measured emotions. In the bus, on the way back, he explained to me:

'I dislike tumult. Perhaps you find it exciting, but it doesn't agree with me. Heavy symbols, unfinished verses, confused images, what good are they? I find it all a bit twisted, and it unsettles me, makes me uneasy.'

'You want to feel at ease?'

'I do. Is that shameful? Every individual does, if they have any self-respect. I certainly do want to feel at ease and don't wish to be subjected to random bursts of lyricism, whether in life or books or painting. I won't have myself swooning, so why stand for it in others? You can only get along with those who can keep a grip on themselves, who are in control of their ideas, who keep an eye on their feelings and keep their emotional turmoil to themselves. I'm a Frenchman. And a Breton, furthermore. I have no patience with Teutons and Jews.'

'An anti-Semite?'

'Yes. Not in politics, but in psychology, certainly. I hope you understand and are not offended.'

'Dear Maurice, in my career as a Jew I've known so many furious anti-Semites. You, as anti-Semites go, are just a dabbler, an amateur. Far from being offended, it is an honour.'

'Thank you, that's very kind, but I have to warn you that it's unmerited. Whether dangerous or not, I'm still an anti-Semite. Or, to put it better, I'm against certain expressions of Judaic sensibility and psychology. I detest the agitated, convulsive, fevered aspect of the Jewish spirit. There's a Jewish way of looking at the world that distorts the proportions of nature, disturbs its symmetry, attacks its reality. The dreamlike tendency you were praising in Chagall is exactly what I denounce. My eyes are wide open. I don't like those who are only half awake. Your Chagall stumbles about between sleep and wakefulness, which disqualifies him from making art. A clear-headed Jew is a phenomenon. The great majority are sleepwalkers.'

'Perhaps, before I respond, we should agree on what the term "clarity" means. Do you believe there's a single way of being clear? A notary can be clear, or a poet, but they don't seem to me the same thing.'

'Perhaps. But I'll take the clarity of the notary. A notary thinks along the purest line of the French tradition: a word for each idea.'

'And so? This is more a stylistic virtue, not one of life. Clarity can be sterile, while tumult can be fertile. Some things are created in upheaval, at high temperatures, which the frozen eye of clarity can't take. There are things you understand with your blood or not at all.'

'I object, most strenuously. You're committing a major anatomical error. The organ man understands with is the head. Blood has other functions. This absurdity about "thinking with your blood" is Teutonic, Slavic or Jewish. A Frenchman would never say that. An Anglo-Saxon still less. I'm grieved to see you becoming emotional, which is synonymous with being Jewish. What a pity: I'm in danger of losing a friend.'

Here I am, defending the claims of spiritual tumult against lucidity. Ştefan Pârlea, if he could see me, would rejoice. To him, I'm a monstrous sceptic. Before Maurice Buret, however, I become a metaphysician.

I think in the Jewish spirit there is a continual open struggle between nature and intelligence, a struggle between extremes which none among us have reconciled. Because of this, to some we seem monstrously lucid, and to others we seem monstrously emotional. There will always be a Ştefan Pârlea to condemn our critical spirit. And a Maurice Buret to detest our tragic spirit. A golden mean should be found, but it's hard to find, and once found it's hard to hold on to. We commit ourselves carelessly, throwing ourselves down one road or another, and pay for this excess later through exhaustion and the antagonism of others.

Naive of Maurice to imagine he's telling me anything new. Haven't I made the same criticisms much more fervently? There's a character in me who loves tension and the whirling tumult of raging winds. And there's another that likes cold ideas, precise distinctions, reserve and waiting. Agreement is difficult between these two characters, but all my personal efforts are directed towards finding this agreement, which needs to be arrived at and maintained.

Michel Buret's 'anti-Semitism' is, basically, nothing but an attitude of reserve – the only type of anti-Semitism possible in France. In the same way I might be anti-French or, more accurately, anti-Cartesian. It's the marking out of an intellectual position, not an antagonism. There's a buffer zone between the Jewish spirit and French values which time may well erode or the passage of generations overcome, but at the first meeting it is clearly very strong. Breaking through this wall of coldness is a problem for the individual, just as each of us has to overcome difficulties relating to personality or temperament.

In my case, I think I could manage the journey were it via Montaigne and Stendhal.

*

I said to Maurice Buret:

'Do you never tire of your own intelligence? Has it never seemed wearying, demanding or inadequate? Having discussed everything, clarified everything and understood everything, isn't there still a shadow or a light beyond your reach?

'It is for remembering far too much that I would criticize you and the French spirit. You all have everything classified and assigned its place, as if in a laboratory, where every test-tube demonstrates a formula, a series of known reactions and certainties. It's a barren landscape. Safe, but barren.

'Your lives lack mystery and I wonder that you're not bored of life. Life, in any case, Maurice, must be terribly bored in your company. You're a person for whom there are no surprises. A "tactful person", you would say. Perhaps. You'll never let out a roar, never break anything, never jostle anyone. Politeness is your philosophy.

'You guard yourself like a public institution. Policing yourself is your vocation. You have floors and apartments inside yourself for every feeling or thought, stairs and lifts which take you from one thought to another. You're the doorman: you check who enters and leaves, close the doors, put out the lights, tidy up. You tend the houseplants, pruning any unruly branches, correcting drooping stalks, lopping off any shoots that rise too high. You can't stand forests, you only feel good in parks. You yourself are your own park.

'I'd like to know if, beyond the little certitudes that you cultivate, you ever stumble across the shadows of the dead . . . If you have ever shuddered at the feeling that what you do is petty, useless, vacuous, that all these "experiences" are barren, that you're missing out on life . . . I'd like to know if you've ever had a sudden, irrational urge to throw everything to the wind and surrender to chance, letting fate take you where it will ...

'You're a sane, well-balanced person, but you're too sane. You lack that little grain of instability without which life never reveals itself to us, without which our immediate horizons never open further. You lack a sense which is less precise than sight, but more essential: "a sense of the tragic".'

6

S.T. Haim got into Paris two days ago. He's staying in Rue Daunou, in that sparkling little hotel where I promise myself, in my sumptuous dreams, to live some day. His suitcase has been around Europe a few times and is covered with coloured stickers. He has been in Paris previously in recent months, though never alone. Without a doubt there's a woman in his life, but the voluble S.T.H. clams up and becomes sombre whenever the topic arises.

We had a long wander together, from the Louvre to Abbesses by foot, and from there up towards the Place du Tertre.

I was afraid he might not like this quarter, which I love more than any.

'You can't imagine how provincial Paris seems, when coming from elsewhere in Europe. You get the feeling of having stumbled into a station where the express trains don't stop. It smells of 1924, or 1928 at most. And here we are in 1931. Never mind Berlin or Vienna, where things are at their most fevered, even Bucharest is livelier, more up to date. When you cross the border at Bale, heading for Paris, the clock goes forward an hour, but you go back in time several years. You'll see what I mean this autumn, when you leave. In Europe, anywhere you go, you'll feel something simmering that isn't felt here and isn't even guessed at.'

'I don't know that I will leave in the autumn.'

'Yes, you will. The Dieppe project won't happen. You'll see.'

'How do you know?'

'I don't. I can see. I see times are changing and I see what's possible and what isn't.'

*

I was surprised to learn that old Ralph T. Rice is well enough acquainted with S.T.H. The pair of them had a two-hour discussion up in the office in Boulevard Haussmann. S.T.H. did some work in the past year for Rice Enterprises in Berlin, where he has business information and openings that are of value to old Ralph.

It amuses me to think of the expression of fear the old man had while listening to S.T.H., who paced back and forth across the office floor, waving his index finger in the air to illustrate the scale of the catastrophe.

'It's all over, sir, it's all over. You can shut up shop.

'We're heading for revolution. It's plain for all to see. Germany can't hold out any longer, Austria certainly can't either, the Far East is simmering. It's not a matter of a seven- or an eleven-year recession, as you read in the books on economics, it's a general calamity. I could demonstrate it with figures, but I'd rather not. I've too much respect for the businessman I sense you to be. I've come from Europe. Tell me: haven't you noticed the whiff of dynamite tickling that nose of yours when you went sniffing after petrol?'

Old Ralph frowns at the ink bottle, as if that first stick of dynamite S.T. Haim evoked were there on his desk.

*

I've introduced him to Maurice Buret. Fed up with conversations about social problems, which he has had already with myself and Rice, S.T.H. was admirable. He becomes a good-humoured fellow as soon as he gets off the subject of the fate of the universe.

The three of us went to the Colonne concert. Honeger's *Horace victorieux* programme was playing, a serious, flowing, precise piece with its great complexity tamed by a deceptive air of simplicity. I left refreshed and serene. Princely order rules the world – I reflected to myself – as long as such victories are possible.

Our evening continued in Montmartre, where some time ago I discovered a miraculous Anjou. S.T.H. was in fine high spirits. He gave us the inside story on the Oustric scandal, which he turned into a full-length novel involving women, affairs, successes on the stock exchange and in the boudoir, all arranged wonderfully and tumbling out at speed, as in a film. He has a wealth of knowledge, but he also knows how to spin a yarn, which he does rather oddly but in a way that's logical and hard to discredit. His explanations have something of Ponson du Terrail; they're melodramatic and sensationalist but are plausible at least, even if not strictly accurate.

'With your talents, you're going to end up working for the Intelligence Services.'

'It's the only job that could interest me. The only one, certainly, if it wasn't that something more decisive, more thrilling, exists. I'm sure top-level police work is highly engaging. But it's limited, poor stuff. It's a job requiring relationships, connections, hierarchies. I need something else. Let me whisper it in your ear, so we're not overheard.'

He leaned over the table and whispered confidentially: '*The ab-so-lute.*'

'*Rien que ça?*' asked Buret.

*

I haven't seen S.T.H. for four days. I open the paper today and on page three see: *Major arrests of communists in Romania*. S.T. Haim is listed among the top names. I'm stunned. I called the hotel. Indeed, it's so: S.T.H. left Paris on the 12th. Today is the 18th. Enough time for him to have reached Bucharest and been arrested.

I've written home for news, to Pârlea and Marin. I've no idea what could have happened. He was so sure of himself, so calm in his heart. It seems like some kind of detective story. I find it disturbing to think that the man I was walking around with only a few days ago in Paris is now locked up in Bucharest. It's a whole different order and level of events. How can it be? I walked alongside him, sat with him at a table, we talked, smoked, drank, and there was nothing about him to suggest his fall was near. Not even a distant sign announcing that somewhere, in that hour, his fate was being decided.

I'm unable to accept this ordinariness and every detail of our evening comes back to me, as though each one might contain a clue.

His grey suit, his blue tie with white dots, the Chesterfields he'd bought on the way from the tobacconist's beside Châtelet ...

*

No reply from Pârlea, none from Marin either. On the other hand, a grocery-store envelope, with the address hurriedly scrawled. I open it: it's from S.T.H.

You'll remember the hour of crisis we spoke of once. It has arrived.

He has an extraordinary memory. I had forgotten.

PART FIVE

I

At the upper end of Şerban Vodă, where the houses begin to thin out, a motor car provokes something of a stir, as in a provincial town. You see the faces of the curious at the windows, doors opening as we pass, children trooping after us.

'Are you going to the crematorium?' a woman leaning in a doorway asked the driver. 'Go to hell,' he replied, furious at the potholes we'd just landed in.

To our left was a sad, dirty wasteland, with broken crates, rags, tin cans and smouldering heaps of rubbish. A tree that had shed half its leaves, a sheepdog with nothing to do and, in places, tufts of grass that had endured until early November.

... Perhaps my visit is a mistake. What can I say to him? What can he say to me? Nothing makes me feel more powerless than a solemn situation, since ordinary phrases seem insufficient and I find serious declarations embarrassing. For three days, since obtaining a visitor's pass, I can think of nothing but the moment of farewell.

I've imagined every gesture dozens of times, and each time it strikes me as either excessive or inadequate. I'm even uneasy about the tin of cigarettes I'm bringing him: I don't know how to give it to him. I'd like to manage the casual gesture with which you ask someone to help themselves by proffering a cigarette. I'd like to shake his hand simply, as I would in the street, to make it seem nothing has changed, that our meeting here is nothing out of the ordinary, that his presence here in jail isn't a catastrophe ...

'Stop!'

The driver braked hard, jolting us yet again.

'We've arrived,' he tells me and points to an imaginary line ahead, past which you could only see the points of three bayonets.

'Jilava Prison?'

'Yes. It's underground.'

The ringing of the bell, the repeated shouts of the sentries ('Changing of the guard!' ... 'Changing of the guard!' ...), the document checks, the suspicious looks from the officer on duty, are all simple, bearable. The only dark and oppressive thing, my old friend S.T. Haim, is this small wooden door at the end of a stone alley, this threshold I will, within minutes – seconds – cross. From here on I am powerless to avert my gaze. From beyond, strange, distant footsteps can be heard, as if from another world. There, the door is opening. I have to come up with a smile. At all costs, I must find it in me to smile.

Blessed S.T.H.! He appeared in the doorway as stormily as ever, blond, agitated, impatient, his whole face illuminated. He stopped there for a moment to seek me out from twenty metres, from the other side of the bars. How many steps does he take to reach me? One, I think.

He talks quickly, hastily, with animation, with eyes and hands, with the lock of hair that always flops over his forehead, with his whole being, as though under fierce internal pressure, exulting now with the joy of release.

'If you could know how great it is here! People, the first people I've met. Centuries of prison are behind the door, no? Thousands of years. And it's still not enough, because these people can take it without complaint. I would've been ashamed to feel sorry for myself, for my twelve-year sentence. If it weren't for the lawyers and Mother, I wouldn't even have appealed. Because this is where I'll end up in any case. For us in here, there's no review board, no appeal. I don't delude myself with that nonsense. But the biggest appeal of all is coming – and coming soon, you might as well know. I don't know what it'll be like on Calea Victoriei, but here in the cells there's a great smell of revolution. Don't laugh. I can feel it. It's a definite, physical feeling. There's not a night I don't fall asleep thinking that in the morning we could find the doors swinging open. We could be out before the first snowfall.'

His absurd confidence astounds me. No, I'm not going to grab his shoulder and shake him awake. What good would that do? It's better if he believes and waits, even if he's only waiting for a pathetic shadow, a chimera he has taken with him on his journey into a land guarded by machine-guns and rifles.

Farewell, S.T.H. Ten minutes have passed, and Jilava's clock is more exact than the clock of history. Jilava measures minutes and seconds, you count out decades and centuries.

*

I dropped into the Central, where I was sure to find Ştefan Pârlea. He doesn't move from here from dawn until after midnight. He has a table at the back, on the right, beside the bar, which everyone recognizes as his domain. It's been a long time since he's been at the ministry. He resigned in order to be free. Free to do what? I don't know. Free for 'the new dawn'. I'd have liked to tell him that his new nihilist hangout – unkempt and tatty – is ridiculous. But I was afraid he might explode with his old cry: 'Shut up! You're an aesthete!'

I'd gladly avoid him, but he's the only person who can really tell me what's going on with S.T.H., why he was arrested, why he was convicted and what his prospects are. His file contains a German police report, which identified him in Berlin three months before his arrest, speaking at a neighbourhood communist meeting. There's also the evidence of a senior functionary, who heard him speaking loudly on the Orient Express about 'important secrets about arms'. In addition, depositions, allusions, presuppositions. The whole thing is flimsy and insubstantial. What's true, though, is that it concerns S.T. Haim, an eager revolutionary any day of the week. It would have been no surprise had he been caught with nitro-glycerine in the pocket of his waistcoat. The man is as capable of carrying a bomb as an umbrella and of calmly depositing it at a cloakroom: 'Please, put this bomb under my number; though mind it doesn't go off.'

Pârlea finds my questions irritating.

'Why did they arrest him? Why did they convict him? Blather and nonsense. They arrested him because they had to. Him yesterday, me today, tomorrow everybody. That's the only way you can have a revolution: with everyone sent to jail. Is he guilty? Innocent? He gets five years? Fifty-five years? His problem. For us, there's only one question: is the state at the point of collapse or is it not?'

'I hadn't taken you for a communist.'

'And I'm not one. What does that mean? Communist, reactionary, left, right . . . Superstitions, man, half-baked ideas. There's only an old world and a new one. That's all. A world that's at breaking point and one that's being born. Am I supposed to sit here lamenting S.T. Haim? I've no time. Full stop. We're all stumbling through the night, pell-mell, some falling, others not, each to his fate. When morning comes, we'll see who's still standing.'

Not even here in the café, between two drained glasses of beer, dominating all the tables around with his baritone voice and scaring his timid young listeners, is Mr Ştefan D. Pârlea ridiculous. He has an inspired visage and a firm fist. When he speaks, his gaze moves about the surrounding faces, as though seeking a target. A group of adolescents flanks him like a permanent guard, all awkward in their civilian clothing, their first since leaving school. They smoke a lot and badly, sometimes with too great a show of bravura, sometimes with a nervous twitch that betrays the recent memory of furtively lighting up in water closets. Various pamphlets circulate among them, and they read them avidly, commenting aloud, reciting verses, proclamations, manifestos. They all speak with exaggerated familiarity although they've never shaken hands, and never met each other before. Between one and two o'clock, the hubbub suddenly ceases. Everybody is looking for the 26 lei needed for the lunchtime special. Coins pass from table to table, coughed up either amicably or with a bit of swearing. The girls are fewer in number, the occasional one lost amidst a group of boys, jaded waifs in trenchcoats, bareheaded, stubbing out half-smoked cigarettes. It's hard to know what they are: perhaps students, perhaps cabaret dancers, perhaps just streetwalkers.

Then there's one who looks surprisingly like Louise Brooks, in *Lulu*. All the boys address her by name – Vally – and she responds to them all with the same sweet, bored smile. She wears a green sweater pulled in boyishly at the waist by a belt and on her head a scrap of a beret – also green – that leaves her three-quarters bare head rounded off with a fringe. She visited our table and greeted Pârlea with a vague gesture, raising her index finger to tip the brim of an imaginary hat.

'Got a smoke?' she asked me in passing, and I proffered my pack of Regalas. She took one, frowning for some reason.

'You look like the heroine in Wedekind.'

'I know. Lulu.'

'How do you know?'

'It's what they tell me.'

She went away, her gait more casual and indifferent than lazy.

I've discovered why Vally turned up her nose while accepting my cigarette. At the Central they only smoke 'workingman's' cigarettes, cheap cigarettes made with black tobacco. Mine was a bourgeois cigarette. Poets, revolutionaries, free people, those with imagination, visionaries, only smoke proletarian tobacco. My poor 30 lei pack was bad manners, an affront. The frown of the girl who looks like Lulu in Wedekind meant: 'So that's the kind you are.'

There are other rules of conduct at the Central. Don't do more than raise a finger to greet someone. Under no circumstances, if you wear a hat, must you take it off. Everybody on first-name terms. But don't formally introduce yourself to anybody. As a rule, everybody here knows everybody. There's no time for politeness, lies, frivolity. We're tired – right? – we're fed up. Rich people, important people, people with pot bellies can fool about all they like. They've the time and inclination for joking around. Not us.

There's a heavy air of boredom and futility at the Central, despite the constant hubbub. If these fellows aren't busy being passionate, then they're pretending to be, if they're not discouraged, then they play at it. Some of them are very young, aggressive and loud, with pubescent rashes on their faces, young agitators who still haven't found a job to do. Scattered among them is the occasional attractive adolescent face. There are also a few recent beards and moustaches that are deliberately unkempt, sombre and prophetic. (The abundance of beards in periods of social unrest, times of revolt or upheaval, should be noted. It's the handiest way people have of making themselves mysterious.)

Once inside, it's hard to leave the Central. Indolence grips you, the dishonest notion that you're waiting for someone when in fact you're expecting nobody, you're just fed up with walking the streets aimlessly. The revolving door spins endlessly, bringing in the same characters. They come and go, then five minutes later they're back at the same table they left. There's an air of somnolence, stuffiness, dissipation, a taste of ash, a memory of cigarette-ends.

Occasionally there's a heated exchange of ideas or fists at one or other of the tables, and everyone is briefly shaken from their torpor. Then the passing fuss subsides again in the constant dull din of voices.

There's a bearded twenty-year-old from Bessarabia who's supposedly a blacksmith's son and a genius. He's translated Alexander Blok and from time to time he comes to life by trumpeting a verse from 'The Scythians'.

*

I came across Vally on her own, leaning back against the bar and watching nothing in particular through half-closed eyes, as though through a thick cloud of cigarette smoke. She's a beautiful girl and her sleek fringe gives her an amiable air which the cigarette doesn't entirely dispel. I went up to her and made a proposal that caught her off-guard.

'How about taking a walk?'

For a moment she seemed not to comprehend. ('A walk? Why?') She stopped before the doorway, hesitating once more. Rain.

'I hope you're not put off by a drop of water?'

She slowly turned up the collar of her trenchcoat, stuck her hands in her pockets and set off with a slightly heroic attitude, as if confronting a storm.

The old pleasure of strolling in the rain. The shining wet asphalt, the twinkling of distant neon signs, people rushing by, taxi horns blaring and the steady, general, generous rain falling on the rooftops . . .

We walked for a good while without speaking. I listened to her footsteps on the asphalt, sounding a little too forced and energetic for her, as though ready for a race of several kilometres. She wore a lightweight raincoat and the rain struck it noisily, making what was little more than a drizzle sound like a storm.

'Why do you come to the Central?'

She didn't reply for a moment. She continued walking, bent forward slightly to spare her cheeks from the falling rain. Finally she spoke.

'It's cheap. Lunch costs 26 lei.'

'So you stay all day? I took you for a student.'

'I am. Kind of. I'm in my third year but I still have exams to repeat from the first year. But I get bored, bored to death . . . I find it hard to sit at home. Nothing I do works out, I'm sick of it.'

'And you find the Central amusing?'

'Amusing! . . . No . . . Well, I don't know. I can't seem to avoid it, that's all. Wherever I'm coming from, wherever I'm going, I drop in. I step in to see what's new and get talking with someone or other. Next thing you know, time has passed.'

She talks in a jaded, indifferent tone, either from great boredom or great tiredness.

'But have you never tried to get away from there?'

'Yeah, sure, but I've never managed it. In the end, I'm happy the way I am. You think it's a big deal if you manage to stay away from the Central?'

'Why are you speaking as if we know each other? You met me three days ago. You don't know who I am or what I want.'

'So what? That's how I talk with everyone. I think you're smart enough not to let it bother you.'

'Thanks for your faith in me. But it's about you, not about me. Doesn't being over-familiar put you at a disadvantage? A more formal way of speaking doesn't just mean you're being polite, it's also a way of protecting yourself.'

'How subtle. But I don't get it. "Protecting yourself." You're funny, you really are. What should I be protecting?'

We walked on in silence. Later, I hailed a cab.

'Where are we going?'

'I don't know. Wherever you want.'

I embraced her and she did not object at all. She let herself be kissed and kissed back, but coolly, without conviction, absently, as if she were smoking a cigarette. I thought of taking her back to my place, but the driver was heading in the direction of Calea Victoriei and I couldn't be bothered telling him to turn around. I dropped her off at the Central. She gave me a soldierly salute from the doorway, her finger to the usual imaginary cap. A smile that communicated nothing flickered on her lips.

I went back to the Central yesterday out of curiosity and stayed the whole evening. I had nothing else to do. It was too early to go home and the weather was too bad for walking around. Five minutes, another five, another five. Someone came and asked me for 26 lei, someone else for a cigarette, someone else for 3 lei for a newspaper. I had the feeling I knew everybody and perhaps I did in fact know them, from the street, the tram or somewhere else.

'I should go,' I said to myself several times, but felt too lazy to stand up. Vally, going from table to table, acknowledged me with a few words in passing.

'Still here?' she asked casually, not pausing for a reply.

In Ştefan Pârlea's group they were discussing 'disintegration'. The boys followed the conversation with great concentration, as though each had personally borne witness to the stages of this breakdown. Watching them falling under the narcotic spell of the discussion – some of them pale, others earnest and tense – made me want to bang my fist on the table to snap them out of it. 'They need to be stampeded,' I thought. 'They need to be cleared out of here urgently; they'll never get out of their own volition.' As if putting up a weary struggle against sleep, I was myself unable to arise from my seat. 'Oblomov,' I reflected, recalling that lazy Slavic hero. 'A café full of Oblomovs. And me, among them, on the way to becoming one.'

We left late, all together. Outside, they bid each other farewell at various street corners, taking the unfinished debate on to their neighbourhoods in smaller groups. After Lipscani Street a fellow happened to be walking alongside me.

'You live around Carol Park.'

'Yes . . . more or less ...'

I felt awkward walking alongside someone I didn't know and to whom I had nothing to say. I tried to make conversation, as the silence was intolerable, but it was no good. I couldn't find much to say and he didn't feel much like replying.

I turned right at the Church of the Holy Apostles, thinking he would carry on ahead towards Antim Street. But he turned the corner with me. I made one last attempt on Emigratului Street, too insignificant a street for his route to coincide with mine. He followed me. I was furious with him and would have liked to stop there and then and demand to know where he was going. But I restrained myself, as there weren't more than a hundred paces left to my door, and once there I quickly extended my hand, taking him by surprise, thereby leaving my farewell half-accomplished.

'What? . . . You're going?'

'Yes. Goodnight.'

He stood there on the footpath, in front of my gate, leaning against a lamppost with his hands in his pockets, suddenly disoriented, as though he'd just missed a train. I took several steps into the yard, unsure whether I should turn around. I had an intense feeling of relief, which an inner voice summed up nicely as: 'He can go to hell.' But I also felt I was doing something 'one ought not to do'. I felt a vague sense of shame, and I foresaw that it would not let me be. I know how I am. I'm not incapable of committing certain minor infamies to protect my personal peace. But once committed, the memory of them nags at me like a speck of dirt in my eye.

I turned back to him, fed up, and snapped:

'What are you doing here? Why don't you go and sleep?'

He shrugged and smiled (probably at the naivety of the question).

'Where do you live?'

'Hmm! Wherever.'

My first thought was this: 'How good it would be to be upstairs already, in my room, alone in bed, making myself at home, turning on the bedside lamp to read.' To be alone at that moment seemed the greatest happiness possible.

'Come on, you can sleep here.' I went on, cursing him in my thoughts with utter fury and cursing myself for this bit of unforeseen bad luck. We undressed in silence, me furious, he unperturbed.

What an odd thing a stranger is. A stranger sleeping next to you. I listen to his breathing as if it were his entire life, with its hidden processes, the pulsing of the blood in the tissues, with thousands of tiny hidden decays and combustions, which together create and maintain him.

I won't be able to sleep. There's no point shutting my eyes, I won't sleep. It's better if I accept insomnia and resign myself to wakefulness. He's worn out. What has happened this evening probably happens to him every evening. Nothing that need bother him.

A stranger sleeps next to me, like a stone beside another stone.

He's the first person ever to enter my life without knocking. Everyone I know, I know on the basis of an implicit pact of solitude. 'Look, this is me, that's you, I can give this much, you that much; we've shaken hands and have thereby sworn comradeship as regards certain things, ideas, memories – the rest is off limits, remains within ourselves, we're well brought up and will never overstep the boundaries or open the doors which we have closed.' The pact is clear, the parties well defined: me, you.

A single stranger sleeps next to me and I feel like a whole crowd has come in with him. He hasn't said anything to me, I haven't said anything to him, but I feel I have nothing else to say to him, nor to hide from him.

*

'Revolution . . . Could be. Within a month, two, three,' say the boys at the Central. Ştefan Pârlea is more specific:

'By George's day the gallows will be busy.'

Perhaps they've got the dates and modalities wrong. But they're not wrong about the atmosphere, which is suffocating.

Where do they come from, these crazy, homeless, superfluous, empty-headed, empty-handed boys, with their undefined roles and blind expectations?

They sleep here tonight, there tomorrow, the night after that they don't sleep at all. They spend their lives passing from one table to another, looking for a penny, a cigarette, or a bed for the night. From time to time one of them finds a rallying call, a message for everybody, an absolute truth, and he elbows his way to the front. After a day or two, after a weekend or two, they lose their way out of boredom or the boredom of those around them.

'We're going to put them up against the wall.' I've heard that expression a thousand times. I bump into an avenger at every street corner.

Who is it they're going to put up against the wall? That hasn't been clearly established yet. The bourgeoisie, the old, those with paunches, the complacent? It's all confused, blind, chaotic. They're all discouraged and strung out. They're worn out with waiting. This endless wait that consumes hours, days and years and still has room in its belly. This goalless, limitless, aimless waiting, a pure state of expectation, composed of nerves and tension.

'It has to collapse, it absolutely has to collapse ...'

'What does?'

'Everything.'

2

I accompanied the master and Professor Ghiță to Snagov to take a look at the professor's plot. It's a small site belonging to the association of teaching staff, in which Blidaru has reserved 200 square metres with the idea of one day building himself a house. He doesn't seem at all inclined to build now. The site is well positioned, on the side furthest from Bucharest, with a vantage above the lake that would allow us to create a superb terrace. I'd like to build the house just for the pleasure of such a terrace. The master and I both tried to convince him, but the professor appears determined not to begin anything.

'Please, don't insist. I feel there's nothing more ridiculous these days than beginning something – whatever it might be. I'm certain the earth will quake tomorrow, so I'm not going to start building a house today. You're well aware how ridiculous it would be. It's out of the question. This is a time for demolition, not construction.'

*

He's lived in the same house since 1923. Everything is as it was when I met him first, the long rectangular curtainless window, the camp bed, the books, the small Brueghel on the wall . . . And he himself, in a long house coat, under the light of his desk lamp, seems unchanged. He speaks slowly, defining as he goes, checking each hypothesis, responding to his own questions, overturning his own objections.

As he is calm and self-controlled, who can judge how pressing the problems preoccupying him are? Listening to him, I often have a sense of being with a chemist who, with a vial of ecrasite in his hand, declaims on the explosive qualities of the human body. And that this cold person is the most passionate and tumultuous of men.

I reminded him of our first conversations here, of the 1923 course on 'the development of the idea of value', the indignation of the specialists, and how amazed we students were . . . I pulled an atlas from the shelf and opened on the map of Europe to mark with a pencil the very centres of crisis, which now validate the predictions he made back then.

He took the pencil from my hand and pointed to the centre of the map: Vienna.

'This is the pressure point. From here everything will fracture. Observe how from a clearly trivial matter, like the Anschluss, a totally disproportionate point of tension is created. Everybody takes a side in the game, everybody joins in, and the more deadly the stakes, the more desperate the pressure. When things collapse, they will collapse completely.'

Leaning over the map, he looked like a general reviewing the course of a battle that is imminent.

*

There's not much to do in the workshop, so I almost always attend Ghiţă Blidaru's course. The slide in the British pound has for the last three weeks fuelled his lectures and given them the vivacity of a serialized novel. From one lecture to the next, a new set of monetary certainties falls apart. The professor receives the latest reports on the disasters with professional detachment, but I find it hard to credit that the general collapse provides him with any satisfaction. However, I don't think the monetary phenomenon interests him except insofar as it is a symptom and an element of disintegration. A strong currency means, in any case, a focus of value, which automatically guarantees the stability of all values, at whatever level you care to look, whether in economics or culture. A provisional stability, obviously, but real nonetheless. Conversely, monetary inflation provokes instability in every aspect of life, and first of all in the collective mind. (Isn't revolutionary Germany a result in large measure of the years of inflation? – this is a question for Blidaru.)

Sometimes at the professor's course I feel like we're gathered together in a kind of ideological headquarters of an immense world war, waiting from hour to hour for telegrams about the catastrophe, dreaming of the new world that will be born from its ashes.

For the moment, beneath the surface, the old strata silently shift. Ghiță Blidaru has a fine sense of hearing.

3

The first telegram from Uioara didn't look too serious. 'Men at Well A 19 refusing to work.' It's not the first time. The only thing that strikes me as odd is the sending of a telegram when so many telephone lines are free. At the offices in Piaţa Rosetti, however, everybody was calm.

An attempt was made in the afternoon to make contact with Uioara, but it proved impossible. The operator in Câmpina gave the same response for an hour: 'Uioara is not replying. Probably there's a fault with the line.' It was quite plausible, but I found it suspicious. 'Perhaps you should warn old Ralph,' I suggested half seriously. They laughed. 'Where will we look for him? We'd have to search all Europe. Anyway, we can't trouble him for every trifle.'

At seven that evening Hacker, from accounting, burst into the office. He'd come straight from Uioara, with two punctured tyres, an overheated engine about to ignite, a shattered windscreen and the half the hood torn away. I was at the workshop and was immediately called to Piaţa Rosetti. En route, the master was silent and pale.

Truth told, Hacker's news was less alarming than the figure he cut. He had been imprudent enough to pass through New Uioara, where people protested with a bit of stone-throwing, which is really nothing serious. The real danger, should it arise, is Old Uioara, where the wells and refinery are. But at that point there were just the beginnings of a more than usually contentious strike.

'I fear for the refinery,' said Hacker. 'They'd all gathered there in big groups, talking. The ones from the refinery were still working when I left, but who knows what's happened since then? Or even if anyone's left at the factory, so that we have electricity. Lord preserve us from darkness! I think it's just what the plum brandy drinkers of New Uioara are waiting for. It was them who cut the phone lines.'

I waited all night for news. Not from Uioara, which we were definitively out of contact with, but from the Interior Ministry and Prahova Prefecture. There was a terrible commotion at the office. Marjorie had come too, with Marin. She was very concerned, yet self-controlled. She was absolutely determined to leave immediately for Uioara, with Hacker's car, which she said she'd drive on her own.

The master had a faraway look. Just once he said to me: 'I'd be sad if they went and destroyed Uioara on us.'

*

The morning papers are alarmist and confused. Nobody knows exactly what's going on. Two directors from the office have gone to negotiate, accompanied by a Ministry of Labour representative and preceded by platoons of police. Certainly, things could settle down if it were just a labour dispute. Is that all it is? I doubt it.

However vague the information we've received is so far, it seems there are two distinct movements in Uioara, though they're both caught up in the same storm. The first group is made up of refinery, factory and oil workers, all from Old Uioara. Then there are the viticulturists in New Uioara. The first group have wage demands, while the second group ask for nothing. They just want to go down to Old Uioara and destroy it. The oil revolt and the plum-tree revolt.

There's unanimous enthusiasm at the Central. On Calea Victoriei, a rumble of war. It's coming! It's coming! It's coming! What is? Revolution, obviously.

This morning, speaking to me, Ştefan Pârlea looked transfigured.

'You know, I feel our moment has come. I feel we're about to leave mediocrity behind. Leave it behind, even though we pass through blood, through flames. There's no other way. We'll be stifled otherwise. When you're suffocating in a house filled with gas fumes you don't waste time opening the windows: you smash them.'

*

The master, Dronțu and I tried to slip off to Uioara in Hacker's Ford, which has nothing to lose anyway. But it was impossible. At Câmpina we were turned back by the police.

What has happened beyond there? Nobody knows. The most sinister rumours are going around. That the peasants from New Uioara have burned down the refinery, that they've emptied the fuel tanks, flooding the whole internal line with crude, that they've barricaded the Americans in the offices, that they've attacked the police with rocks, that the police opened fire, that sixty people are dead . . .

A moment of crisis! A moment of crisis! It's as though I hear S.T.H.'s voice.

*

Vieru is depressed. He believed the project at Uioara was something enduring, and now this unexpected brush with disaster disorients him. So many years of work wiped out in a night, in a moment. If the reports of a fire are confirmed, then what will be left for those who built it? A few plans, a few photographs . . .

Ghiță Blidaru is triumphing. But he is not acting proud and I don't believe he's pleased. He came to the workshop to see the master and I was surprised by his anxious expression.

'Have you won?' Vieru asked him, trying to laugh.

'Not yet, unfortunately. It takes more than a fire to make a revolution. What's happening now in Uioara is certainly in the natural order of things. For ten years the wells have spoken, and now it's the turn of the plum trees. Their voices are older, and so they had to make themselves heard. But let's not fool ourselves. It's still not enough. We need to burn down a whole history, not just three oil wells. There are so many things left to destroy that Uioara resolves nothing. We're only at the beginning.'

*

Eva Nicholson turned up at the offices in spectacular fashion. She came on her own in a two-seater car and in two hours will head back. She's wearing a sports suit over which she's thrown a mackintosh. She's pale, calm and very tired, but completely un-emotional.

'I've come to buy cotton wool, iodine lotion and bandages. There's a need for them there. I couldn't buy them in Ploieşti, where I would have caused suspicion.'

'My dear lady, are you siding with the insurgents?' asked some-body from management.

'They're not insurgents; they're the injured.'

In any case, things at Uioara aren't so bad after all. Eva Nicholson has reassured us. First of all, nothing has been destroyed, or almost nothing. Things have been stolen here and there, and there's been a disturbance. The police opened fire. The workers locked themselves into the factory and refinery. If they don't leave within twenty-four hours, the police will open fire again. Within three days, it'll all be sorted out.

*

Peace. Old Ralph T. Rice arrived yesterday. The latest bulletin from Uioara announces the evacuation of all the buildings. For now, the 'instigators' are being weeded out and made an example of. Work could restart next week at the wells and the refinery. Work has begun already at the power plant with a reduced staff. An Interior Ministry statement mentions four fatalities and several injured. But terrible things are whispered of.

4

Several times I've attempted to work, but it all feels irrelevant. You're on a sinking boat. What's the point of keeping to your post? Disasters aren't organized events – you just have to manage.

Never have my room, my books and my maps seemed more intolerable to me. I've always believed that the only defeats and victories that matter in life are those you lose or win alone, against yourself. I have always believed it my right to have a locked door between me and the world, and to hold the key myself. Now look at it, kicked open. The doors are off their hinges, the portals unguarded, every cover blown.

The dignity that solitude affords is gone. The vice has been cured, perhaps. We're going to remember our natural obligations and will live thrown together with our fellows. Some will be crushed, others saved, as we are pell-mell ploughed back into the savage order from which we once fled as individuals. Who knows? Perhaps a field that for decades has yielded only special plants – chrysanthemums or tubers – needs a furious outbreak of weeds, nettles, henbane and wild laurel for it to regain its fertility. The season of bitter plants has come.

For too long I have played on the stage of lucidity, and I have lost. Now I need to accustom my eyes to the falling darkness. I need to contemplate the natural slumber of all things, which the light calls forth, yet also causes to tire. Life must begin in darkness. Its powers of germination lie hidden. Every day has its night, every light has its shadow.

I cannot be asked to accept these shadows gladly. It is enough that I accept them.

*

To surrender to the wind and the rain, to submit to the coming night, to lose yourself in the passing crowd – there is nothing more restful. I will no longer seek the path that leads me to myself. But nor can I expect horizons now hidden to arise out of nothingness. Despair is a sentiment I have long suppressed, knowing how oppressive it is in a Jewish sensibility. I will not go back to the ghosts I have left behind. Is a 'new dawn' on the way? It surely is. But until then, the dusk will be slowly gathering over all I have loved and love still.

I will build the house at Snagov. I have to. If necessary, even if Blidaru does not wish me to. I have to build a house of gracious, simple lines, with great windows and an open terrace – a house for sunlight.

I have spoken at length with the professor and, though he is unconvinced, he will consent. I have asked him for full freedom to decide and to work. He has sworn he will not set foot there until I give the word.

Ştefan Pârlea always talks of the great historical conflagration that is drawing ever closer. Very well, then. I will have something to offer up to this conflagration.

PART SIX

I

I was on my way to the workshop, to meet the master. We seldom see each other now I've begun work at Snagov. I decided to go to town no more than once a week, on Saturdays. I'd have trouble finishing by September otherwise.

At the corner, towards Boulevard Elisabeta, was a group of boys selling newspapers. 'Mysteries of Cahul! Death to the Yids!'

I have no idea why I stopped. I usually walk calmly by, because it's an old, almost familiar cry. This time I stopped in surprise, as if I had for the first time understood what these words actually meant. It's strange. These people are talking about death, and about mine specifically. And I walk casually by them, thinking of other things, only half-hearing.

I wonder why it is so easy to call for 'death' in a Romanian street, without anyone batting an eyelid. I think, though, that death is a pretty serious matter. A dog crushed beneath the wheels of a motor car – that's already enough for a moment of silence. If somebody set themselves up in the middle of the street to demand, let's say, 'Death to badgers', I think that would suffice to arouse some surprise among those passing by.

Now that I think about it, the problem isn't that three boys can stand at a street corner and cry "Death to the Yids', but that the cry goes unobserved and unopposed, like the tinkling of a bell on a tram.

Sometimes, sitting alone at home, I realize I can suddenly hear the ticking of the clock. It has been beside me all along but, either because I wasn't paying attention or because I'm accustomed to it, I don't notice it. It has got lost, along with many other familiar little noises, in a kind of silence that swallows the sound of things around you. Out of this stillness, you get suddenly caught off-guard by the clock ticking with unsuspected violence and energy. The ticks strike in short, clipped beats, like the blows of tiny metal fists. It's not a clock any more, it's a machine gun. The sound covers everything, fills the room, grates on your nerves. I hide it in the wardrobe – it resounds even from there. I smother it beneath a pillow – the sound continues, distant and vehement. There's no cure but to resign yourself. You have to wait. After a while, by some miracle, the attack is over, the cogs settle down, the second hand relaxes. You can no longer hear it: the ticking has blended back into the general silence of the house, merged with the general hum of all the other objects.

Exactly the same thing happens with that age-old call for death, which is always present somewhere on Romanian streets, but audible only at certain moments. Year after year it resounds in the ear of the common man, who is indifferent, in a hurry, with other things on his mind. Year after year it rumbles and echoes in street and byway, and nobody hears it. And one day, out of nowhere, behold how it suddenly pierces the wall of deafness around it, and issues from every crack and from under every stone.

Out of nowhere? Well, not really. What is required is a period of exhaustion, of stress, of tense expectancy, a period of disillusionment. And then the unheeded voices are audible again.

*

In Snagov, on the site, on scaffolding, among workmen, amid stones and cement and girders, there are no problems. The problems begin once I return to the city.

Something has happened in recent months. Some invisible mechanism which allows people to keep going has broken down. I see only exhausted people, I meet only those who have given up. The revolution was on its way, but did not arrive. The episode at the two Uioaras was a brief outburst, a lick of flame.

They had been saying: 'This is the end of everything – here's where it all begins.' But here we are, nothing has ended, nothing has begun.

St George's day is long past. The hangings Pârlea envisaged for the holy day have not materialized. All the appointed days have come and gone, all the deadlines have expired.

Something must be done for those at the end of their tether, fresh prospects are needed for those frustrated expectations.

A few boys on a street corner cry out 'Death to the Yids'. It'll do, for now.

*

It is extremely difficult to follow the progressive hardening of enmity from one day to the next. Suddenly you find yourself surrounded on all sides, and have no idea how or when it happened. Scattered minor occurrences, gestures of no great account, the making of casual little threats. An argument in a tram today, a newspaper article tomorrow, a broken window after that. These things seem random, unconnected, frivolous. Then, one fine morning, you feel unable to breathe.

What is even harder to comprehend is that nobody involved in any of this, absolutely nobody, bears any blame.

*

A terrible moment at the workshop. A quarrel with Dronțu.

We had been squabbling. Not for the first time, he not being the kind to mince his words and me not being slow off the mark either. It's usually over quickly; he swears, I swear back – and then we shake and make up.

I don't know how it started this time. I think it was over a bottle of ink I'd hidden away somewhere that Marin needed urgently. We scuffled, in jest of course, spoke rather roughly, then somehow found ourselves face to face and genuinely furious. There was a look in Marin's eyes I'd never seen before. For a moment, a single moment, I thought he was joking and about to burst out laughing. I was going to extend my hand but, fortunately, I hadn't a moment in which to make the slightest gesture, because he blew up:

'Don't act the Jew. I'm from Oltenia. Don't speak that Jew-talk with me.'

I went pale. There was nothing I could do; everything between the two of us – memories, friendship, our professional relationship – turned to nothing. I had a powerful sense that the man standing before me had become a total stranger. He had become so distant, so foreign and inaccessible, that responding to him would have seemed as mad to me as conversing with a block of stone.

I should be sad. I'm surprised that I'm not. It's as though I've been hit in the shoulder by a bullet, and now I'm waiting for the pain. But it doesn't come.

I have a strange feeling that the name Marin Dronțu belongs to a stranger. It's like a name from a book. I never imagined that I could forget a person, so deeply, so suddenly, so entirely.

I slept well, dreamlessly. I worked all day.

*

Marjorie came to Snagov. I was on the scaffolding and when I saw her in the distance, in white, it gave me a jolt, as though I were seeing her from years before, in Uioara; the likeness of Marjorie Dunton. I invited her to my room, a hundred paces from the building work, by the lake. Only now have I realized how much this room resembles our cabin from the old days.

Marjorie came on her own initiative.

'What happened yesterday was awful. Marin told me all about it. It's ridiculous. Two serious people like you ... You must understand. A moment of irritation, of distraction. One doesn't break off an old friendship over something like that. You understand, don't you? Tell me you do!'

'Dear Marjorie, I understand. I understood from the first moment.'

'So the two of you will make up?'

I shrugged.

'Obviously! You said it yourself, for God's sake: we aren't kids.'

*

212

Evening boating on the lake, with Marjorie and Marin. We were awkward with each other for a time. We shook hands and skipped the explanations. It's easier that way.

There was a fine view of Blidaru's house from out on the water, with only the straight lines of the walls discernible in the dark. The scaffolding, carts loaded with lime and the heaps of stone were immersed in shadow. It soothes me just to look at this house. I only wish I could postpone the day I will complete it.

We'd been silent too long, and Marjorie sensed this. She asked Marin to row back towards the shore.

'I'm tired, fellows. Come on, carry me. Do you remember? When we were in Uioara?'

Do we remember . . . I lifted her to 'Rock-a-bye Baby', and Marjorie, recalling a moment from that September day long past, took her hat from her head and, waving it like a flag, began to sing as she did then:

> It's a long way to Tipperary
> It's a long way to go.

I was well aware that this was nothing but an effort to invoke among us the shadows of the past, but it didn't prevent a familiar emotion from taking hold of me.

As I accompanied them to the bus, Dronțu said to me, with a certain languor, a certain heart-weariness, which made up for a lot:

'You know, life is rotten. We manage to do a heap of rotten things and don't even wonder at it. It really is rotten. Nobody's to blame.'

Indeed, nobody is to blame. This is the point we find ourselves at, sooner or later. I know this so well, from the past, from the profound sense that there is nothing that can be done about it. I know that things can't happen in any other way . . .

2

Sami Winkler has departed. In a workman's shirt, bareheaded, a little knapsack on his back, looking out of the window of a third-class compartment like someone going to the mountains for a couple of days.

I asked him, jokingly:

'Aren't you travelling light for a man who's making history?'

'No. It's all I need. I'm leaving the rest behind.'

'Isn't that tough?'

'Pretty tough. So it's better to make a clean break. To say goodbye to the lot rather than to one thing at a time.'

He was on his own. He'd forbidden his relatives from coming and his travelling companions had gone ahead to Constanța, to await him on the ship. Next Thursday they'll be in Haifa.

'And then?'

He replied by spreading his arms, probably meaning that the answer was too great for a single word: 'everything', 'life', 'victory', 'peace' . . . He was very calm, unexcited, unhurried.

Two boys selling a right-wing newspaper happened along. 'Take one, gentlemen, it's against the Yids.' Their timing made us smile. Sometimes symbolism is too obvious.

Winkler called them over and bought a paper.

'I brought nothing to read on the trip.'

Indeed, he had brought no books. Not a single one. Then again, books were never really his thing.

We shook hands. I would have liked to embrace him, but I was afraid of the disruption such a show of feeling would have injected in our self-controlled parting. We shook hands.

*

I would like him to prevail, but I find it hard to believe in his victory. I hope he finds peace among his Palestinian orange groves, the peace we have sought in our own ways; S.T. Haim in Jilava Prison, Abraham Sulitzer through journeys and books, Arnold Max through poetry, me on the site, building. The boat cutting through the waves to Haifa will perhaps mark the direction towards a new Jewish history. Will it take him towards a Jewish peace? I don't know. I don't believe so. I don't dare to.

Two thousand years can't be overcome by leaving for somewhere. They would have to be forgotten, the wound cauterized, their melancholy cut to the ground with a scythe. But the truth is that there are too many years for us to be able to forget them. We live always in the troubled memory of them. The memory reaches far back and hangs like a haze over the horizon of our future. Only rarely, through this history of warfare, victories and kingdoms, does any light pierce the mist. Is it possible to build a new history from such material?

*

Winkler has many fights ahead – and he will win them all. But there is something he must let go of also, and I don't know if he will succeed. He must let go of his habit of suffering, he must let go of his vocation for pain. This aptitude is too well developed and the instinct too entrenched to yield even before such a simple life. This bitter root can withstand every season and will always be ready to bear its sad fruit, even in the gentlest summer, with the soul lulled by dreams of eternal peace. You will face yourself again in a moment of terror and will learn once again that old lesson you keep forgetting: that you can escape from anywhere, but you cannot flee your own self.

3

I wish I could reproduce word for word, like a stenographer, the discussion I had yesterday evening with Mircea Vieru.

He had visited me at work. Blidaru's house is of interest to him too. Mostly he's interested in it as my building – the first one I've done alone. He doesn't want to make any criticisms. He very much wants to see me bring it all to a conclusion, on my own – which both delights and intimidates me. I'm not certain that I'm really getting it right. Sometimes it all seems inspired, clear and coherent. At other times, the contrary; it's all lifeless, cold and schematic. I invited the professor, but he didn't want to come.

'No. Carry on, do what you want, work how you want. That's what we agreed. When you're finished, let me know. Until then, the house is yours.'

From the site, I went with Vieru to the Bucharest road to have dinner. It's been a full five weeks since I've been out of Snagov.

'I never see you in town any more. Why?'

'Because I'm fed up with it. It's the tense, poisonous mood. At every street corner, an apostle. And in every apostle, an exterminator of Jews. It wears me out, depresses me.'

He didn't reply. He reflected for a moment, hesitating, a little embarrassed, as though he wished to change the subject. Then, probably after brief private deliberation, he addressed me in that determined manner people have when they want to get something off their chests.

'You're right. Yet there is a Jewish problem, and it needs to be solved. One million eight hundred thousand Jews is intolerable. If it was up to me, I'd try to eliminate several hundred thousand.'

I was startled. I think I failed to hide my surprise. The one person I had believed utterly incapable of anti-Semitism was he – Mircea Vieru. So, him too. He noticed my distress and hurried to explain.

'Let's be clear. I'm not anti-Semitic. I've told you that before and abide by that. But I'm Romanian. And, all that is opposed to me as a Romanian I regard as dangerous. There is a corrosive Jewish spirit. I must defend myself against it. In the press, in finance, in the army – I feel it exerting its influence everywhere. If the body of our state were strong, it would hardly bother me. But it's not strong. It's sinful, corruptible and weak. And this is why I must fight against the agents of corruption.'

I said nothing for a few seconds, which was not what he had expected. I could have responded, out of politeness, to keep the conversation going, but I failed to.

'Do I surprise you?'

'No, you depress me. You see, I know two kinds of anti-Semites. Ordinary anti-Semites – and anti-Semites with arguments. I manage to get along with the first kind, because everything between us is clear-cut. But with the other kind it's hard.'

'Because it's hard to argue back?'

'Because it's futile to argue back. You see, dear master, your mistake begins where your arguments begin. To be anti-Semitic is a fact. To be anti-Semitic with arguments – that's a waste of time, a dead end. Neither your anti-Semitism nor Romanian anti-Semitism has need of arguments. Let's say I could answer those arguments. What then? Would that clarify anything? Taking into account that all the possible accusations against Romanian Jews are just local issues, while anti-Semitism is universal and eternal. You don't find anti-Semites only in Romania. They're also in Germany, Hungary, Greece, France and America – all, absolutely all, in the context of interests, with their own methods, with their own temperaments. And there haven't only been anti-Semites now, after the war, there were anti-Semites before the war, and not just in this century, but in the last one and all the others. What's happening today is a joke compared to what happened in 1300.

'So, if anti-Semitism is indeed such a persistent general fact, isn't it useless to seek specific Romanian causes? Political causes today, economic causes yesterday, religious causes before that – the causes are too numerous and too specific to explain such a general historical fact.'

'You're very crafty,' interrupted Vieru. 'Aren't you trying to make anti-Semitism inexplicable by making it eternal? And declaring Jews innocent?'

'God forbid! Not only does anti-Semitism seem explicable to me, but I believe Jews alone are to blame. Yet I wish you could recognize at least that the essence of anti-Semitism is neither of a religious, political nor an economic nature. I believe it is purely metaphysical in nature. Don't be alarmed. The Jew has a metaphysical obligation to be detested. That's his role in the world. Why? I don't know. His curse, his fate. His problem, if you like.

'Please believe me. I don't say this out of pride or defiance. On the contrary, I say it with sadness, weariness and bitterness. But I believe that it's an implacable fact and know that neither you nor I nor anybody else can do anything about it. If we could be exterminated, that would be very good. It would be simple, in any case. But this isn't possible either. Our obligation to always be in the world confirms it over so many thousands of years, which you know have not been merciful. And then you have to accept – look, I accept it – this alternation of massacres and peace, which is the pulse of Jewish life. Individually, each Jew can ask in panic what he has to do. To flee, to die, to kill himself, to receive baptism. Resolving one's personal affairs involves endless pain which you, certainly, as a man of feeling, will not ignore – but this is nothing more, however, than "resolving one's personal affairs". Collectively, though, there is only one path: waiting, submission to fate. And I think this, rather than being an act of reneging on life, is one of reintegration with nature, with the awareness that life goes on after all these individual deaths, they too being part of life, just as the falling of leaves is a fact of life for the tree, or the death of the tree to the forest, or the death of the forest for the vegetation of the earth.'

'Once again, you're being very crafty,' he replied. 'You're changing the subject completely. Forgive me, but the problem of the Jewish people doesn't interest me. Their own affair, as you put it so well. What interests me is simply the solution to the Jewish problem in Romania. Not from a metaphysical point of view, which I refuse to enter into, but from a political, social and economic point of view, however that may alarm you. I maintain that the Jewish threat to Romania is real – a reality which must be understood and contained with tact and moderation, and yet firmly.

'You reply by talking about pogroms in 1300. Well, that's running from the argument. That anti-Semitism, as a religious phenomenon, is one thing, and my so-called anti-Semitism, which is political and economic, is another. There's absolutely no connection between the two. They're on different planes. I'm surprised at you intentionally making such a logical confusion. Let's return to what is plainly called "the Jewish problem" in Romania. There are a million eight hundred thousand Jews in Romania. What are you going to do with them? That's all there is to it.'

'Let's go back, then, if you want, and I'll make a small, very small, observation on my logical confusion. If you'll allow me.

'The nature of today's anti-Semitism seems so different to you to that of 600 years ago. Religious then, political now. Do you really think these phenomena are unrelated? How mistaken you are. Think about it and tell me that they're not two faces of the same thing. Of course, the anti-Semitism in 1933 is economic, and in 1333 it was religious. But this is because the defining element of that society was religion, while in this century it's economics. If tomorrow's social structure centres neither on religion nor economics, but instead on – let's say – bee-keeping, the Jew will be detested from the point of view of keeping bees. Don't laugh, it's true. What changes in anti-Semitism, as an eternal phenomenon, is the plane on which it is manifested. Not its origin. The viewpoints, yes, are always different: but the essence of the phenomenon remains the same. And this is, however much you may protest, the requirement that the Jew must suffer.'

'Forgive me, please forgive me, but I refuse to reply. Essences, first causes, metaphysics – I don't accept any of this. I'm calling you to order. I'm a thinker: it appears you're a mystic. We won't reach agreement if we continue.'

'We're less likely to if you don't reply. Look, I'll indulge you and deal with your arguments. So you'll see how confused things have just got. What you call "arguments" are in reality nothing but excuses. You're not an anti-Semite because you believe in certain Jewish threats, you believe in certain Jewish threats because you're an anti-Semite.'

'Observe how this rather resembles the story of the chicken and the egg. Which came first? Anti-Semitism or the Jewish threat? Talmudism, my friend, Talmudism.'

'Then it's Talmudism, if you wish. But listen to me in any case. And, so as not to generalize, let's take a concrete example. A moment ago you said there were one million eight hundred thousand Jews in Romania. Where did you get that figure from?'

'Where did I get it from? I know it. It's common knowledge.'

'"Common knowledge" is rather vague. How was it arrived at? Who arrived at it? Who verified it? Nobody, obviously. According to the Jews themselves, there are calculated to be between eight hundred and nine hundred thousand. At most, a million. According to authorities, in taxation, local government, electoral registers – there are slightly more than a million: a few tens of thousands more. But you bluntly say, simplifying the controversy, a million eight hundred thousand. Why? Is it not perhaps because this extra seven or eight hundred thousand satisfies your anti-Semitic feelings, which precede any figure and any danger?'

'It's wrong of you to abuse the argument in this way. I don't of course have the means to determine how many Jews there are. Let's say there are only a million. So what? Do you think if there's a million, they no longer constitute a threat?'

'You see, dear master, now it's your turn to be crafty. Because that's not the issue. It's not about how many of them there are, but how many of them you think there are. Why do you – so critical in architecture and so rigorous about every fact and affirmation, so severe in your own thinking and conscience when it concerns artistic matters – why do you become suddenly negligent and hasty when you start to speak about Jews, casually accepting a ninety per cent approximation, when in any other domain you'd baulk at an approximation of 0.01? Why does your intellectual probity, which I have so often judged to be too exacting when you foolhardily stake everything you have for the tiniest truth – why does this probity no longer apply here, in our conversation about Jews?'

He said nothing for several moments. He stood up, took several steps across the terrace, stopped before me, perhaps wanted to say something, thought better of it, and then continued pacing the terrace, steadily, lost in thought. Then he spoke, very calmly, without the usual abruptness to his statements.

'You were right just now. It's very hard for us to see eye to eye. Every fact and argument can be construed and misconstrued in a thousand ways. It'll never end.'

'Well, if you reject metaphysical explanations ...'

'No, be serious. The truth is, we're not statisticians. If we were, it would be as easy as pie. We'd say: there are so many Romanians and so many Jews. So many good Jews and so many Jews who constitute a threat. And we'd be completely enlightened. But as we can neither count them nor judge them, we have to be satisfied with certain impressions, certain intuitions. I know, for instance, that there are two Jewish bankers in Romania who manipulate our politicians, our government, our apparatus of state. Well, I have the feeling that these two examples represent an entire intolerant and domineering Jewish mentality. You want me to give you figures, when it's a matter of intuition? Who are we? People who enumerate or people who think?'

'Neither, in this case. We're people who feel. You said it yourself: "I have the feeling that . . ." Well, we're in agreement here. It's a matter of a feeling, not of reason. That's why the discussion seems superfluous to me. Bear in mind that I tried to avoid it. But I was accused of dealing in metaphysics. I'm so convinced that this feeling of yours, this "intuition" if you prefer, is unassailable, that I know in advance that every argument, good or bad, will fail. I could contrast those two Jewish bankers you spoke of with two thousand or two hundred thousand unfortunate miserable Jewish workers struggling against hunger to earn their daily bread. But what of it? Would this shake your faith in your intuitions? God forbid! Do you not see that what you call "intuition" and what I call your "anti-Semitism" select examples that can nourish it and ignore those which can refute it?

'There has always been something in the Romanian sensibility which has driven it to count the deserters and to disregard the dead and wounded. Out of bad faith? No. I'm convinced that that's not it. From suspicion and doubt, from being accustomed to dealing with an old feeling of repulsion in others.

'Believe me, I'm not blaming you for anything. I tell you this with my hand on my heart: There's an inevitability to this against which there is nothing to be done. As it happens, your arguments are unjust. Even if they were excellent, we would still get nowhere. I believe, with great regret and equanimity, that there's nothing to be done about any of this. That with all the goodwill in the world, on both our parts, it's a lost cause from the start. I feel awkward talking this way about myself but, having arrived at this point, it's best to speak unreservedly. You know, I'm certain that some day, if necessary, I'll die on a Romanian front line. Heroism? Certainly not. But I don't believe I'm a shirker. I'm not the kind to run from a place where something decisive is being played out. I believe that wherever I find myself, in life, in war, in love, I will stay and fulfil my destiny. Our many years of friendship and acquaintance permit me to tell you this simply. Well, do you think this last hour is going to prove anything? Because, one way or another, won't I always be an outsider, always under suspicion, always kept at arm's length?

'No, no, believe me, it's all useless. And, anyway, my sense of this futility is also my only consolation.'

Again he was silent, for a long time, thinking. I couldn't tell if he had been able to follow all I had said or had absently continued his own line of thought. Then he addressed me, with a certain weariness.

'You dispirit me. I don't know why, but I have the impression that every door you close opens ten more. Certainly, I'd find it difficult to reply to you. We would move still further from the heart of the matter. The heart of the drama, if you like, if that pleases you. You're far too passionately Jewish and I'm far too self-restrainedly Romanian for us to agree. In argument, of course, as elsewhere in life, permit me to be less sombre than you are and to say that with Jews like you peace will always be possible. Even more than peace: love.'

'"With Jews like you . . ." I've heard this expression before. "If only all Jews were like you . . ." It's a familiar old way of being friendly. And so humiliating. I'm tired of it, believe me.'

'Tired and intolerant. You don't let me finish, you don't let me explain myself. You'll admit you're a difficult person to converse with. I firmly believe that your "metaphysical" despair introduces too much complexity into what is a difficult practical problem, but one to which a solution exists. The fact that I believe this is the beginning of the solution. It remains for you to believe it too – all of you – and the job is done.'

'You have a naive spirit.'

'Yours is tragic.'

We both lit our cigarettes. We tried to talk, but it didn't work – and it was late when we separated, a little embarrassed, with a truly warm handshake.

4

Ştefan D. Pârlea's conference at the Foundation on the values of gold and the values of blood. An enormous crowd, on the balconies, on the stairs, on the steps to the stage. Pârlea had to struggle to the lectern. He was pale and resolute, as though bearing the burden of the masses, though at moments his gestures assumed such violence and directness that he seemed to hold everybody's breath suspended in expectation with his upraised arm.

I don't know what he said. I tried several times to shake free from drowning in the sea of people beneath his waves of words, some whispered, some shouted. I looked for a single island amid the shipwreck, to stem for a moment the insistent thundering flow of questions, to retain a thought, a judgement, a direction. It all seemed overwhelming, urgent, unstoppable, like an earthquake. I could no longer recognize the person who was speaking. He was glimpsed from afar, an unsettling apparition from a dream, something out of a legend.

I was brought back to the moment by the cheering and shouting and the thunder of applause. A familiar song arose from the galleries:

> The foreigners and the Yids
> All suck us dry, always suck us dry.

Obviously.

*

A moment of crisis, a moment of crisis ... A world that's dying, a world being born ... History split into two parts ... a dead epoch ... a living epoch ...

Don't be afraid, dear old gentlemen. You have nothing to lose. Neither what you've been believing, nor your head, nor your money, nor your little certainties, nor your little doubts. Everything will remain in place, everything will stay as it was. As it happens, there is a cry that arises again on time to calm the fever of indignation and to take the sting out of great revolutions. There is another death, which can be demanded more easily than your own precious death. There is a race of people ready to pay up on time for you. To pay for the overfed, for the starved, for the white, for the red, for the thin, for the fat. Haven't you always said they're a race of bankers? So, let them pay.

*

No, no, no, a thousand times no. I mustn't reproduce my 1923 notebook all over again. If I don't immediately choke my taste for martyrdom, I'm lost.

I know: it's incomparably easier to accumulate disappointments and to live on their embers, to immerse myself in stagnant pools and the warm waters of sadness, and to believe in the pride of that sadness – it's much easier than remaining on guard, and being comprehending of others and harsh with myself. I will keep watch, even if I am keeping watch over my final hour.

('Keeping watch over my final hour' is still too rhetorical. Almost a slogan. My dear friend, there are enough sloganeers. If you can't manage to speak, keep quiet.)

*

I asked Pârlea:

'Aren't you afraid it's going to end again with cracked skulls and broken windows? Don't you ask yourself if it's going to end up with an anti-Semitic disturbance, and go no further? Don't you think calling this thing of yours a "revolution" is just using a new word for an ancient wretchedness?'

He frowned, and answered:

'There's a drought, and I await the rain. And you stand there and tell me: "A hard rain is what we need. But what if it comes with hail? If it comes with a storm? If it ruins what I've sowed?" Well, I'll tell you: I don't know how the rain will fall. I just want it to come. That's all. With hail, storm, lightning, as long as it comes. One or two will survive the deluge. Nobody will survive drought. If the revolution demands a pogrom, then give it a pogrom. It's not for me, or you, or him. It's for everybody. Whose time is up and whose isn't, I don't care, even if I myself die. I only care about one thing: that there's a drought and rain is needed. Apart from that, I want nothing, expect nothing, wonder about nothing.'

I could reply. I could tell him that a metaphor is inadequate in the face of a bloodbath. That a Platonic inclination for dying doesn't balance out the serious decision to kill. That through the ages there has never been a great historical infamy committed for which there couldn't be found a symbol just as big, to justify it. That, in consequence, we would do well to pay attention to great certainties, to great invocations, to the great 'droughts' and 'rains'. That the temper of our most violent outbursts might benefit from a shade less enthusiasm.

I could reply. But what good would it do? I have a simple, resigned, inexplicable sensation that everything that is happening is in the normal order of things and that I am awaiting a season that will come and pass – because it has come and passed before.

*

'Your presence is harmful,' Pârlea tells me. 'You're too lucid. We need a generation of men who have had enough of always being intelligent. A small band of men capable of throwing caution to the wind.'

Pârlea isn't joking. Like any missionary, he can't stand those who wait and watch. Several times he's hit me with: 'Answer, man, black or white? Yes or no?' The intolerance of the inspired is dreadful. I used to believe it was a Jewish defect, but I was wrong: the defect arises from fervour. S.T. Haim, at one time, criticized me for exactly the same thing as Ştefan Pârlea today: a deliberate lack of enthusiasm. Were I to tell him I have my own demons, he wouldn't believe me. The only difference between us is that he lets his excite his fever while I keep watch over mine.

I'll always resist invitations to fervour, and will resist the more tempting ones all the more resolutely. Letting yourself be swept along on the current is too attractive to be trusted.

It has been my fortune to have grown up by the Danube, where the humblest boatman working the oar must continually read the waters. I don't know any inspired boatmen, only those who take care. All your nebulous intuitions are worthless on the Danube. What you need is good judgement.

Were I less wary of over-analysing myself, I'd try to establish to what degree I'm above all a native of the banks of the Danube. That is my country. It has always been hard for me to simply say those two words – 'my country'. Since childhood I've become accustomed to having my good faith doubted. Sensitive to ridicule, I haven't insisted on making affirmations that nobody would accept.

We, Romanians . . . It was almost inevitable at school, in history lessons, recounting a war, to employ this first person plural: *we, Romanians* ('which Romanians?' someone on my bench shouted at me once, forbidding me for a good while from sympathizing with the story of Ştefan the Great). I was careful to avoid terms that might be judged affected, though I was at an age when solemn words provide a certain pleasure. Country, fatherland, nation, hero – a whole forbidden vocabulary. As an intellectual exercise, it wasn't bad, as I was forced from early on to monitor my words and to make them mean exactly what was required. But, no matter how much consolation you get from the feeling of being wronged, the game isn't all fun. A shadow of terror hangs over all my memories of school and childhood.

Today I regard with asperity any tendency I have towards feeling persecuted and I'm rather unforgiving of my emotional outbursts.

But I will not soon forget my first night on guard duty years ago, in the regiment, when they told me that position number 3, in the adjutancy, could not be assigned to me. ('There's a special regime for Jews,' explained the lieutenant, a little embarrassed.) In this way, as far as they were concerned, even if I wasn't a proven traitor, I was in any case a potential one. A 'special' regime annulled in that moment the life I had lived on this soil, the lives of my parents, the lives of my grandparents and great-grandparents, a 'special' regime with a serial number erased nearly two centuries of history in a country which, of course, was not 'my fatherland', since I might betray it in the course of a night on guard duty.

Writing, I have the feeling that I'm getting pathetic about 'my sad fate', and this is not my intention at all. It's good to remind myself anew that I decided once and for all not to be a martyr, which is too serious a role for me to play. All I am doing here is explaining to myself my plain inaptitude for certain grand words, certain solemn ideas. Probably it will always be difficult for me to speak of 'my Romanian fatherland' without a feeling of sudden awkwardness, being unable to conquer through willpower a right which the slow passage of time has not let me conquer, in the face of good faith ignored and sincerity scorned. But I will speak of a land that is mine, and for her I will risk appearing ridiculous, and I will love that which I am not allowed to love. I will speak of the Bărăgan and the Danube as belonging to me not in a legal or abstract sense, under constitutions, treaties and laws, but bodily, through memory, through joys and sorrows. I will speak of the spirit of this place, of its particular genius, of the lucidity I have distinguished here under the white light of the sun on the plain and the melancholy I perceive in the landscape of the Danube, drowsing to the right of the town, in the watery marshes.

It's time for me to stop. I've let myself be carried away and have started making speeches. I'll start again tomorrow, with less sentimentality.

*

There is in the landscape of the Romanian character a particular region, a particular sensibility, where I feel at home: Muntenia. It's the point from which the culture of the country can be observed, analysed and judged. Moldova is more fertile, but also more confused: her creative resources are infinitely more complex, but imbalanced, mixed chaotically. There is a coolness to the Muntenian spirit that I gladly recognize to be the rather sterile yet commanding play of intelligence. There's much more metal in the soil on this side of the Milcov river.

I think there's more to Pârlea's hostility than Romanian–Jewish discord. There is also the Moldovan–Muntenian split. I said this to him, and it made him laugh. 'So, now you're a Vlach, too.' I took the joke without offence and decided to think about it properly. If Wallachia is as much a psychological category as a geographical one, and there's a Wallachian people as well as a Wallachian climate, then I am, in Romanian terms, a Wallachian, a Muntenian. The chaos of Pârlea's thinking, its obscurity, its leaps, its generous naivety, all derive from an unbridled, lyrical, rhetorical sensibility with which S.T.H., being from Fălticeni, can sympathize directly but which, in the light of day on the Danube plain, looks like the chasing of a mirage.

*

I will never cease to be a Jew, of course. This is not a position I can resign from. You are or you're not. It's not a matter either of pride or shame.

It's a fact. It's not necessary to forget it. It would be just as unnecessary for someone to contest it. But nor will I, in the same way, ever cease to be from the lands of the Danube. This too is a fact. Whether someone recognizes me as such or not is their business. Their business entirely.

The difficulty does not reside and never has resided in legal recognition of my situation, which is a detail that has nothing to do with me, since I'm not trying to lay claim to anything or have my rights recognized. (I imagine a gathering of willows from the Brăila marshes, asserting their right to be willows.) I know what I am, and the difficulties, if they exist, can only concern what I am, not what is written in the state's registry books. The state may declare me what it will, but I won't stop being a Jew, a Romanian and a Danubian. 'You might be overdoing it,' whispers my anti-Semitic voice (as I have an anti-Semitic voice, with which I converse in moments of reflection). Certainly, I might be. I'm not saying that the blend is free of any dissonance, I don't claim that peace between these tendencies is immediate. On the contrary, I know that this agreement is hard-earned, that this cohabitation has personal, internal difficulties. For me, a political discussion of the Jewish problem is completely sterile. I'm only interested in one solution, and it is psychological and spiritual. I believe the only way in which I can clarify any of this ancient pain is for me to try, alone, for my own sake, to comprehend the knot of adversity and conflict with which I am bound up in Romanian life. And I don't believe this solitariness is an escape, a lack of solidarity with my people. On the contrary, as it's not possible for the experience of one person who sincerely accepts and lives a drama not to be of some use in lighting the way for all the others. It seems more urgent and effective to me to achieve a harmony in my own life between the Romanian and Jewish parts of my character than to obtain or lose certain civil rights. I would like to know, for instance, what anti-Semitic law could erase from my being the irrevocable fact of having been born by the Danube and loving that place.

Has anybody had greater need of a fatherland, a soil, a horizon with plants and animals? Everything abstract in me has been corrected and, for the most part, cured by a simple view of the Danube. Everything fevered has been soothed and ordered. I don't know what it would have been like to have been born somewhere else. But I am convinced I would have been different. The example of the regal indifference of the river has risen against my Judaic taste for personal catastrophes. The simplicity of the landscape has countered my inner complications. And insecurity and worry have been shown the ephemeral yet eternal play of the waves.

The image is cheap. Yet, cheap or not, it consoles me still.

5

I stayed until very late yesterday at Snagov, until everything was finished; the parquet varnished, the windows cleaned, the locks put in the doors. I waited until the people had left one by one and remained alone in the doorway, the last one left.

It is the house I dreamed of. A house built for sunlight. Evenings, its shadow falls across the water, like the shadow of a plant.

Ghiță Blidaru passed without speaking through every room. We stopped on the terrace, where the September morning spread into the distance, beyond the lake, white in the declining autumn light, as though exhausted by its own splendour.

I was happy that he said nothing to me and I understood from his silence that he felt at home.

It's a pleasure to build and it's an even greater joy to say farewell to what you have built.

We will forget each other, my white house in Snagov, you to receive the sun each day through your wide windows, me to put up other walls, just as likely to be forgotten.

Look, this is where our paths separate: you are what I have always dreamed of being – simple, clean and calm, your heart accepting of the coming of every season.

PENGUIN MODERN CLASSICS

THE OUTSIDER
ALBERT CAMUS

'This new version ... treats Camus' text with respect, directness and an unexpected delicateness. She reveals, and permits, an original edgy strangeness in the prose' Ali Smith, *The Times*

'The sky seemed to rip apart from end to end to pour fire down upon me'

Meursault will not conform. When his mother dies, he refuses to show his emotions simply to satisfy the expectations of others. And when he commits a random act of violence on a sun-drenched beach, his lack of remorse only compounds his guilt in the eyes of society and the law.

Albert Camus' portrayal of a man confronting the absurdity of human life became a classic. Yet it is also a book filled with quiet joy in the physical world, and this new translation sensitively renders the subtleties and dreamlike atmosphere of The Outsider.

Translated by Sandra Smith

PENGUIN MODERN CLASSICS

LOVE AND EXILE
ISAAC BASHEVIS SINGER

'An astonishingly intimate record of a writer's inner wanderings' *San Francisco Chronicle*

From pre-First World War Warsaw to the New York of the 1930s, Isaac Bashevis Singer traces the early years of his life in this autobiographical trilogy. In *A Little Boy in Search of God*, he remembers his bookish boyhood as the son of an Orthodox rabbi, equally absorbed in science, philosophy and cabbala. Later, the pursuit of women came to obsess him almost as much as the pursuit of knowledge, and in *A Young Man in Search of Love* he chronicles the intricacies of his first love affairs. When he emigrated to the United States from Poland on the eve of the Second World War loneliness and depression overwhelmed him, and he relives these dark years in *Lost in America*. From beginning to end, *Love and Exile* sheds new light on Singer's own life and the fictional lives mirrored in it.

PENGUIN MODERN CLASSICS

HUMBOLDT'S GIFT
SAUL BELLOW

With an Introduction by Martin Amis

'Bellow at his best ... funny, vibrant, ironic, self-mocking, and wise'
San Francisco Examiner

For many years, the great poet Von Humboldt Fleisher and Charlie Citrine, a
young man inflamed with a love for literature, were the best of friends. At the
time of his death, however, Humboldt is a failure, and Charlie's life has reached a
low point: his career is at a standstill, and he's enmeshed in an acrimonious
divorce, infatuated with a highly unsuitable young woman, and involved with a
neurotic Mafioso. But then Humboldt acts from beyond the grave, bestowing
upon Charlie an unexpected legacy that may just help him turn his life around.

WINNER OF THE NOBEL PRIZE FOR LITERATURE

PENGUIN MODERN CLASSICS

ONE DAY IN THE LIFE OF IVAN DENISOVICH
ALEKSANDR SOLZHENITSYN

'It is a blow struck for human freedom all over the world ... and it is gloriously readable' *Sunday Times*

This brutal, shattering glimpse of the fate of millions of Russians under Stalin shook Russia and shocked the world when it first appeared.

Discover the importance of a piece of bread or an extra bowl of soup, the incredible luxury of a book, the ingenious possibilities of a nail, a piece of string or a single match in a world where survival is all. Here safety, warmth and food are the first objectives. Reading this book, you enter a world of incarceration, brutality, hard manual labour and freezing cold – and participate in the struggle of men to survive both the terrible rigours of nature and the inhumanity of the system that defines their conditions of life.

Translated by Ralph Parker

WINNER OF THE NOBEL PRIZE FOR LITERATURE